WHAT YOU DESIRE

ANYTHING FOR LOVE - BOOK 1

ADELE CLEE

For Paul, Dan and Matty
With love

CHAPTER 1

*S*ebastian Ashcroft, fourth Marquess of Danesfield, thrust his hand under the seat and grabbed the mahogany box.

"Bloody hell." The curse burst from his lips as his carriage swerved left and right to shake his pursuers.

Ramming the heel of his boot against the seat opposite to act as a brace, he flicked the catch on the box and removed the pistol before pouring powder into the muzzle and tamping it down with the rod. The scoundrels would make their move before the next turnpike. All he needed was one clean shot to even the odds.

Keeping a firm grip on the loaded weapon, he peered out of the viewing window.

The principal rider wore his collar raised to cover the lower part of his face, his wide-brimmed hat pulled down at the front to shield his eyes. He rode with the deportment of a gentleman. Yet, his horse's dull black coat and clumsy gait suggested he'd been hired in the dark or out of sheer desperation.

Swamped by his driving-coat, the second rider was smaller in frame. A length of material covered his mouth to mask his identity. It was obvious he lacked experience as the gentleman kept glancing back over his shoulder urging him to maintain the pace, often dropping back to wait.

The possessive act suggested a kinship, that of a brother or son—or even a lover.

"Damnation." Sebastian yanked down the window and yelled up to his coachman, Haines. "Stop the carriage."

"But, my lord," Haines shouted from his box seat.

"I said stop the carriage."

As the carriage rattled to a halt, Sebastian flung open the door and jumped down to the ground. Holding his pistol firmly in front of him, he marched to the rear of the carriage to greet his assailants.

"You wanted my attention and now—" Sebastian skidded to a halt, frozen by the sight of the gentleman's agitated horse. Teeth bared, the animal snorted loudly and came up on its hind legs.

"Stay back. Do not come a step closer," the gentleman ordered, pulling the horse's head tightly round to the left until its nose almost touched the top of his polished boots. There was an air of authority in the rider's voice.

The second rider gave a high-pitched shriek and slapped a gloved hand over the fabric to mask any further sound.

The elegance and mastery with which the gentleman settled his horse confirmed he was a skilled rider and most definitely of good breeding, which made the whole encounter even more puzzling.

Sebastian aimed his pistol at the gentleman. "If you're lucky enough to escape without a lead ball in your back, your horse will be the death of you."

"Let's hope I'm fortunate enough to escape both," the gentleman sneered with a level of arrogance demonstrated in elite circles.

"Even if that were possible, the punishment for robbing a member of the nobility is death. You'll both hang."

"I doubt it."

There was something familiar about the man's arrogance and polished repartee. Perhaps it was time to make things a little more interesting, Sebastian thought, and so aimed his pistol at the second rider who'd sat motionless throughout the whole exchange.

"Get down," Sebastian said. A quick glance at the shapely thighs encased in a pair of breeches confirmed his suspicion.

The rider was a woman.

Alarmed, her head shot up towards her associate. Sebastian could feel the tension in the unspoken words passing back and forth between them.

"He … he cannot hear you. He's deaf."

Sebastian chuckled to himself. "That is unfortunate," he said, feigning surprise. "If he's deaf you must be blind. I know a woman when I see one, and this is the most ridiculous robbery I have ever witnessed. You're not even armed."

Sensing his master's irritation, the horse grew restless once again. It shuffled backwards and pawed the ground as though the earth had crumbled away beneath him and he was unsure where to place his feet.

The gentleman muttered an angry curse.

Suppressing a grin, Sebastian pressed him further. "What sort of man allows a woman to act as his right hand in a robbery? You obviously care little for her welfare."

"It was not my idea," he replied through gritted teeth. "Trying to get her to listen to anything I say is like trying to trap lightning in a blasted bottle."

Sebastian could not hide his amusement. He could not recall the last time he laughed aloud. In the last six years, he had been involved in many dangerous encounters, but this one had to be the most bizarre encounter of his entire life. To Sebastian's surprise, the gentleman sniggered, too.

"How dare you laugh at me," the woman scolded. Straightening her back, she appeared more robust than Sebastian first thought. She'd yanked down her disguise to reveal a pert nose and a pair of rosy pink lips. "And if you think I'm going to sit here any longer and be ridiculed for … for caring, for wanting to make sure you didn't end up dead in a ditch."

She swung her horse around, dug her heels in and cantered off across the field towards a small wooded area in the distance.

"For heaven's sake, Annabel, wait. Damn it, woman. Do you want me to shout your name out for all to hear?"

Sebastian studied the man's frustrated countenance and almost felt sorry for him. "Now it's just the two of us, let's get back to this business of robbery."

The gentleman sighed loudly. "This is not a blasted robbery." His gaze flitted back and forth between Sebastian and the woman in the distance.

"Then why in hell's name were you following my carriage?" Sebastian asked as he watched the woman head for the woods.

The gentleman swung his horse around ready to ride out in pursuit. "You may lower your pistol for I am here on an errand." With one hand gripping the reins, he reached inside his greatcoat and removed a red velvet pouch. "Here, take this." He threw it down and Sebastian caught it with his free hand. "I trust you'll keep it safe, and if this damn horse kills me, you'll know what to do." The gentleman straightened and raised the brim of his hat. "And I suggest you get some sleep, Dane. Your eyes are as red as the Devil's."

Only his closest friends called him Dane.

Sebastian stared at the familiar face. "Beaufort?" he said, wondering why his friend felt it necessary to conceal his identity.

"And keep an eye on Sophie for me. I'll be home as soon as I can."

Before Sebastian could utter another word, Beaufort galloped off across the field as though his life depended on it and disappeared into the woods.

Sebastian stood there, his eyes wide, his mouth hanging open. Had it not been for the piece of red velvet lying in his palm, he would have believed he'd drifted off to sleep and imagined the whole damn thing.

As he strolled around to the carriage door, he glanced up at Haines' hulking figure perched on his box seat like a stuffed bear. "It's always good to know when trouble strikes I can count on your assistance."

"I thought you were handling things just fine, my lord," he replied, keeping his eyes fixed firmly ahead.

Sebastian arched a brow. "And you knew that without moving a muscle."

Haines turned to face him, his weather-beaten face expressionless. "Like you said when you hired me, my lord. People see what they want to see. Just 'cause you didn't see me move doesn't mean I wasn't leaning over the top of the carriage pointing a pistol of my own."

Sebastian grinned. His man had a fair point.

"Perhaps it's time I listened to my own advice." He looked out across the field before turning back to Haines. "Did the whole thing not strike you as rather odd?"

"Can't say as I can remember being chased by masked riders desperate to give me something," he said, pushing the front of his hat up to scratch the top of his head. "And looking at the piece of cloth in your hand I'd say it's something right important."

Lost in thought, Sebastian stared at the velvet pouch, his attention caught by the initials RB embroidered in gold thread.

The sound of a cart rattling down the road disturbed his reverie and Haines gave a polite cough.

"Beg your pardon, my lord, but we need to be on our way. We've got a good day's journey ahead, and there's no telling what state the road's in."

"Very well." Sebastian sighed, unable to resist one last glance over his shoulder.

He had missed Beaufort during the six years he'd been away. He had missed his witty banter and arrogant drawl. And he felt a stab of guilt for being absent during what was obviously a time of great need.

Returning to his carriage, Sebastian placed the pistol in the box, settled back into the leather seat and untied the string on the velvet pouch. There was another roll of velvet inside, and he opened it to reveal an elaborate gold and ruby necklace.

He had seen many enchanting things on his travels but had seen nothing quite like this. The chain consisted of a row of oval rubies encased in gold and joined together by a fine filigree design. It was so intricate and delicate in detail that it could have been spun by a spider. Transfixed by its beauty, Sebastian simply stared.

Why would Beaufort give him such a precious antiquity?

Perhaps his creditors were chasing his heels, and he wanted to hide the heirloom. It would certainly explain the shabby state of his horse. Yet he knew Beaufort still owned the estate that bordered his and he'd not been told of any money worries.

The thought of going home to Westlands brought a hard lump to his throat, and he swallowed deeply to dismiss the years of guilt.

The past no longer mattered.

All the years of pain and hard work had been worth it. His estate was thriving. Now, he intended to take his rightful place, to relax and enjoy the peace and tranquillity.

He glanced down at the necklace in his hand, the weight of its burden pressing down on his shoulders. Whatever problem Beaufort had, Sebastian could not get involved. Then he felt the familiar stirring in his chest, the thrum of excitement that always lured him towards dangerous and mysterious escapades.

Damn it.

The quicker his friend returned to claim the pretty necklace the better.

CHAPTER 2

"*M*r. Potts, I think he's here, Mr. Potts."

Sophie Beaufort watched the old woman scurry out through the door behind the glass counter and then continued to examine the box of ribbons.

"Your mother seems rather excited today," she said, pulling out a length of red satin.

She did not need new ribbons, or threads, or buttons, but her regular walks to the village made the days seem shorter.

"She has been like it all morning," Emily said, shaking her head. "She thinks the marquess is going to come in and buy her whole stock of gloves. I've told her he probably buys all his apparel in London, but you know how she gets."

Sophie swallowed a few times hoping it would help to correct the problem with her hearing. "I thought I heard you say the marquess," she chuckled. She really was spending far too much time on her own.

"I did." Emily bent down, removed another drawer and placed it on top of the glass counter. "I know how you hate to tie it up, but I think the dark green would look wonderful with your ebony hair."

Feeling an odd flutter in her chest, her mind oblivious to whatever it was Emily had just said, Sophie placed her hand on the counter and inhaled deeply through her nose.

"Why … why would your mother think that?"

Emily glanced back over her shoulder and then leant forward. "Mother said it's the least he can do. She's spent the last six years moaning and complaining about him, and there she was yesterday morning, a smile spread right across her face, waving her handkerchief at him as his carriage rattled by."

A hard lump formed in Sophie's throat. "The marquess has come home?"

"Yes." Emily beamed. "Isn't it wonderful? Lord Danesfield has returned to Westlands."

"Wonderful," Sophie repeated, fear and loathing hiding within that one feigned word.

Emily gave a teasing wink. "He'll probably call on you today, what with you being his closest neighbour. Course, he'll be expecting your brother to be home."

Sophie's stomach twisted into gut-wrenching knots as she recalled her last encounter with Sebastian Ashcroft. The image conjured was so real she smoothed her hand down the front of her dress, expecting to feel the evidence of the dumpy fourteen-year-old girl.

"Just make sure there's someone with you," Emily said as her gaze drifted over Sophie's hair. "You know what the gossips say about him, although I don't believe it myself."

Sophie smiled and nodded in acquiesce; a bid to maintain her fragile composure. Her heart thumped violently in protest, desperate to tell the world that he was everything people imagined him to be: a coward, a rake, and a debauched fool.

"He's here. He's here. I knew he would come." Mrs. Potts rushed to the window. She turned to Emily. "Don't just stand there. Make yourself presentable, girl."

Emily skittered over to the window. "Mother's right," she

said as her eyes grew wide. "The marquess is here, and he is heading toward our shop."

The world suddenly tipped off its axis. Sophie gripped the counter to steady her balance. Little lights flashed before her eyes and the room melted into a hazy mist.

Emily rushed over to her. "The marquess is here," she said, her mother's excitement obviously contagious.

Sophie thought to put her handkerchief to her mouth lest she caught it, but there was no danger of that. Excitement was definitely not what she felt.

She gripped Emily's hands, the blood rushing from her face and pooling at her feet as though expecting an army of heathens to burst through the door.

"I don't want to see him," Sophie cried. "You must hide me, Emily." Fearing she sounded like a raving lunatic and in a bid to infuse an element of logic to her plea, she added, "I don't want him to ask about my brother. I don't want him to know I am on my own. At least, not yet."

Emily gave her a knowing look. "Well, there's no sense in taking chances," she said. "Quick, you can hide behind here." She directed Sophie to the concealed dressing room, pulled back the red curtain and ushered her inside. "Wait in here until I come and get you. Mother is too busy flapping to notice."

Emily closed the curtain, leaving her alone in the shrouded space.

The sound of scraping wood and the tinkling of a bell preceded the dull thud of booted footsteps.

"Good day, my lord," Mrs. Potts chirped. "May I say what a pleasure it is to have you home at last?"

"Good day to you, Mrs. Potts. It is certainly a pleasure to be back."

Sophie closed her eyes tight and placed her palm over her stomach to stop her traitorous body responding to the warmth of his tone, to the slow, purposeful drawl.

You hate him, she cried silently, chastising her fickle heart.

"Indeed, I am in desperate need of new gloves," he continued, no doubt much to Mrs. Potts' delight. "And I can see you have an excellent selection."

In the small confines of her curtained prison, Sophie did not hear the rest of the conversation. Her mind drifted back to the study, to the young girl hiding behind the drapes desperate to hear more from the handsome buck.

"I will speak to Sophie," her brother James had said. "Every time I turn around she is nipping at your heels like an annoying little dog."

He spoke then, and she remembered her tummy flipping somersaults. "That's what country girls do, James. They are tedious and tiresome and will not rest until you die of boredom. I can picture your sister married to a vicar, listening to him drone on about the righteous and eating supper at six. She will sit with her hands in her lap and only speak when spoken to."

James chuckled. "What you desire is someone more *seasoned*."

"Precisely. Did I tell you about the lady I met in London recently? She had the sweetest mouth …"

Sebastian Ashcroft broke her heart that day.

And the irony of her current situation was not lost on her.

With a deep breath, she opened her eyes and glanced at her reflection in the mirror.

Her long black curls were tied loosely at her nape as opposed to the ridiculous knots she'd worn as a girl. Her slender, shapely figure no longer resembled an over-sized dumpling. No one thought her weak and insipid; the whole village knew her to be strong and fiercely independent. The silly little girl had grown into a woman, and she did not need to hide behind curtains anymore.

With renewed confidence, she straightened her back, lifted her chin and threw back the velvet curtain. "The bonnet is divine, Emily," she said, striding out of the dressing room. "I shall call and collect it tomorrow." As she approached the door, she could feel the heat of his gaze, and he rushed forward to hold it open. She refused to look at him directly but decided to be civil. "Good day, Mrs. Potts. Good day, my lord," she said, resisting the temptation to run all the way home.

CHAPTER 3

*S*ophie sat behind the large mahogany desk, staring at the crumpled pieces of paper scattered over its surface.

Her brother, James, should have been home over a week ago. Despite writing numerous letters to his forwarding address, she had not received a reply.

She thought of writing to a great-aunt, but the lady never ventured as far as London. Then she wondered if James had met up with friends, but she didn't know where to send her missive. They had a cousin in Kensington; though he enjoyed gloating over other people's misfortunes and would turn a simple misunderstanding into something far worse.

Then there was Sebastian Ashcroft, the Marquess of Danesfield, known simply as Dane to his male friends.

She would rather walk the plank and dive into shark-infested waters than ask for his help. She would rather stand naked in a field dodging a shower of barbed arrows. She would—

A loud rap on the door broke her reverie.

"There is a gentleman to see you, miss," Rowlands said, struggling to hide his surprise. He offered the salver, the pristine calling card in the centre proof he spoke the truth.

A visitor?

Panic flared.

The marquess had called.

Her heart fluttered up to her throat forcing her to gulp as her hands shook and her mind tried to rouse a coherent thought.

What on earth was wrong with her? Why wouldn't he want to visit an old friend? She did not have to invite him to dinner or partake in a lengthy conversation. Struggling to control the warm feeling blossoming in her chest, Sophie stood abruptly and snatched the card from the tray, expecting to see Dane's pompous script.

She stared at the crisp white card. "Who is the Comte de Dampierre?"

"I have no notion, miss," Rowlands replied, his expression somewhat vacant. "The gentleman mentioned an acquaintance with his lordship."

Sophie's hand flew to her chest. "He is acquainted with the Marquess of Danesfield?"

A deep furrow appeared between Rowlands' brows. "I was referring to your brother, miss, to Lord Beaufort."

Her face flushed. Of course, he meant her brother. Since Dane's return her brain had turned into a wobbly pile of mush.

"Very well, you may show him in," she said, trying to hide her embarrassment. Perhaps the gentleman had come to offer an explanation for her brother's absence.

Sophie could not recall ever meeting a comte before though she must have done. When her parents were alive, they threw many house parties with all sorts of interesting and flamboyant guests.

Then a sudden sense of foreboding gripped her.

She could think of only one reason why an acquaintance would take the trouble to travel such a long way. The grave thought was too bleak to contemplate.

Rowlands opened the door and stepped forward. "The Comte de Dampierre," he announced.

Sophie could hear the slow, methodical thud from his heeled

boots echoing along the hall like a death knell. When he entered the room, he kept his eyes fixed firmly ahead before coming to an abrupt halt a few steps away from the desk.

The gentleman was a walking monument to foppish fashion. The lapels of his green tailcoat were trimmed with black velvet, his cravat tied in a fussy, complicated style. The collars of his shirt finished just above his chin, creating a contradicting impression: one of flamboyancy yet utter rigidness.

The comte gave a dandified wave while his other hand gripped the silver top of a black walking cane. "Miss Beaufort. It is a pleasure to meet you, finally."

His English was impeccable. And while there was a hint of a soft French burr, his tone lacked the warmth his words implied.

Fighting the urge to cower under the desk, Sophie walked around to greet him. He took her hand and raised it to his lips. His small pointed beard brushed over her skin, sending a cold chill through her body. As he straightened, his gaze roamed over her loosely tied hair, and one corner of his mouth curved up in amusement.

Gently retrieving her hand from his grasp, Sophie gestured to the small seating area in front of the fireplace. "Would you care to sit? Rowlands will arrange for tea to be brought in."

Rowlands bowed gracefully and walked out into the hall, taking care to leave the door wide open.

The comte's assessing gaze swept the room before drifting over her body as though she wore the flimsiest of gowns and not the plain muslin day dress. "Your brother, he has told me much of your beauty. But I fear he has been modest in his appraisal."

Were all Frenchmen so bold?

"You are too kind." She feigned a smile as she took a seat. "I must say I am relieved to have some news of my brother. I was beginning to feel a little apprehensive."

He sat down and continued to stare at her, running his fingers over his bearded chin, sculpting it into a point. His eyes were dark, almost black, and she felt them bore right into her soul.

"Am I to understand that you have not heard from your brother?" he said with a frown. "That he has not corresponded?"

Sophie shook her head. "No. I've not heard or received anything. I assumed you had brought news of him."

The comte's aquiline nose twitched, and he ran his fingers over his chin once again. "Please forgive me for being the bearer of such news. But I fear the city does not suit him. A gentleman with such weaknesses would be better served in the country, away from all temptations."

"Temptations!" she cried, somewhat bewildered. Weak was the last word she would use to describe her brother. James was so honest, so reliable, so dependable.

"Do not worry your pretty head. He has made his affairs known to me, and I will assist him where possible."

"I do not wish to sound ungrateful, but it is difficult for me to believe that my brother could be in some sort of trouble."

He raised a brow and gave a look to suggest she was rather naive. "Men seldom confide in those they feel duty-bound to protect. And I do not wish to cause you any further distress. However, your brother he has … how shall I say … exhausted his funds."

She felt a sharp pain in her chest. James had promised her he wouldn't sell the necklace. He promised her he would only obtain a valuation and then return it to the bank.

The comte opened his mouth to speak but paused when Mrs. Hudson entered with the tea tray and remained silent until she had left the room.

"There is a gentleman who is interested in purchasing a certain family heirloom," he continued, "which would, of course, greatly ease your brother's burden. I would be happy to assist in such a task." The corners of his mouth curled upwards into a contrived smile. Deciding to press his case he sat forward, resting both hands on his cane to support his weight. "You may place your trust in me. You may be certain your necklace will be perfectly safe in my hands."

Sophie had no idea how this man knew of her brother or the necklace, but instinct told her he was not a man to be trusted.

"I fear you're mistaken if you believe I am in possession of such an item. I'm sure my brother explained our ... situation."

Like Lucifer rising from a fiery grave, the comte shot up. His eyes were piercing, the planes of his face as hard and as rigid as stone. "Do not play games with me," he cried, raising his cane and thrusting it in Sophie's direction.

Feeling a frisson of fear shooting through her, she should have screamed. But she didn't.

This was exactly the sort of situation a woman of independence could expect to find herself embroiled in. What use would she be to anyone if at the first sign of trouble she turned into a quivering wreck? She was the mistress of the house and would stand strong, a figure of authority, of superiority. Suppressing all doubts, she rose abruptly from the chair to face him.

After all, what could he do?

Murder her in her own home?

"I am not the one playing games." She lifted her chin. "If you know my brother, as you claim, then you must be aware the necklace is in London. But rest assured, even if I had it in my possession, I would not hand it over to a man who professes his loyalty while trying to terrify me with his stick."

The comte glared at her, and the room felt decidedly chillier. Then the corners of his mouth twitched, and he laughed. Taking a step back, he grasped the engraved handle of his cane and with one swift movement drew the sword.

Sophie heard the slicing sound, saw the glint of the blade.

Placing the sharp tip on her shoulder, he let it fall slowly, tracing a line over the front of her dress, over the curve of her breasts and the flare of her hips.

Frozen to the spot, Sophie sucked in her breath as her cheeks burned.

He lowered the sword and with his free hand grabbed her chin, the pad of his thumb following the outline of her lips. "I do believe you may turn out to be much more of a prize than some ancient necklace. There is nothing I enjoy more than a fighting spirit."

Tiny drops of saliva hit her cheek, and she suppressed the urge to flee the room and scrub her skin until it bled. Never in her worst nightmares had she expected to deal with such a shameless rogue. This gentleman made the Marquess of Danesfield look positively saintly.

The comte paused for a moment, then took a deep breath and stepped away. "But I am a fair man. So I will make it easy for you," he continued in a less threatening manner. "Your brother no longer has my necklace. Of this, I am certain."

Sophie swallowed a gasp.

His necklace? What had her brother done?

"We were to make an exchange. A deal of sorts. The necklace for, well, for something I value greatly. Now, he has my treasure and has simply disappeared. I do not take kindly to betrayal, and so seek some form of recompense."

"Recompense?" Sophie tried to keep calm. "But I cannot help you."

"Oh, but you can." He raised his sword to circle her breasts once more.

Sophie shivered, then straightened her back in protest.

He smiled at her reaction. "I am certain you hold the key to a host of hidden treasures. And I am most reluctant to leave without so much as a glimpse. But I am, after all, a gentleman and so will give you time to make the necessary arrangements." With a sigh of resignation, he replaced the sword back in its sheath.

Sophie swallowed deeply to dislodge the lump in her throat. "I have nothing to offer in recompense."

There was a small flicker of excitement in his black eyes. "Ah, but you do, Miss Beaufort. It is simple. You will find the necklace and bring it to me. I have business on the Continent and my ship sails eight days hence. You will come to me and hand

17

over the necklace. Or I shall be forced to take you with me on what I am sure will be a most enlightening journey."

Sophie could hardly believe her ears. Surely this must be some ridiculous dream and any moment she would wake up in a cold sweat, grateful it was all over.

The comte took a few steps closer and the smell of stale tobacco filled her nostrils. He raised his hand, and she flinched as he took hold of her chin, tilting her head from side to side as though looking for a sign of imperfection.

"Exquisite!" He released her and stepped back. "I anticipate our next meeting will be far more … pleasurable. I shall leave you, madame, to consider your options." The comte strode over to the desk, straightened one of the crumpled pieces of paper, dipped the nib of the pen in the inkwell and scratched away. He turned to Sophie and gestured towards the scrawled note. "Here are my directions. We shall meet at midnight." He took a few steps towards her as his coal-black eyes explored her body. "I am somewhat shy, you understand, and prefer to examine my goods away from prying eyes."

"You forget yourself." Sophie tried to muster an ounce of courage. "My family will have something to say on the matter."

Rather than appear offended, he looked amused. "Ah, but you forget, Miss Beaufort. You have no family. But never fear. I shall take great pleasure in rectifying your position personally."

Without uttering another word, he bowed gracefully, turned on his heels and marched towards the door. He came to an abrupt halt and swung around to face her, his unforgiving gaze searching her face. "Do not make me come back for you," he said in a tone as lethal as his sword. "You would not like the outcome."

Sophie wrapped her arms around her stomach, as though reeling from a succession of brutal punches, and listened to the echo of his boots along the hall. Only when she heard his carriage rattle down the drive was she able to breathe a little easier.

A whimper escaped from her lips when she imagined the comte returning. His threats made her more aware of her vulnerability. But she could not think about that now. Perhaps the comte had no intention of carrying her off on a sordid journey. However, his eyes—cold black pools of nothingness—suggested otherwise.

How on earth had James ended up in such a mess?

She was grateful for one thing. If James had taken an item belonging to the comte, at least he'd had the sense to disappear.

All she needed to do now was find out where.

There was a far more pressing problem to consider.

What had happened to her mother's necklace?

Pacing the room, Sophie tried to imagine what she would do if faced with her brother's predicament. It proved to be a fruitless task for he had never in his life done anything she'd suggested. He always did the opposite.

Then inspiration struck.

Sophie pulled on the cord and waited for Rowlands to enter.

"Rowlands, I wonder if you can help me." The butler simply bowed in response. "I know Mrs. Hudson likes to keep abreast of all the comings and goings in the village, and I wondered what news she has regarding the return of the Marquess of Danesfield."

"By news, I suspect you mean gossip, miss," Rowlands said respectfully.

"Gossip, news, it is all the same to me," Sophie replied with an impatient wave of the hand.

"Forgive me. I must disagree, miss. The news is that the marquess returned home to Westlands three days ago. It is a fact. The gossip, which supposedly came from one of his lordship's staff, is that he has spent the last few weeks in London enjoying its delights before returning home for spiritual recuperation."

"He has come home to revive his spirits?"

"I cannot say, miss, as I do not believe gossip."

"No, of course. Thank you, Rowlands. That will be all."

Sophie walked over to the window, folded her arms across her chest and looked out over the manicured lawns.

So, if one believed the gossip, Dane had spent time in London before returning home so suddenly. It could not be a coincidence, and she knew James would trust the marquess with his life. Perhaps James had given him the necklace, knowing he was coming home.

The comte's evil grin flashed before her eyes, and she felt nauseous at the thought he may return.

She would have to find a way of searching Dane's house without arousing his suspicion—without having to partake in a conversation. Without looking into those wicked brown eyes she always found so unnerving.

CHAPTER 4

*S*ebastian had taken shelter in the garden temple: a Grecian-style building at the end of the lawn, watching the rain as it poured in torrents, whipping and splashing off the stone steps.

The weather in England always amazed him. Minutes earlier, he had been basking in the sunshine, and now he could barely see the grass in front of him.

Indeed, the impulsiveness of it all made his senses jolt with excitement. The feeling reminded him of his wild escapades in France.

It took him a moment to hear the pounding of the horse's hooves as it cantered up the drive, mistaking the sound for the faint grumble of thunder. He struggled to see through the heavy downpour and assumed the rider had misjudged the weather and simply sought refuge from the storm.

When he narrowed his gaze, he could just make out the figure of a woman slumped forward, her arms draped loosely around the horse's neck as it charged towards the front portico.

Instinctively, he vaulted the steps in one swift movement and ran across the sodden lawn, ignoring the squelching sound underfoot as he tried to maintain his balance.

He almost collided with the chestnut mare in his attempt to reach the woman before she tumbled from her horse. She clung to its neck, her long black hair hanging loose, obscuring her face. She made no protest when he placed a hand on her shoulder, the other on her back, and eased her down into his arms.

Dripping wet tendrils of hair stuck to her face. Her lips were a pale shade of blue. He glanced at the fine muslin dress plastered to her body and wondered why the hell she was out riding in such flimsy attire. Bellowing for the servants, he held her more firmly as he carried her up the stone steps, suppressing his frustration at the state of his new boots.

When the butler failed to answer, he kicked the solid wooden door as hard as he could and eventually heard the slow clip of shoes on the tiled floor.

As Dumont opened the door, Sebastian barged past him into the hall, almost knocking down Mrs. Bernard, who'd heard the commotion and come running.

"Good gracious, my lord. What have you done to her?"

Sebastian groaned inwardly. What was the woman thinking? That spending six years abroad had turned him into a heathen. That insisting on eating his breakfast in bed meant he was a cold-hearted debaucher.

"We've been frolicking about in the river, and I thought it would be rather entertaining to bring her back here," he replied with some sarcasm.

All the life drained from Mrs. Bernard's face until it was as white as the hair at her temples.

Sebastian sighed. "I'm joking. I merely found her on the steps."

Mrs. Bernard placed her hands on her hips. "Well, what to you intend to do with her?" Her displeasure at such improper conduct was evident in her tone.

"If I knew that, I would not be standing at the door in a pool of water."

Sebastian tapped his toe in the puddle to reinforce his point.

Mrs. Bernard's head moved swiftly between the puddle and the woman in his arms, and he could not decide which one she found more distressing.

"Are you bringing her in, my lord?"

"If I do not put her down quickly, I'm certain we'll both end up in bed."

Mrs. Bernard made the sign of the cross and muttered something about needing help from the Lord.

"With a fever!" he said. "We will both be in bed with a fever. I am cold and wet, and my back feels as though it is no longer attached to my body."

Sebastian glanced down at the limp woman in his arms, at the sodden dress that clung to her like a second skin.

He had always preferred a curvaceous figure. Not that this woman was plump, on the contrary, he had felt her narrow waist when helping her down from her horse. She had the sort of figure artists dreamed of painting: soft and round in all the right places, and he had a sudden desire to brush away the tangles of hair from her face.

With an open mouth, Mrs. Bernard continued to stare at him.

"What would you have me do?" he continued. "Leave her to die on the steps?" He knew he sounded overly dramatic, but it had the desired effect.

Finally, Mrs. Bernard turned to Amy, the housemaid who'd been hovering in the background waiting for instruction. "I'll need blankets. In the drawing room. No. In the library. And some tea. Ask Tom to light the fire."

He carried his mystery maiden through to the library and waited while Tom moved the chaise nearer to the fire. Amy covered it with a blanket, and he lowered her gently down.

Mrs. Bernard's gaze drifted over him, her white-flecked eyebrows meeting in the middle. "You need to get out of those clothes, my lord, or you'll catch your death."

"Yes, in a moment." He stared at the woman as water

dripped onto the Persian rug, wishing one of them would move her damn hair.

As though the Lord had heard his prayers, Mrs. Bernard knelt down and lifted the wet tendrils from the woman's face, smoothing every piece of hair away until left with nothing but pale, porcelain skin. Then she placed the back of her hand on the woman's forehead and peered beneath her closed eyelids.

"Well?" he asked with a shrug, not bothering to hide his impatience.

"Oh, there's no damage done. Nothing that a cup of tea and a good night's sleep won't cure."

"I didn't mean that. Who is she?"

Mrs. Bernard stood and called Amy and Tom over to the chaise. They all gathered around to study the woman's face.

Amy spoke first. "Well, I can't be sure. Her dress is all ruined and with her eyes closed it's hard to tell, but it looks like Miss Beaufort to me."

Mrs. Bernard squinted. "You know, Amy, I think you might be right."

Sebastian considered the lady lying on his chaise. Her cheekbones were delicate, her dress clung to long shapely legs, and the beautiful curve of her—he shook his head. "You're obviously mistaken. Miss Beaufort is just a girl."

They all turned and looked at him as if he was completely mad.

"No, she must be what … one and twenty now, my lord." Mrs. Bernard looked up at the ceiling as though she expected to find the answer there.

Good God, had he been away that long? He glanced down at the lady in question. What the hell was she doing riding about the countryside half dressed?

Mrs. Bernard, Amy, and Tom were all staring at him, eyes agog while waiting for his response.

"You must remember Miss Beaufort, my lord," Mrs. Bernard

said in a tone that suggested he had been involved in a terrible accident and had lost all cognitive abilities.

"Of course, I remember her. She's just grown somewhat since we last met."

Now that he thought of it, she appeared vastly different from the girl he remembered.

Sophie Beaufort had been the most irritating child imaginable. She had an annoying habit of popping up at the most inopportune moments. At one particular party, he was in a secluded area of Beaufort's garden, about to indulge in a passionate clinch with Melinda Albright when they heard a cough coming from the bushes. The sound brought the lady to her senses. His lasting impression was an image of Miss Albright dashing across the lawn, followed by a plump girl wearing a ridiculously frilly dress.

Once again, his gaze fell to the lady stretched out on his chaise, to the raven-black hair cascading over her shoulders, to the swell of full breasts as her chest rose with each deep breath.

Mrs. Bernard interrupted his reverie. "We need to get her out of those wet clothes, my lord."

For once, his housekeeper's thoughts echoed his own.

In a desperate attempt to focus on anything other than the removal of Miss Beaufort's clothing, he said, "Give me a moment to change and I'll ride over to Brampton Hall and collect dry clothes."

The figure on the chaise murmured. Her eyes fluttered briefly before closing again.

"But she can't stay here, my lord, not while you're in residence," Mrs. Bernard whispered.

"I have heard James Beaufort is away," he said, and they acknowledged him with a collective nod. Perhaps when Miss Beaufort woke, she could tell him why her brother found it necessary to give him a priceless family heirloom. "There must be someone staying with her, a chaperone or someone in charge. I'll simply bring them here."

They all turned and stared at him. Amy put her hand over her mouth to suppress a giggle.

Sebastian threw his hands up. "And pray tell me what is so amusing?"

"Begging your pardon, my lord," Amy said, offering a curtsy, "but it's just the thought of someone trying to take charge of Miss Beaufort. Everyone knows she takes care of things when his lordship's away."

Takes care of things? What was Beaufort thinking, leaving her alone while he gallivanted about town?

"Well, in that case, no one need know she's here. It's more than likely she'll be fit to return home after dinner and in the meantime, I shall have her maid brought over."

Mrs. Bernard sighed. "Well, I suppose a few hours can't hurt." She turned to Amy and Tom and wagged a plump finger. "And that means no loose talking down in the village. If I hear so much as a whisper, I'll know where to come."

CHAPTER 5

*S*ophie raised her head off the pillow and peered into the darkness. Other than a growl from her stomach, she could only hear a strange snorting coming from her maid as she slept in the chair.

Thank God.

After lying awake for hours waiting for everyone to go to bed, her patience had all but up and left.

It was not easy feigning an illness in the hope of gaining unrestricted access to Dane's house. Thankfully, the rainstorm had provided the perfect excuse. Even so, she really did feel cold to her bones, and her nerves were in tatters after the comte's departure, which all added credence to her distressed state.

The memory of Dane holding her tightly in his arms flashed into her mind, the blood rushing to her cheeks when she recalled feeling a flicker of desire. Damn him. Scoundrels had a way of rousing unwanted feelings. Luckily, she'd had her eyes closed, making them much easier to suppress.

Peeling back the coverlet, Sophie eased herself out of the bed. Taking the chamber candlestick from the side table, she edged her way past her snoring servant and lit the wick on the fire burning low in the grate.

She tiptoed over to the armoire in search of her clothes but found it empty. It was too dark to go rummaging around for them now, and she didn't want to wake the whole household. Besides, should she be discovered wandering about in her night-dress, she could say she'd woken up dazed and disoriented from her illness. And in her bare feet, she had less chance of anyone hearing her footsteps.

Sophie turned the knob and opened the chamber door, glancing over her shoulder to ensure her maid still slept, before slipping out into the corridor and down the stairs.

After numerous attempts to locate Dane's study and concealing a groan when she stubbed her toe, Sophie's hand settled on another door in the hope she had found the right room at last.

Taking a deep breath to calm her racing heart, she eased the door away from the jamb. The candle flickered as she entered and she sheltered it with her hand before closing the door softly.

Breathing a sigh of relief—for she had accomplished the most difficult part of her task—she stared through the muted light to the large, imposing desk sitting squarely in front of the window.

She moved closer, her footsteps light and slow, placed the candle on the desk and flicked through the neat stack of papers in the hope there might be a letter from her brother.

There was nothing.

Such a solid sturdy desk must hold a whole host of secrets. Where better to hide a letter or a necklace?

With that thought in mind, she moved around to the drawers, feeling a sudden rush of excitement as she trailed her fingers over the hard mahogany planes. The thrill of stepping into dangerous territory caused a nervous flutter in her stomach, and her hand shook as she touched the cool, metal handle.

In the corner of her eye, she glimpsed a shadow but had no time to react as a large hand closed firmly over her mouth.

"Why, Miss Beaufort, I had no idea you were such an early riser," the Marquess of Danesfield whispered, his tone rich and languid. Sophie struggled to break free from his grasp, and he pulled her back against his hard chest. He lowered his head, his cheek brushing against her hair. "Now, I am going to release you, and then you will tell me what the hell you are doing in my desk."

Sophie suddenly became aware of the state of her undress as the heat from his body penetrated the thin fabric, caressing and warming her skin until it burned.

When he released her, it took her a moment to remember how to breathe. But if he was expecting her to cower in fear, to offer an apology or explanation for her conduct, then he was sorely mistaken. Instead, she thrust her elbow into his ribs with all the force she could muster.

She heard him groan, and she swung around to face him. He was hunched over, one hand cradling his chest the other braced against the wall for support. Sophie took a few steps back, to place some distance between them.

"How dare you manhandle me in such a manner," she cried, brushing her hand down the front of her nightgown.

"Manhandle you! I fear I am the one with a cracked rib."

He winced as he straightened and she braced herself for the verbal onslaught. But he just stood there, staring, the corners of his mouth twitching in amusement.

He had altered somewhat during the last six years.

He seemed taller, his shoulders stronger, more powerful. His hair was far too long, she decided, as she watched him push back an ebony lock from his brow. However, his character still posed the same contradiction: extreme arrogance infused with a playful, boyish charm. Those wicked brown eyes stared back at her, and she noticed the faint shadows beneath.

The life of a rakehell had taken its toll.

The thought caused a series of lascivious images to flood her senses. Images that had no place in the mind of an innocent woman and her gaze fell to the opening of his shirt, to the dusting of dark hair. She swallowed deeply and bit down on her bottom lip by way of a distraction.

A subtle smile played on his lips. He dragged the chair from the desk and dropped into it with casual grace. His gaze settled on her face before drifting down over the front of her nightgown, lingering in all places he should not dare to look.

"Were you in such a hurry to see me that you neglected to dress?" He stretched his legs out in front of him and crossed his arms behind his head. "Or do you consider this appropriate for the occasion?"

"Do not be ridiculous," Sophie replied, trying to sound annoyed rather than embarrassed for she did not want him to think her prudish. "You know very well why I'm dressed like this. Someone has stolen my clothes."

"How utterly inconvenient," he replied. "However, it appears the only person intent on stealing is you, Miss Beaufort."

Now she truly was angry.

"How dare you. I have never stolen a thing in my life." She raised her chin in defiance. "And I certainly have no intention of doing so now."

Well, it was not a lie. One could not steal something that already belonged to them.

He sat up and folded his arms across his chest. "No, you just sneak around in the middle of the night in a state of undress, for what, Miss Beaufort? Who or what were you hoping to find?"

His slow, seductive voice caressed her skin like a gentle breeze. She cursed inwardly. It didn't matter what she said. Being so skilled in the art of flirtation, he could twist her words, was capable of stirring strong emotion.

Taking a deep breath, Sophie placed her hands on her hips. "Let us stop these childish games. I believe you have something I need. Something upon which my life depends."

Dane gave a lascivious grin as he stood and took a step towards her. "I'm not used to a lady being so forward. But I'm more than happy to give you everything you need, and more."

Sophie stared at him, shocked at such barefaced arrogance and in a moment of frustration cried, "You … you debauched fool."

Dane straightened and placed his hand over his heart. "Now I am offended. I have it on good authority that I'm one of the most intelligent men in all of England."

He stood there like a shrine to conceit and Sophie knew he was right about one thing—he was no fool. Why did he make her feel like a helpless animal ensnared in a trap? Why did she feel so intimidated, so useless, so pathetic?

If she could not deal with Dane, how on earth would she deal with the Comte de Dampierre?

Dane probably expected her to run back to her room in fear of her virtue or crumble into a weeping wreck. Well, if nothing else, she would wipe the smug grin off his face.

Gathering every ounce of courage she possessed, she stepped closer until she felt the warmth radiating from his body. He looked surprised when she stretched out her hands and placed them gently on his shirt, letting her palms glide over the hard planes.

His muscles flexed beneath her touch. It took every ounce of self-control she possessed to stop her fingers from exploring, to curb the sweet fire heating the blood in her veins.

She would take great pleasure in putting this rogue in his place.

"Perhaps it was wrong of me to judge you so harshly," she said softly, dismissing all fears and doubts. She stood on her tiptoes and whispered in his ear. "I'm sure you are regarded as highly intelligent by your peers." When she moved her hands up over his shoulders, she heard him suck in his breath, heard his groan of appreciation. "But I don't think half the whores in

31

London count," she yelled as she pushed him back into the chair with all the force she could muster.

Sophie swung around, crossed the study and was at the door when he grabbed her arm and brought her back around to face him. Like Lucifer, he glared at her, his dark eyes penetrating her soul. Anyone else would have expired on the spot. But Sophie was swimming in the sea of success, and he was drowning in turbulent waves of emotion.

"I see some things never change," he growled. "You are just as bloody irritating."

She shrugged her arm out of his grasp. "How strange. It did not seem to bother you a moment ago when you were panting like a dog."

He jerked his head back as though he'd been stung. But when he spoke, his words were calm, measured and dripping with sarcasm. "What an eloquent turn of phrase. Do all the ladies of your acquaintance share your unconventional habits?" His gaze roamed over her hair, over the front of her nightgown and Sophie crossed her arms over her chest in defiance.

"Do you always lose control so easily?"

The corners of his mouth twitched. Was he angry or amused? She could not tell. But she could feel the restrained tension emanating from every muscle in his body.

"Do not mistake me for a fool, Miss Beaufort. I have been in control of this situation from the moment you entered my house, from the moment you began prowling around in a state of dishabille to snoop in my desk."

Sophie opened her mouth to protest, but he raised his hand to silence her.

"Let us stop this game," he continued, "and let us examine why you find it necessary to behave like such a hoyden."

Hoyden?

The man had the nerve of the Devil. He'd spent the last six years entertaining his mistresses on the Continent without a thought for his tenants.

He strolled over to the chair next to the fireplace, sat down and tugged on his boot.

"What on earth are you doing?"

"Undressing," he uttered casually. "I know what you've come for. I know what you desire."

CHAPTER 6

*S*ebastian took great pleasure in watching her reaction.

She twiddled her fingers and shuffled from one foot to the other. Her eyes, as blue and as inviting as the Tyrrhenian Sea on a hot summer's day, were wide with uncertainty, her gaze flitting between his boot and his face. He really wished she would stop biting her bottom lip as it caused a tightening in his abdomen he found far too distracting.

Miss Beaufort was an enigma.

She had been correct in her observation although he would never admit it. As soon as she'd put her hands on his chest, his pulse had quickened, his usual steely reserve melting. Remarkably, those ripples of desire still flowed beneath the surface, like the constant course of a stream. Perhaps that was why he felt so annoyed, so irritable, yet highly aroused at the same time.

Placing his hand into his boot, he removed the small silver key and almost chuckled when he heard her sigh with relief.

"One can never be too careful with thieves about," he remarked, thrusting his foot back in his boot.

With purposeful strides, he walked around the desk, unlocked a drawer and retrieved the red velvet pouch. Ignoring her gasp, he placed it on top and removed the necklace.

"It's exquisite." He held it above the candle. The oval rubies appeared more vibrant from the glow of the flame. "I do not believe I have ever seen anything quite so enchanting." It was time to start subtly probing for information, and so he added, "I'm just surprised you want to sell it."

"Is that what James told you? I should have guessed that was his intention."

"Obviously, you do not agree with his decision."

"The necklace has been in our family for generations. My mother refused to part with it," she said softly, rubbing her fingers along her collarbone as though remembering the coolness of the metal on her skin. "And I must admit I feel the same way."

Sebastian swallowed. He had a sudden urge to see it draped around her neck, to see the rich, red stones set against perfect porcelain, to see it cast a warm glow over the curve of her breasts.

Good God!

"I cannot believe James would go against my wishes," she continued. "I cannot believe he has agreed to sell it."

"Do you need the money?" He forced his mind to focus. It was an impertinent question. Under the circumstances, he felt justified asking.

"I'm sure James has already explained. He has some ideas for developing the estate and well, it was something we were going to discuss after the valuation."

"But you do not agree."

"It is not my estate." She put her hands on her hips. "What I fail to understand is why the necklace is in your desk."

Trying to ignore the way the thin fabric clung to her body, he replied, "A question I have wondered myself."

Dropping her hands, she stared at him blankly. "You are not making any sense."

"What would you say if I told you two masked riders followed me from London?" Sebastian placed the necklace gently onto the velvet cloth. "Their sole intention was not to relieve me of my purse, but to give me a necklace worth a king's ransom."

"Masked riders?" she repeated as tiny furrows appeared on her brow. "Who were they? How did they come to have the necklace?"

"Your brother was the principal rider. He had gone to a great deal of trouble to hide his identity, which I believe was not entirely for my benefit."

Sebastian studied her reaction carefully.

She should have been shocked. A whole host of questions should have tumbled from her lips. However, they did not. It obviously came as no surprise to her, meaning she knew exactly why James found it necessary to wear a disguise. After having a lengthy discussion with her housekeeper, he had an idea, too.

"Did James mention me when he gave you the necklace?"

"Only that he wishes me to act as your guardian in his absence and keep the necklace safe." It was not a lie, just a slight manipulation of the truth. Someone needed to take her in hand.

She thrust her chin in the air. "I do not need anyone to take care of me."

"No? Do you think your brother would approve of you being alone here with me, wearing nothing but a nightdress?"

"Well, he is not here," she said, a trace of resentment evident in her tone. "You mentioned another man, another rider. Do you know who he was?"

Although she tried to remain expressionless, he could almost hear the little wheels whirring in her head. She wanted information. But why?

"This is where it gets even more intriguing," he said, pausing briefly for dramatic effect. "The other rider was a woman."

"A woman!" she exclaimed unable to hide her shocked expression.

Well, that answered his next question. James must have met the woman in London, and recently. Their verbal exchange suggested a level of intimacy, yet James had made the mistake of underestimating her character—a feeling currently plaguing Sebastian.

"Do ... do you know who she was?"

"Thankfully, no," he chuckled, remembering the way she had ridden off in a tantrum. "For some reason, I seem to have developed an ability for attracting hotheads." Indeed, between Miss Beaufort and Mrs. Bernard he did not know if he was coming or going.

"And what is that supposed to mean?" Sophie put her hands on her hips again, causing the thin fabric to stretch across her stomach.

"Please," Sebastian said through gritted teeth. "If you value your virtue, do not do that again."

For some obscure reason, he was in a state of semi-arousal and she was certainly not helping matters.

She glanced down and then dropped her hands, her cheeks flushing a pretty shade of pink.

In a desperate bid to change the subject and dampen his desire, Sebastian decided it was time she gave him some answers. "So, now I have been kind enough to tell you all I know regarding your brother and the necklace, I feel it only fitting that you show me the same courtesy."

"I do not know what you mean."

Sebastian sighed. "Very well, let me put it plainly. How did you know I had the necklace? Why would you risk your reputation by coming here, and what does the French comte have to do with it all?"

She appeared astounded and so Sebastian decided he would make it easy for her. Besides, the sooner he dealt with this, the sooner he could go back to some semblance of normality.

"I shall let you into a little secret," he continued. "Your housekeeper was quite forthcoming on the subject of foreign visitors."

"You spoke to Mrs. Hudson?"

"Of course. I called to collect your nightdress," he said, gesturing to the garment. Although considering the effect it was having on his current disposition, he wished he had let her sleep in wet clothes.

She tilted her head to the side and considered him for a moment, no doubt calculating what he knew and what secrets she was willing to divulge.

"Yesterday, a few hours before I arrived at your door, a gentleman who called himself the Comte de Dampierre came to Brampton Hall," she said in a measured tone, as though making a statement at the monthly assizes. "It appears James is in trouble. Apparently, he made a deal to trade the necklace and has since disappeared. The comte suggested the matter might be concluded if I were able to discover its whereabouts. Hence, the reason I am here."

While he knew she spoke the truth, such a curt and concise recital omitted one vital ingredient: emotion. Such lack of feeling, either in tone or in the relating of events, told him there were parts of the conversation she had neglected to mention.

"Did Dampierre tell you to come here?" he asked. He had spent a considerable amount of time in France and yet had never heard of the Comte de Dampierre.

"No, that was my idea. You're the only person James trusts. But, as the rightful owner of the necklace, I shall relieve you of your burden so you may continue your quest for spiritual recuperation."

Her pretty blue eyes sparkled with amusement. The corners of her mouth curled up into a mischievous grin.

"Spiritual recuperation—is there such a thing?" he asked, a little confused. "If there is, I can assure you my spirit does not need to recuperate."

"Really?" she mocked. "I heard you had lost your vitality and had come home to rediscover it."

Sebastian placed his hands on the desk and leant forward. "There is nothing wrong with my vitality," he answered defensively. "And I am afraid that somewhere along the way you have made a frightful miscalculation. I think you will find your brother is the heir. The necklace belongs to him."

She moved to put her hands on her hips but changed her mind. "Yes, but in choosing to place it in your hands, he obviously meant for you to return it to me."

"I do not believe that to be the case. Your brother obviously doesn't want this Dampierre fellow to have it, and I doubt he would want to place you in any danger. Whilst I agree there is something strange about the whole affair, perhaps he gave it to me knowing how I thrive on intrigue." He gave her a wicked grin. "And believe me when I tell you, Miss Beaufort, intrigue is not the only feeling thrumming through my veins."

At first, she appeared a little flustered. Her eyes shifted around the room, and he could hear her breathing more deeply. He would have given anything to know what she was thinking.

"I'm afraid I must insist, my lord. The necklace must be returned to London as a matter of urgency. It is not a topic for negotiation."

It was the first time she had addressed him with the respect befitting his station, but she had done so by way of a reprimand.

Sebastian walked around the desk, closing the gap between them and perched on the edge. He had a newfound respect for Miss Beaufort. Such fortitude in a man was commendable. For a woman, it was remarkable. However, he'd be damned if he would allow her to do something so foolish. In granting him guardianship of the necklace, it appeared James had inadvertently granted him guardianship of his sister.

"So let me understand your situation," he said, rubbing his chin. "You, an unmarried woman of gentle breeding, insist on riding alone to London carrying an extremely expensive necklace. Once there, I believe you intend to trace your brother or meet with a French comte."

"Yes," she replied with a firm nod.

"And you expect me to hand it over and wave goodbye at the

door." He straightened to his full height and said in a stern voice, "Have you ever been to London, Miss Beaufort?"

"That is of no consequence," she replied, unperturbed. "I am perfectly capable of taking care of myself."

Sebastian snorted. Her argument had no basis for she had probably never ventured more than ten miles from her own front door. "I will not deny that your courage appears to have no bounds, but you could not possibly be aware of what danger lies ahead."

The mere mention of the word *danger* should have been enough to create doubt over such a ludicrous plan, but Miss Beaufort was either deaf or oblivious to the meaning of the word.

"I have a theory, my lord." She straightened and raised her chin. "Those not courageous enough to take risks, will accomplish nothing in life." She gave a little shrug. A coy smile played on her lips. "Sometimes you just have to take a chance."

It appeared there was only one way to put a stop to her ridiculous notion of heroism. "I believe I am about to put your theory to the test."

He did not wait for a response. In a few strides, he covered the distance between them, moved his hand to the small of her back and pulled her to his chest.

"Where is your courage now, Miss Beaufort?" he whispered as his lips met hers.

CHAPTER 7

*S*ebastian knew why he was kissing her.

From the moment she had stood on her toes, pressed her soft body up against him and teased him with her wandering hands, he had struggled to think of anything else.

He expected the kiss to last mere seconds. But this was a woman who defied his expectations. Foolishly, he'd convinced himself the kiss was simply a way of highlighting her naiveté. To demonstrate the dangers an innocent woman might face once alone in the city.

Then a sigh left her lips, and the thought left him.

Relaxing his grip, he let his hand roam over her lower back as his lips moved slowly and smoothly over her sweet mouth. She responded to his touch, pressing herself against him, moulding herself into him. He could feel the swell of her breasts through the fine fabric, could feel the heat radiating from her body.

He continued slowly, curbing his desire, telling himself she would come to her senses and break contact. Then her hand drifted up over his chest, up to caress the back of his neck, her fingers stroking in a slow, seductive rhythm. Her lips parted on another soft sigh, and he could not hold back.

His tongue traced the line of her lips, desperate to taste her, to possess her. She opened for him, her untutored tongue meeting his with a need that matched his own. Their breathing became shallow and rapid, and he let his hands move further down her back, cupping her and drawing her closer to ease his throbbing manhood.

Desire gripped him like a whirlpool, pulling him down, sucking him under.

Good Lord. What had happened to Beaufort's sister while he had been away?

The thought caused a jolt of awareness, jerking him to his senses, as though he'd just stepped on a carpet of nails with his bare feet.

What the hell was he doing?

He should be acting like a respectable guardian, not a scoundrel in need of sexual gratification. He tore his lips away and tried to shake the desire raging through him.

What had started out as a plan to enlighten her had turned into one of the most stimulating experiences of his entire life.

He looked down at the delectable Miss Beaufort. Her cheeks were flushed, her lips slightly swollen. Her dark, silky locks hung wildly over her shoulders, and he fought the urge to lift her into his arms and carry her off to his bed.

Pinching the bridge of his nose, he closed his eyes, telling himself this could not happen again, not with his friend's sister. This was supposed to be about reining in the wayward Miss Beaufort. He needed to put some distance between them. And he knew exactly how to do it.

Sebastian stepped back and folded his arms across his chest. "As the exercise proves, the only thing protecting your reputation is my respect for your family. And, as you are now aware, courage is a useless weapon against a man's voracious appetite."

Miss Beaufort inhaled sharply, her eyes wild with contempt.

"As a woman you will always be weak in that regard," he

continued calmly. Arrogance dripped from every word, yet inside his body still burned for her. "To place yourself at risk accomplishes nothing."

Had it been any other inexperienced woman, he would have expected tears—the uncontrollable sobs of shame and mortification. Unsurprisingly, Miss Beaufort stood frozen to the spot, her tightly clenched fists hanging by her sides. The bright pink glow warming her face reflected anger rather than embarrassment.

She turned away from him, her head moving left and right, searching the room.

Perhaps he was wrong, and she was about to cry. Guilt flared as he knew he'd sounded cold and unfeeling.

Straightening her back and raising her chin, she walked gracefully over to the side table. With a clinking sound, she removed the crystal stopper from a decanter of brandy and poured a measure. In two gulps she drained the glass. He watched her shake visibly as the liquid fire trickled down her throat. She gave a little cough and a short exhale before slamming the glass down on the table.

When she swung around to face him, her countenance appeared much improved, but her eyes looked as though they could turn a man to stone.

"I fear I am inclined to agree with you," she said calmly.

He could hardly believe his ears. Finally, the lady was listening. He could not help but feel smug. A sense of masculine pride enveloped him and patted him on the back.

"You see, I have always believed I had a passionate nature. Indeed, I did not know how passionate until a moment ago when you kindly conducted your little experiment." She strolled around the room, picking up objects: a paperweight, a book of sonnets, a pipe tamper in the form of a naked woman. Examining them, she placed them down again. "I must say I found the experience quite overwhelming."

There was something different about her voice. It had lost all traces of innocence; her tone held a seductive, alluring quality that sung to him. Sebastian straightened as he fought against the memory of their passionate exchange.

"Indeed, I am aware such a passion spills over into all aspects of life," she continued. "If I am to be so easily coerced and dissuaded from my path, then I am not being true to my nature." She looked up to meet his gaze, her sapphire-blue eyes piercing his soul. "But you are correct, my lord. As a woman, I fear I shall attract entirely the wrong sort of attention."

"Precisely, Miss Beaufort," Sebastian said, swallowing deeply. "Which is why—"

"Which is why," she interjected, "I shall strive to find another solution. As the saying goes, to those that will, ways are not wanting."

He coughed into his fist and then said rather smugly, "I'm afraid you are missing the point, Miss Beaufort. I think you will find the saying goes, to *him* that will, ways are not wanting."

She smiled; the wry expression made him feel like a silly child who had missed an obvious piece of information.

"Let me speak plainly," she replied abruptly. "I do not intend to sit around like a simpering miss, eating supper at six and hoping for news from my brother when he could be in need of my help. Believe me when I tell you, I am in just as much danger here as I am in London. Dampierre will call again. So," she continued a little more calmly, "I am going to find my brother with or without your help, with or without the necklace."

Had he been thinking with his rational mind, Sebastian would have considered his words carefully. He would have used his talent for manipulation to overpower her in this verbal battle. However, logic and rationale had forsaken him.

"Not before hell freezes over."

Rather than appear annoyed, Miss Beaufort looked amused. "I think it is you who is missing the point." She stood in front of him, raised her left hand and examined both sides. "I see no wedding band, and I'm certain you are not my father or my brother. You have no authority over me, my lord."

Sebastian had a good mind to take her over his knee and tan her luscious behind.

"Do not try my patience," he barked. "I may be forced to call your bluff." The thought left him feeling slightly aroused and so he quickly changed the subject. "Besides, London is not Marchampton. You cannot go knocking on every door in the hope of finding your brother. You wouldn't know where to start."

She raised a brow. "You'd be surprised, country mice can be very resourceful," she replied, sarcasm evident in her tone. "James obviously left directions. I have the address. I have money. I know I can find the Comte de Dampierre."

What the hell was she trying to prove?

He stared at her, somewhat dumbfounded as he pondered the dilemma. When had she become so obstinate, so spirited and so damnably appealing? She seemed to have the upper hand in this game of wits, but he would be a fool to let her do something so reckless.

"You have left me with no other choice." He sighed, acknowledging defeat. "I shall leave this afternoon and bring that wastrel of a brother of yours to heel." He swallowed deeply as his eyes roamed over her flimsy nightgown, over her swollen lips and mussed hair. "I fear he has an awful lot to answer for."

"Am I to understand that you refuse to give me the necklace?" When he nodded, she said gracefully, "Then I concede. I am confident you will find a reasonable way of explaining us riding out together."

Sebastian snorted. "I intend to travel alone."

"Well, that presents a problem. You see, if you leave without me, I will be obliged to follow."

Bloody hell!

Why would the woman not yield?

"Without the necklace your journey would be a waste of time," he retorted.

"Without information regarding the whereabouts of my brother and Dampierre, so would yours, my lord."

That was not entirely true. Once in London, he could find that information within the hour. "Let us suppose for a moment I agree to your proposal. I cannot allow an unmarried woman to travel in a closed carriage with a man half the village believe to be a dissolute rake. Mrs. Bernard would have a fit of apoplexy."

"Well, I would not want to be responsible for the death of your housekeeper. So, let me make my position clear." She stood before him and looked him straight in the eye. "I do not worry about my reputation for I have no intention of ever marrying. I fear I am far too headstrong to make some quiet country squire a suitable wife." Her eyes perused him from head to toe as though he was some dowdy old dress in a shop window, then she added, "Or any other man for that matter."

"I am sure Marchampton will be relieved to hear it," he scoffed, although a part of him would enjoy the challenge of trying to tame her.

She appeared resolute rather than offended. "You may jest, my lord, but as I am sure you have gathered, I could not play the docile wife and marry for convenience. And I have yet to come across a man interesting enough, a man who excites me enough," she said as her gaze moved to his lips and lingered there for a moment. With a sigh of resignation she added, "So if you are concerned with your own reputation, I suggest you come up with a plan. Either way, I am leaving at noon."

"I could always say I am carting you off to an asylum. The whole village would believe *that*," he replied, somewhat amused by the thought.

She took a step closer and said with a seductive purr, "Oh, I am not mad, my lord. I have what you would call an adventurous spirit, and I am afraid there is no cure. Now, if you have finished being stuffy." She walked around the desk, picked up her candle and used it to light his before walking slowly, yet purposefully, towards the door.

"Where are you going?" he asked, sounding somewhat like a neglected mistress.

She glanced over her shoulder. "To wake my noisy mare of a maid and find my dress. I have things to attend to if I am to return at noon."

Sebastian watched her walk out into the hallway. He did not go after her. What was the point? He could not reason with a woman who appeared to act only on impulse, even if he did find that rather intriguing. Besides, he needed time to think of a solution to the problem without the constant barrage of witty remarks.

He walked over to the table, picked up her brandy glass and turned it over in his hand. Although it was empty, he lifted it to his lips. Something deep within him stirred, some raw and earthy masculine need to conquer, to claim, to have Miss Beaufort completely at his mercy. The more she defied him, the more powerful the urge to control.

An image of her lying beneath him flooded his mind, her hair splayed across his pillow, her hands clutching his shoulders, of her begging him for more. Shaking his head in a bid to erase it, he poured a large measure of brandy and drank it down.

Whatever happened, he could not touch Miss Beaufort again. As the closest friend of her family, it was his responsibility to offer his protection. He gave a weary sigh. Trying to protect the woman would be like trying to fend off a lion using nothing but a piece of string.

He could not take the risk of leaving for London without her, and he could not risk riding with her in such proximity. That part of the problem was easily solved. Miss Beaufort would ride in his carriage, and he would ride Cronus. She would need a maid, of course. Perhaps Amy would oblige.

When they arrived in London, he would take her to the house

in Red Lion Square and lock her in the bedroom while he hunted down her poor excuse for a brother.

Then, he would hand over the damn necklace and the tempting Miss Beaufort before returning home to continue his quest for a peaceful existence.

Simple.

CHAPTER 8

"*D*on't worry, Mary. Just cut it," Sophie said, pushing aside all doubts as she sat at her dressing table.

"But surely there must be some other way, miss," her maid replied, holding a glossy ringlet as if it were the crown jewels and to let go would mean facing the hangman's noose.

Sophie feigned a smile. "It's just hair. It will grow back."

"I still don't see why you need to cut it," Mary said with a sigh.

"It will be far safer to travel about if people think I am a man. And I have never seen a man who has hair to his waist."

Dane was right about one thing. As a woman, she would be vulnerable on her own in London. As a man, she would be free to do as she pleased. His silly experiment had given her the idea.

She was still rather proud of the way she'd handled him. Perhaps her encounter with the comte had given her a renewed confidence. Indeed, everything Dane said or did paled in comparison to Dampierre's threatening manner.

When Dane had pulled back from their kiss and informed her it had been nothing more than a way to prove his point, she knew he was lying. Shockingly, she had felt the evidence of his arousal; she had felt the way his body responded to her and it spurred her on to be bolder.

The fact she had kissed him back proved to be a little worrying. But then she told herself she also had a point to prove. She was not the silly country girl anymore. As a woman, she would do everything in her power to show him he'd been wrong about her. She would have him spinning around in such a tizzy he wouldn't know a bray from a bark.

The sudden snipping of scissors caught her attention.

"Well, there's no going back now, miss," Mary said as the first few tendrils of hair fell to the floor.

Sophie glanced at her maid's reflection in the mirror, observing the deep furrows between her brows. The lines had been a permanent fixture for the last two hours.

"Mary, if you do not stop worrying, those lines will be as deep as trenches. All the mice will come scurrying along thinking it a place to bed down for the night."

Mary stopped snipping and placed her hand on Sophie's shoulder. "It's not the hair, miss. It's just the thought of you out there, all alone."

Sophie covered Mary's hand with her own. "There is no need for concern. I shall be under the protection of Lord Danesfield and you know the marquess is a dear friend of the family," she said, attempting to sound sincere. Perhaps it was best not to mention the fact that she planned to steal her necklace and head off on her own.

"I know, miss. But you'll be all alone with him, and you know what they're saying about him in the village."

"What, that he's a rake and a debaucher?"

"I know it's not my place to say, but there's no trusting a gentleman like that."

"And what sort of gentleman do you believe Lord Danesfield to be?"

"You know," Mary said as her face flushed a deep shade of

crimson, "one with a saucy tongue and a devilish grin. A man whose heart is as hard as his muscles."

Mary certainly had the measure of him.

"Well, it would not do to tempt such a man, so all the more reason for me to cut my hair. Besides, his lordship doesn't think of me in that way. He is simply fulfilling the role of a protective sibling in Lord Beaufort's absence."

"Whatever you say, miss." Mary shrugged her shoulders. "I just hope you know what you're doing."

"Trust me. I am perfectly capable of handling Lord Danesfield," Sophie said, praying she was right.

The ancient cedar tree on Keepers Lane, with its low sweeping branches, offered the perfect cover for a discreet rendezvous. Clad in beige buckskin breeches and a conservatively cut coat, Sophie sat astride Argo, a beast of an animal belonging to her brother.

She had ridden Argo many times over the last few years, and while he looked rather menacing, he was quite easy to handle. She leant forward and gave the horse a reassuring pat, and he responded with a snort.

The thud of horse's hooves pounding the dirt track caused her to look up just as Dane came thundering into view.

He did not look pleased.

He reared up in front of her on a large black stallion, which looked far more menacing than Argo. However, the horse paled into insignificance when compared to the magnificence of its rider.

Dane's greatcoat hung loosely at his sides, revealing muscular thighs that his breeches struggled to restrain. Beneath the midnight-blue tailcoat, he wore a yellow waistcoat which accentuated the hues of his warm brown eyes. His top hat was possibly the tallest she had ever seen and when accompanied by his dark scowl, made him appear rather ominous.

He did not speak, but his hard, assessing gaze darted between her horse and her clothes.

Sophie smiled, as she refused to be intimidated. "Good afternoon, my lord. I see you received my note."

His breathing appeared a little ragged, and when he eventually spoke it was through gritted teeth. "Over the years, I have been shot at, sliced with a blade, and chased from one country to the next. But I have never been angrier than I am at this moment. You should be thankful I am not your brother, else you would be dragged from that horse and thrown over my knee." His eyes shot to her breeches as if contemplating doing just that, but then he shook his head as though he found the image disturbing. He took a deep breath. "Now, you will follow me to Westlands where there is a carriage waiting and—"

"I'm afraid that won't be possible," Sophie interrupted.

Sensing his master's agitation, the black stallion became restless, and Dane brought him firmly to heel.

"As you can see," Sophie continued, waving a gloved hand in the direction of her newly cut hair, held off her shoulders in a loose queue. "I have gone to an incredible amount of trouble to appease your rather overcautious nature. Indeed, poor Mary has spent hours sewing me into these breeches."

He looked down at her breeches and muttered a curse. "My overcautious nature? What the hell are you talking about?" His voice sounded more irritated than angry.

Sophie was more than pleased to enlighten him. "Perhaps you do not recall your little experiment. The one where you attempted to prove how vulnerable a lady can be. The one where you kissed me in order—"

"Enough." He raised a hand to silence her. "I remember, Miss Beaufort. But what's that got to do with this scandalous display?"

By everything holy, Sophie had never heard such hypocritical drivel. Scandalous display, indeed. The man was a rake, a rogue, a degenerate who bought his mistresses baubles while his tenants rotted in squalor. If it were not for the necklace, she would not even be having this conversation.

"At least, I do not shirk my responsibilities," she countered in a tone full of self-righteous indignation.

"At this present moment, Miss Beaufort, you are my responsibility," he bellowed, ignoring the insult. "And I'll be damned before I allow you to ruin your already fragile reputation." He glanced at Argo. "It appears stupidity is in the blood. I am confident your horse will be the death of you before the day is out."

"I am more than capable of handling Argo."

Oh, how she wanted to prove this gentleman wrong.

She was not a dullard, not a meek country chit too scared to step over her own threshold. Nor was she an elegant lady who would rather die than tarnish her precious reputation.

Family was what mattered to her—and love and loyalty. She was passionate and generous of spirit and if that meant being reckless and impulsive, then so be it.

Sophie edged Argo out from under the cover of the tree and onto the well-trodden lane. "Once again you seem to have left me with little choice." She saw the brief look of victory on his face: a grin that was all smug and self-congratulatory, a look quickly replaced with one of doubt and mistrust.

Without another word, without another glance, Sophie took a firm hold of the reins, dug her heels in and was soon galloping down Keepers Lane on her way to London.

Dane would follow, of course, she was sure of it. For some unfathomable reason, he felt duty-bound to protect her. He considered her his responsibility, and he was most definitely taking his role seriously.

Why the sudden change of heart, she wondered?

Why insist upon that which he had spent years avoiding?

Duty and responsibility were not words she had ever associated with the Marquess of Danesfield.

Not until now.

CHAPTER 9

*F*or the first time in his life, Sebastian had seriously underestimated his opponent.

It had taken every ounce of strength and fortitude he possessed not to bolt after her, pull her from the blasted horse and drag her off to a nunnery. To a place where such mischief would be punished with lifelong seclusion, ten hours a day of solid prayer and no supper for a week.

Instead, he simply sat in the middle of the lane, his body rigid, his expression stern, his thoughts confused and chaotic. There was nothing simple about dealing with Miss Beaufort, he thought, his eyes transfixed by the movement of her slender thighs as they gripped and rode the spectacular beast out of view.

He recalled telling her how he'd been in control of everything since the moment he'd carried her over his threshold. She must think him a fool. He had not been in control of a damn thing.

When he rode into the courtyard of Westlands, some ten minutes later, he found Haines in his usual position, perched atop the box of his carriage. His hulking frame filled the seat.

Yet it was remarkable how a man his size was adept at making himself appear unnoticeable.

Sebastian caught his gaze and gave him the look that indicated there had been a change of plan. Haines jerked his head towards the carriage, a small inconspicuous nod, and Sebastian led his horse to the door and tapped on the window.

Amy lowered the window and popped her head out, her face alight with excitement. "Yes, my lord," she said, gripping the window like a pauper would a guinea.

"I am afraid there has been a slight change of plan," Sebastian said, watching her struggle to hide her disappointment. "Miss Beaufort has made her own arrangements ... with the family of a friend, I believe. But I would still like you to travel with Haines as we may join her on the journey. Besides, Miss Beaufort may require your services once we reach town."

Had he been discussing any other lady, he was certain his story would have sounded reasonably plausible, but Amy put her hand over her mouth to suppress a snigger.

"You will be perfectly safe with Haines," Sebastian continued, feeling like a buffoon for the umpteenth time, "but I would ask you to draw the blinds as you pass through the village. You may change your mind and stay here if you wish." He would not force his servants to do something that made them feel uncomfortable.

"No, my lord!" she replied, beaming like a child again. "I'm more than happy to go."

"Very well," Sebastian nodded.

As Sebastian brought his horse round to face Haines, he heard Amy close the window. The carriage rocked as if she'd thrown herself back into the seat and he could have sworn he heard her giggle.

"What do you want me to do, my lord?" Haines said.

Sebastian shook his head and sighed. "It appears Miss Beaufort is a thorn to surpass all others." He lowered his voice. "She has taken it upon herself to ride to London dressed in a tailcoat and breeches. In all our wild adventures, I have never witnessed anything so ludicrous. I doubt there is a man alive willing to tame that one. The woman is an utter menace."

Haines did not answer, and while his face maintained its usual stern expression, his eyes held the smallest spark of amusement.

Sebastian curbed his temper. "We'll proceed as planned. But we can't stop at The Three Crowns, not with her dressed like that. It's far too busy."

Haines lowered his head. "We don't need to stop at all, my lord, other than to change the horses. The maid seems happy enough in the carriage. We've done it before." He shrugged. "It's probably best you and the lady avoid the main roads. Well, if you think you can catch up with her, that is."

Sebastian ignored the last remark as he knew Haines was provoking him. He had wasted time returning to Westlands but was more than capable of making up lost ground. Taking out his pocket watch he noted the time. "Give me a twenty-minute start and then I'll meet you at Rockingham Pool. It's just a few miles to the Inn on the Green, which is quieter and more secluded. I'm sure after twelve miles in the saddle and with no padding other than a thin pair of breeches, Miss Beaufort will be only too pleased to ride in the comfort of a carriage."

Every muscle and every bone in her body ached.

Sophie was not used to riding without layers of fabric acting as a cushion, and she rubbed her hand down her thigh to try to alleviate the stiffness. How on earth did a gentleman ride all day with such flimsy material for protection? Then again, she had pushed herself too hard as she didn't want to make it too easy for Dane to catch up.

Oh, what she would give for a nice cup of tea and a hot bath.

She slowed Argo to a walking pace and glanced over her shoulder, wondering if she'd made a terrible miscalculation.

What if Dane had no intention of following?

She had never actually referred to him as Dane, not aloud. The ladies, particularly those simpering misses who batted their lashes and craved an alliance, called him Lord Danesfield. To the gentlemen, he would simply be Danesfield, in deference to his title. Sophie refused to be cast in the role of a desperate debutante as it implied weakness; it implied inferiority and a desire for an emotional connection.

Her peaceful deliberations were disturbed by the sound of horse's hooves pounding the dirt at a considerable speed. She did not give him the satisfaction of turning around, but she knew it was Dane when the horse slowed to a walking pace at her side.

"It was good of you to wait," he teased, patting his horse and commending him for his efforts.

She glanced at him. A faint sheen of perspiration glistened on his cheeks, and his hair looked wavy and damp where it met his collar. His eyes were warm with a vitality that stole her breath, and she wondered if this was the sight his mistress saw amidst the throes of passion.

She looked away sharply, her lips forming a scowl. "Had I known it was you, I would have bolted for the hills. What does a lady have to do to be rid of you?"

"I wouldn't know. I've never found myself in such a predicament," he said with amusement. "Besides, I think we both know you wanted me to follow you. To save you from the dangers of stumbling upon a reckless rogue intent on kissing you."

"You're the only reckless rogue I know."

"Well, then there's no need to worry. As I recall, your little sighs and gasps suggest a fondness for rogues and for kissing."

All the blood rushed to her cheeks, and her tongue felt too thick to form a reply.

They covered the next mile in silence, and she wished she could think of something witty to say, something to divert her attention away from the strange sensations fluttering in her stomach. The air between them crackled, the vibration stirring the soft hairs at her nape, leaving her skin tingling, leaving her breathless.

She did not look at him but became intensely aware of his gaze, on her face, on her legs, gliding over her body. It was as though it held a magical ability to scorch her skin, leaving a hot, burning trail in its wake.

She closed her eyes in a bid to banish the feeling, to eradicate the power he had over her. Once, a long time ago, she had thought herself in love with him. But she was no longer a naive girl. He would never be Lord Danesfield to her. He would always be Dane.

"Considering our current situation, I suppose I should call you Dane," she said with feigned confidence.

"In private, you may call me Sebastian," he replied abruptly.

"But do not all gentlemen of your acquaintance defer to your title?"

He sighed. "Loath me to point out the obvious, but donning a pair of breeches does not make you a gentleman. Besides, only my closest friends call me Dane. My female relatives always call me Sebastian and since I've been forced to act as your guardian, you fall into that category."

"I see," she replied indignantly, for she did not want to be regarded as family.

Besides, she had not forced him to do anything and certainly did not need coddling. Not from a man who always placed his own needs above all others, a man who now had the affront to take the moral high ground.

"But what of your mistress?" she said, attempting to demean his high principles. "What does she call you?" There was a bitter edge to her tone that she could not disguise.

"You are not my mistress."

"Obviously," she snorted, shrugging off a feeling of inadequacy. "I heard country girls bore you to tears."

"Who told you that?"

"You did." She turned and met his puzzled gaze. "Have you ever heard the tale of the prince and the country mouse?"

"I can't say I have," he said, somewhat amused.

"Well, although some thought the prince handsome, he was an extremely poor judge of character. Annoyed with the mouse, he kissed her in an attempt to frighten her away."

"Which evidently proved to be a futile exercise," he interjected.

"Of course. The country mouse simply transformed into a tiger and gobbled the prince right up," she mocked.

Dane laughed. "So, it's not enough to tease me with your wandering hands. Now, you tempt me with your lascivious analogy. I must say, Miss Beaufort, I shall look forward to the event with eager anticipation."

"Sophie," she corrected, a little confused by his reply.

"Excuse me."

"In private, you may call me Sophie."

He was silent for a moment, then said rather abruptly, "I think not, Miss Beaufort. I believe that pleasure is reserved for your brother and your future husband."

"I told you. I have no intention of marrying. I believe marriage would be a somewhat tedious affair."

Particularly if it was to you, she added silently.

He glanced across at her. "I would have thought it all depends on the person one marries. If one finds a partner capable of keeping alight the inner flame, then I do not doubt there are many pleasures to be found in marriage."

Sophie snorted. "Do not tell me you believe in such nonsense, that you of all people desire marriage."

"I am a peer of the realm. It is my duty to marry and produce an heir. It should not surprise you that I hope it will be a pleasurable experience."

The mere thought of him married, of him entertaining a wife, made her feel lightheaded.

She imagined seeing them at social gatherings, imagined him smiling at a beautiful golden-haired temptress as she pushed the rebellious lock of hair from his brow.

"Besides," he continued, "what will you do when your brother marries? What will you do when you are no longer mistress of the house?"

"I shall move to the cottage," she said. Or perhaps far enough away never to have to set eyes on Dane again. "I would much rather be mistress of my own heart than be mistress of a stranger's dinner menu."

He laughed and said in a languorous tone, "But what of the physical aspects of marriage. How do you propose to compensate for that?"

He was teasing her, but she refused to let him have the upper hand. "For an unmarried man who has spent years enjoying such pleasures, you sound very naive." She stared at him with a confidence that made her feel all worldly and wanton.

Dane looked appalled. "If you mean you would take a lover, then I believe you are the one being naive," he snapped. "You would be ruined. Such a stain on your character would affect every female member of your family, including any future daughters born to your brother."

Why did he relate everything back to duty and obligation?

"I would be discreet," she replied with a shrug, but her words seemed to anger him all the more.

"And what of children," he scolded. "Do you have any idea what it is like to be born on the wrong side of the blanket? Or are you going to tell me you intend to deny yourself the pleasure of motherhood?"

"I do not want children." Even as the lie left her lips, she could not hide the tremor in her voice or stop the single tear from forming. She wanted children more than anything. Such a loss was a heavy price to pay for independence. "I believe children should be a precious gift from a blissful union, not a commodity to barter," she spat. "Not some possession simply to continue the bloodline."

"Or something begotten out of duty," he added.

They fell silent. In an attempt to find a distraction she rubbed her aching thigh—an action that received close scrutiny from her companion.

"Beyond the copse," Dane said, pointing out into the distance, "there's a large pool where we can rest and take a drink. We'll stop there and—"

"I am perfectly fine," Sophie interrupted. She did not want to be treated like a child. "There's no need to stop on my account."

"You've been in the saddle for the best part of three hours. If you have no consideration for your own wellbeing, have some for your horse."

Since when had he become the voice of reason?

Sophie could think of no witty retort as one could not argue against common sense. Besides, she needed to find some diversion from these turbulent emotions.

They rounded the bend, and she nudged Argo onto the verge and across the grass towards the pool. As she approached, she could not help but smile, struck by the wondrous vision before her, a vision of perfect beauty.

Like an oasis in the desert, the water was as clear as glass, reflecting the rich, green hues of the surrounding hills. It was a sanctuary, an idyllic refuge, a shrine to new life and new beginnings.

Ignoring her aching muscles, Sophie climbed down and threw her hat to the ground. After shrugging out of her coat, she stood with her hands on her hips and admired the view.

"Oh, Dane, it's spectacular," she exclaimed with delight, glancing back over her shoulder. "I have never seen anything so beautiful."

"Neither have I," he said softly as his gaze locked with hers.

She wandered down to the edge of the pool and knelt beneath the willow tree. Dipping her hands into the cool water, she pressed her damp fingers over her brow and down her neck. The warmth of the sun seemed to relax her muscles, and she repeated her ablutions, relishing the feel of the water as it trickled over her skin. She stood, wiped her hands on her breeches and bent down to pick up a stone, sending it skimming across the pool, watching it bounce four times before it sank with a loud *plop*.

"Did you see that?" she said, clapping her hands. She swung around to find him still sitting astride his horse, his gaze dark, intense. Those sinful eyes stared at her breeches, which were no longer concealed by her coat. They followed the curve of her thigh up over the swell of her hip.

She swallowed deeply.

He dismounted in one graceful movement. Throwing his hat and greatcoat to the ground, he covered the distance between them in a few strides, his gaze never leaving her. "Perhaps you're right," he murmured, his voice deep and rich as he focused on her mouth. "When it comes to you, I am a reckless rogue."

This time, there was no gentle coaxing, no soft teasing. His mouth, hot and demanding, devoured hers in a frenzy that left her panting and clutching at his shoulders. This was not simply a kiss; it was possession, and he drank hungrily and selfishly from her.

She should have pushed him away, slapped him, called him all the things she knew him to be. But her traitorous body ached for him, for his smell, his taste, his touch. She was a Judas to her own cause, and she didn't care.

She was lost, falling fast, and it felt divine.

While his mouth moved wickedly, his tongue plunged deeper to dance with hers. His hand slid seductively around her back, up under her waistcoat, balling the thin linen shirt into his fist. His other hand gripped her hip, and both worked together to urge her closer to his hard body.

He broke contact and sucked in a breath.

"*Good God*," he growled against her ear.

In a daze, she opened her eyes to look at him—and screamed.

The unmarked carriage had stopped on the road directly behind them. The occupant, a woman, was hanging out of the window watching their amorous display. Thankfully, the coachman did not look their way but sat like a solid lump of stone staring out at the road ahead.

"It's just my coachman," Dane said, looking back over his shoulder. He released her and straightened her clothing. "Wait here."

She watched him storm across the grass, raking his hand through his hair and pulling at the sleeves of his coat. The woman threw herself back into the carriage, closed the window and yanked down the blind.

The coachman did not move.

A brief conversation ensued between the two men, the coachman's gaze following his master as he paced back and forth. Then Dane climbed inside the carriage and promptly closed the door.

Sophie hated herself.

She hated the way she felt when Dane kissed her. She hated the way her body betrayed her so easily, succumbing to his touch. She hated that she'd stood there dumbstruck while he climbed into the carriage to offer an explanation to his mistress. Most of all, she hated the jealousy that writhed in her chest.

Allowing anger and frustration to bolster her courage, she decided to confront them. The least she deserved was an explanation. So she stomped across the grass, picking up her hat and coat. As she approached the carriage, the coachman coughed loudly. Before she could raise her hand to knock, the door swung open, and Dane vaulted out.

"I hate to spoil your little *tete-a-tete*." Sophie placed her hand on her hip. "But will someone please tell me what on earth is going on."

"If you'd care to step inside." He pulled down the steps for her to climb in. "Amy will explain everything."

"Why would I—" Sophie began.

Dane did not give her a chance to finish before scooping her up in his arms, dumping her on the carriage floor and folding up the steps. "Until tomorrow, Miss Beaufort." He offered a graceful bow as Amy darted forward and pulled the door shut.

"Wait!"

"Do not stop until you reach town," Dane shouted as the carriage lurched forward.

CHAPTER 10

"The Marquess of Danesfield," Dudley Spencer's butler announced without the slightest inflection.

His friend would most certainly find the introduction amusing, Sebastian thought, as he stepped across the threshold into the study.

As predicted, Dudley walked around the desk and gave a theatrical bow. "My lord, welcome to my humble abode."

Sebastian grasped Dudley's shoulders and pulled him into a welcoming embrace, as though it had been considerably longer than a week since they last met.

"What has brought you back to London so soon? Please tell me you're not missing me already." Dudley's smile faded as he examined Sebastian's dusty, slightly crumpled attire. "Did you ride here directly?"

Sebastian smiled. "You always were extremely perceptive."

"Is that not why we work so well together?" Dudley placed a hand on Sebastian's shoulder. "Come, take a seat. Have you eaten?"

"Not since last night." Sebastian dropped into the leather chair opposite Dudley's desk. "There is someone I wish to avoid, and I could hardly call in at my club looking like this."

Haines had not taken Miss Beaufort to his official London residence, but to a house he used purely for business purposes. A house in a quieter part of town where his neighbours were not members of the *ton*, but doctors, lawyers and bachelors who all struggled to make time to eat and sleep, let alone concern themselves with other people's affairs.

She would be safe there.

Dudley rang the bell, requested a cold platter and a bottle of his best claret. He took a seat behind his desk and focused an inquisitive gaze on Sebastian.

"Now you have my full attention," he said, leaning back in the chair and steepling his fingers, "what do you mean there is someone you wish to avoid? Please tell me this is not about a woman."

After all the years spent working together, they understood the need to be honest with one another. To withhold information often meant putting lives in danger and so they'd made a pact never to keep secrets.

"The person I wish to avoid is the person I brought with me to London," Sebastian said, running his fingers through his hair.

Aware of Dudley's confused expression, Sebastian told him everything—including a rather embarrassing confession relating to an impromptu kiss at Rockingham Pool.

"I could not help myself." Sebastian jumped to his feet, began pacing back and forth in front of the desk. "I don't know what came over me. One minute I am sitting on my horse admiring the view. The next, I am devouring her mouth with the urgency of an opium addict drinking his last tincture."

"Without wishing to cause insult," Dudley said in an even tone, "from what you have told me, Miss Beaufort is hardly gently bred and by your own declaration was a willing partner."

"That does not make it right," Sebastian argued, thoroughly ashamed of himself. The thought of his blatant disregard for propriety caused his temperature to rise. He pushed his fingers down between his neck and collar to allow the air to circulate.

Dudley narrowed his gaze. "Do you care for her?" The corners of his mouth curved into a mischievous grin.

His question was like a slap in the face. Sebastian stopped pacing and placed both hands on the back of the chair for support. "Of course not. I hardly know her. Most of the time I have to stop myself from grabbing her by the shoulders and shaking her until she sees sense." Or from pushing her to the ground, covering her with his hard body and plundering her sweet mouth, he added silently.

Dudley laughed. "I seem to remember feeling the same way about Charlotte, and I married her."

"I am not going to marry Miss Beaufort."

"Yet in the space of a few hours you have kissed her twice." Dudley made him sound like the worst of scoundrels. "You need a wife, and you said yourself, as soon as all financial matters concerning the estate were settled your priority would be to beget an heir." Dudley shrugged. "Why not ask Miss Beaufort? She obviously stirs some grand passion within you. I have never seen you so agitated over a woman. I have never seen you so … so …" Dudley waved his hand in the air as he struggled to find the right word.

"Frustrated?" Sebastian offered.

"I was going to say unbalanced," Dudley replied, unable to hide his amusement. "I assume Miss Beaufort will stay in Red Lion Square. But what about you?"

Sebastian swallowed. "I cannot leave her there alone."

"You intend to stay there with her? Is that wise?"

Sebastian did not answer the question as there was a gentle knock on the door and a footman entered carrying a tray of meats, cheese, and sweet biscuits.

Dudley cleared a pile of papers and asked for it to be placed on the desk. "Don't wait for me," he said, obviously aware of Sebastian's greedy gaze. "You look ravenous. It's a good job Miss Beaufort is not here as you would be in danger of devouring her whole."

"Am I to be the whipping boy for all your poor jokes?"

Dudley patted him on the back and handed him a glass of claret. "I hate to be the one to preach—"

"That's a lie," Sebastian interjected. "You love making me look foolish."

"Well, yes. But as your friend, I feel it my duty to remind you of the potential outcome of your situation. You know I speak from experience."

Sebastian swished his wine around in the glass. "There is only one possible outcome," he said, his tone subdued. "I shall return Miss Beaufort to her brother, untouched and unwed."

Dudley's mouth curved into a sardonic grin. "I think we both know that will not be the case."

Sebastian muttered a curse and popped a chocolate macaroon into his mouth.

They sat for a while in relaxed silence while Dudley dipped his nib into the inkwell and scratched out a few notes.

"Do you want me to enquire into Lord Beaufort's whereabouts?" Dudley asked as Sebastian finished his repast.

"No, I shall see to Beaufort," Sebastian replied, taking a mouthful of wine. "I need you to find out anything you can about the Comte de Dampierre. He must have an address here in town. Miss Beaufort seemed confident she could find him if need be. She seems to think some sort of deal had been struck. Her brother had promised to sell or trade the necklace and then for some reason refused."

Dudley frowned. "Can you trust Lord Beaufort?"

"With my life," Sebastian replied without hesitation. "The gentleman I know would not renege unless something prompted him to do so."

Dudley put a definite cross through one of the scribbled notes. "Is the necklace valuable? Perhaps when Beaufort came to London, he discovered it was paste and did not want to look foolish."

Sebastian laughed. "You're thinking of the time we traipsed

halfway around France looking for Lord Pottersham's mistress after she had run off with his wife's jewels."

Dudley's eyes flashed with amusement. "It would have been helpful if his wife had mentioned she'd swapped the gems for paste."

"Here, you may see for yourself." He removed the pouch from the concealed pocket sewn inside his coat, stepped forward and placed it on the table before returning to his seat. "I could not risk leaving it behind."

Dudley opened one of the desk drawers and removed a rose-wood magnifying glass. Rolling out the pouch, he took the necklace to the window to examine it in the light. "I must say it is a rather fetching piece."

The rubies twinkled like the stars and Sebastian caught his breath as his mind conjured an image of it draped around Miss Beaufort's bare neck. Except in Sebastian's mind, it was not just her neck that was bare.

"Most definitely not paste. There are too many imperfections, too many signs of nature's impurities," Dudley murmured. He returned to his chair and placed the necklace on top of the velvet pouch. "I am not qualified to place any sort of value on it, but even so, the thought of value does raise a very important question."

"I know what you are going to say," Sebastian said, bringing his wayward thoughts to heel. "If no money has changed hands then why would Beaufort negating their deal be so important to Dampierre? Why would he travel all the way to Marchampton unless the deal had already been done?"

"I would wager Miss Beaufort knows more than she is letting on. Else why would she be so determined to relieve you of the necklace?"

"I suspect you're right."

Sebastian knew she had not been completely honest. It took an awful amount of courage to scheme one's way into a person's home. The act suggested an element of desperation. In part, it was the reason he had insisted on accompanying her.

"I think it is fair to assume that Beaufort has something belonging to this Dampierre fellow." Dudley glanced at the rich rubies. "It must be something of great value to send a peer into hiding and a French comte scouring the country."

An image of James Beaufort's female companion flooded his mind: the disguise, the reluctance to call out her name, the need to take cover in the woods. "You're not going to believe this," Sebastian said as recognition dawned. "But I believe Beaufort and Dampierre are at odds over a woman."

CHAPTER 11

*I*t was late afternoon when Sebastian rode Argo into the mews of his house in Red Lion Square. After dismounting, he gave the horse a reassuring pat before handing him over to Peter: an orphan boy of fourteen, whose passion for horses surpassed any young buck frequenting Tattersall's.

"Don't worry. Cronus is safe." Sebastian ruffled the boy's hair in a bid to ease his troubled expression. "He's stabled out of town, but I'll collect him when I return to Marchampton."

Peter sighed. "I thought you'd gone and sold him for this one," he said, stroking Argo's nose.

"I would never sell Cronus." Sebastian placed a hand on the boy's shoulder. "This is Argo, but he's only visiting so don't get too attached." He smiled at Peter's look of wondrous appreciation. "Is Haines about?" Sebastian was curious to know how Haines had fared with his minx of a passenger.

The boy shook his head. "No, my lord. He said they need him in the house."

With some trepidation, Sebastian made his way inside. No doubt Miss Beaufort had been causing all sorts of trouble in his absence. He wondered if she would be waiting for him, ready to pounce, ready to lash out with her sharp tongue and he imagined dodging books and ornaments while trying to calm her volatile temper.

He found Haines in the kitchen, sitting at the oak table in just his shirtsleeves, helping Amy polish cutlery. Mrs. Cox stood at the counter, rolling out pastry.

"Good afternoon," Sebastian said. They were so busy chatting no one seemed to notice he was standing there.

"My lord," Haines replied, looking a little embarrassed as he stood to attention. "I didn't know you were back."

Amy jumped up quickly, knocking over a chair, and Haines walked around and picked it up while she bobbed a curtsy.

The kitchen door burst open. A pale, thin girl scuttled in carrying a tea tray and came crashing to a halt directly in front of Sebastian.

Mrs. Cox rushed forward, wiping her hands on her apron, her plump face dotted with flour. "You do remember me telling you about my niece, my lord?"

Sebastian nodded. "Yes, I do. It is Sarah, is it not?"

The girl attempted a curtsy but looked like she was ducking under a swinging branch. "Thank you, my lord, for giving me this position. There's not many who would take a girl who's got a kiddie."

Sebastian smiled and helped her to steady the tray. "Is that Miss Beaufort's luncheon?" he enquired, noticing she hadn't touched a morsel. Perhaps she was still annoyed with him and this was a form of punishment. Given the option, he'd choose assault with a vase over silent manipulation. "I assume she is still in her room?"

Haines spoke up. "She asked for a bath to be drawn, my lord, and for Amy to press her clothes."

The thought of Miss Beaufort lounging in a bath just a few feet above sent his pulse racing, and he placed his fingers behind the knot in his cravat to loosen it a little.

"Did Miss Beaufort say why she refuses to eat?"

"No, my lord, I tried the door but it was locked," Sarah replied. "I did knock, but she didn't answer. She's probably fallen asleep, and so I thought it best to bring the tray down."

"But she slept most of the journey," Amy added, shaking her head. "She told me herself, it wasn't good for the constitution to sit around idle."

Sebastian narrowed his gaze. "Where are her clothes?"

"Amy took them up an hour ago," Haines replied, a look of suspicion marring his weathered face.

"I cleaned them as best as I could, given such short notice, but Miss Beaufort seemed happy enough." Amy looked proud of her efforts. "She said as long as she looked respectable enough to walk down the street—"

"Bloody hell!" Sebastian cried, turning on his heels and running out of the door.

He mounted the stairs two at a time, aware of Haines' heavy plodding behind him.

"In here?" Sebastian asked, pointing across the landing to the room furthest from his own.

"Yes, my lord." Haines' voice was tinged with remorse and his head hung low.

Sebastian turned the handle and discovered the door was locked.

"Miss Beaufort," he called as he rapped on the door. He felt like smashing the blasted thing down with his fists.

There was no reply.

Sebastian knelt down and peered through the keyhole. She had taken the key out of the door and he could see straight through into the room. His instincts told him she was no longer in the house. Experience told him she had left through the front door. If she had escaped via the window, she would have left the key in the door.

"Shall I barge the door, my lord?"

"No, Haines, that won't be necessary." Sebastian stood and straightened his coat. "I believe Miss Beaufort has already vacated her room. But you may ask Mrs. Cox for the spare key."

"Beg your pardon, my lord, but this is my fault." Haines stood with his shoulders slumped forward. "I've never known anyone as angry as Miss Beaufort when you left her in the carriage," he said, scratching his head. "But she seemed happy when we arrived."

Of course she was bloody happy. No doubt she had been planning her escape from the moment she knew he was not following behind. Thank goodness he had the necklace else he doubted he would see her again. He patted his chest to make sure it was still in his pocket, and Miss Beaufort didn't know of a conjurer's trick to spirit it away.

Sebastian did not know what bothered him most. The fact Miss Beaufort was now wandering around town dressed in those blasted breeches for the entire world to see, or that she seemed to have an innate ability of making him look like a complete idiot.

"I am afraid the blame rests firmly at my door. No pun intended. Foolishly, I assumed Miss Beaufort would seek my counsel before tearing off around town." He was going to have to put an end to this cat-and-mouse game they played.

Haines cleared his throat. "When you give Haines a job to do, my lord, he always does his best. Never let it be said Haines don't do his duty," the coachman proclaimed, as though reapplying for his position. "It's just the lady has a look about her, a way of ... well, let's just say she was mighty cheerful for someone about to bolt."

Sebastian felt sorry for the man. "Miss Beaufort is an unusual lady, Haines. I fear I will never quite understand her motivations or her impulsiveness. I suppose you cannot attempt to cage a tiger and expect it will not try to bite you." He smiled, remembering Miss Beaufort's prince and mouse story and her threat to gobble him up.

"I can't say I know much about tigers, my lord." Haines scratched the top of his head again. "But I know what it's like to catch a butterfly, to trap it in a glass and watch it struggle to break free, to watch it grow tired and flutter to the bottom, all hopeless an' lost."

"You're suggesting Miss Beaufort is struggling to be free of the glass." Sebastian leant back against the jamb and folded his arms across his chest. "I did not know you were so perceptive, Haines."

"Beg your pardon, but there's not much else to do atop a carriage all day long besides think."

"Indeed."

Haines opened his mouth but then snapped it shut.

"Please, continue," Sebastian said. Any information to aid him in understanding Miss Beaufort's psyche was valuable indeed. "I feel I am in need of enlightenment, and I find your analogy quite refreshing."

Haines shuffled on the spot. "Well, you take Miss Amy," he continued a little cautiously. "There'd be those who'd be annoyed by her constant chattering. Some might say no good can come from such foolish talk."

"And you, what would you say, Haines?"

The corners of Sebastian's mouth curved into the beginnings of a smile, for he already knew the answer.

"Well, my lord," Haines began. "I'd say that when she speaks the whole world lights up. If it means my ears have to take a bashing, seems like a fair trade to me."

Sebastian's thoughts were drawn back to Miss Beaufort. He admired her tenacity, her courage. Yet the qualities that intrigued him the most were the qualities he tried to suppress.

In his effort to protect her diminishing reputation, he had forced her to take matters into her own hands. He wondered why he cared so much.

Why did he feel such a desperate need to control and conquer?

What was it about Miss Beaufort that spoke to him in a way no other woman ever had?

Throughout his life, he'd always done what he felt right, propriety be damned. He considered the unconventional methods he'd used to save his father's lands, to restore his legacy for future generations. How was he any different from Miss Beaufort?

Perhaps they had more in common than he first thought.

Knowing her brother was alive and well was not enough. She wanted to find him, to offer assistance and support. It's exactly what he would have done. Woe betide anyone who tried to stop him. Suddenly, the road ahead became clearer. In future, he would treat Miss Beaufort as he would Dudley; as a partner, a friend. He would allow her the freedom to make her own decisions. What choice did he have? It was either that or he feared he'd be a rambling madman before the week was out.

"I can speak to the staff. See if Miss Beaufort gave any clue as to where she was going," Haines said.

"That won't be necessary. It appears Miss Beaufort is quite capable of taking care of herself," Sebastian replied, pushing himself away from the jamb. "As soon as I've changed, I shall scour the streets for her. I'm confident she will return. When she does would you ask if she is free to accompany me for dinner this evening?"

"What, in the dining room, my lord?"

"Yes, of course in the dining room. I shall leave it to you to break the news to Mrs. Cox." Sebastian turned and took a few paces towards his room. "Oh," he said, swinging back round to face Haines. "Dudley Spencer's wife will be sending a few things over for Miss Beaufort." He was going to say he'd rather be damned than let her wear those breeches. But he was no longer in the habit of smothering butterflies. "There'll be a few dresses, amongst other things. Have Amy press them and lay them out in Miss Beaufort's room," he paused and then added, "should the lady wish to wear them, of course."

Haines nodded and made his way to the top of the staircase. He stopped, his calloused hands gripping the rail as he turned to face Sebastian. "I doubt life would ever be dull with Miss Beaufort around."

Sebastian laughed. "No, Haines, life would be far from dull. Of that I am certain."

CHAPTER 12

"*I* imagine Lord Danesfield must have been furious when he discovered I'd gone out," Sophie said as Amy fastened the buttons on her gown.

"He cursed a few times, but I said you would come back."

Sophie's hands drifted down the front of the turquoise-blue dress, tingling at the feel of the soft silk. The elegant style, with its full sleeves and low décolletage, flattered her figure and made her feel feminine and rather bold.

She glanced at the white dress hanging on the door of the armoire. It was the more modest of the two, and she knew she had made the right choice. If Dane intended to berate her over her expedition into town, she needed to feel confident, to feel his equal.

"You look very pretty, miss, if you don't mind me saying," Amy declared as she unpacked the leather portmanteau Charlotte Spencer had sent over. "Blue suits you. I doubt his lordship will have a mind for food when he sees you in that."

"Amy," Sophie scolded, although she could hardly blame the maid for making such an assumption. Not after witnessing their amorous interlude by the pool. "As I explained yesterday, the marquess is simply a friend who lent a helping hand when I stumbled."

Saying it aloud made the whole thing sound even more absurd; a thought echoed by Amy's snigger.

"I thought you said you had something in your eye?"

Sophie cursed silently. She had been so angry with Dane she could not remember what she'd said. Besides, what was the point of striving for independence or fighting against conformity when she did not even have the courage to take ownership of her actions?

"Well, yes, perhaps there was a little more to it than that," she admitted, straightening her back and lifting her chin. "But it will not happen again."

No. It most certainly could not happen again, especially after such blatant disregard for her feelings. Her side still ached from being picked up and dumped in the carriage.

"Besides, the marquess is used to the seductive skills of a mistress," Sophie added honestly. "I doubt I would ever be able to compete."

Amy smiled and arched a brow. "Let me tell you, miss," she whispered. "I know I babble on, and most of the time no one's even listening, but I do know a thing or two. I know a man doesn't kiss a woman the way his lordship kissed you if someone else is warming his bed at home." She gave a little wink.

Sophie could feel the blood rushing to her cheeks.

"Oh, I nearly forgot. There's a letter." Amy rushed over to the dressing table and handed her the sealed note. "Mrs. Spencer sent it with the wardrobe. Are you sure you don't want me to dress your hair for dinner? I could arrange it for you while you read your letter."

"Thank you, Amy, but that won't be necessary." Sophie tried to keep up with Amy's chatter.

"But it's been ages since I've done anyone's hair." She looked a little forlorn. "I promise I won't do anything too fancy.

Mr. Haines said he once saw a lady with a whole bunch of grapes stuck on her head." Amy gave another snigger. "I'll just do a simple chignon with a few curls framing your face. Mrs. Spencer sent over a pretty little pearl comb that would look—"

"Very well." Sophie sighed, raising a hand in resignation. She sat carefully on the stool so as not to crease her dress and turned the letter over to examine both sides. "But nothing too elaborate. Perhaps it would have been wise to do this before I dressed for dinner."

"It won't take long, what with your hair being shorter." Amy's face was a picture of pure joy. "You go ahead and read your letter and don't mind me."

The letter, written in a delicate feminine flourish, began with an informal introduction and conveyed an almost childlike eagerness to become acquainted. Charlotte Spencer went on to explain that the garments were new and as Sophie was in such dire need, she could keep them.

Sophie found herself smiling as she refolded the letter. It was remarkable how a few simple words could convey much of a person's character. She would look forward to thanking Charlotte in person as she had a feeling she would like her immensely.

"There we are, miss, all finished." Amy placed the unused pins into the glass dish on the table.

Sophie looked up into the oval mirror, angling her head to study Amy's work. She had done a good job, and the overall effect was one of ... Sophie struggled to find the right words ... one of rustic simplicity.

Amy had attempted to tame the unruly curls, but Sophie's hair refused to comply. She admired the few straggling locks that had already sprung loose at the nape and decided she loved it. Although the style lacked the finesse required for a more formal occasion, Sophie felt it reflected her character perfectly: downright stubborn and wildly unruly.

"It's lovely, Amy. Thank you."

"Those curls have a mind all of their own," she chuckled. "It's a good job you didn't fancy the fruit. It would never have stayed in there." She waited for Sophie to stand and then helped to smooth out her dress. "You're to meet his lordship in the drawing room." Amy leant forward and lowered her voice. "Mr. Haines said his lordship always takes his meals in his study, says he can't remember the last time he sat down to dinner."

Was she supposed to be impressed by the effort? Or did he plan to hide behind formality when he berated her for her conduct? No doubt he planned to use his debaucher's repartee to unnerve her.

"Well, I had better not keep his lordship waiting."

Sebastian stood at the window, his arms folded as he stared out across the street. He was not looking at anything in particular. In fact, had there been a mugging outside his front door he would not have even noticed.

He was too busy contemplating Miss Beaufort's reaction to being thrown into his carriage. He was too busy trying to calm the heat flooding his body at the thought of seeing her again.

The door creaked open, and he heard the patter of slippered feet coming to a stop in the middle of the room. His heart thumped loudly in his chest.

"Good evening, my lord."

Her warm voice brimmed with arrogance, as though she commanded the opposite side of the battlefield and intended to use every tactic possible to demean his position. She would be disappointed. His new approach to her unconventional manner placed him one step ahead. Or so he thought until he turned around.

"Miss Beaufort."

He greeted her with a slight bow which afforded him the opportunity to mask his initial surprise, to mask the rush of desire that gripped him around the throat determined to rid him of his breath. He'd expected her to wear the breeches: to annoy him, to prove a point. He'd not expected her to wear a gown or for the neckline to fall so deliciously low. Nor had he thought to see her hair piled on top of her head in such a wild and wanton display.

"I wasn't sure you'd join me."

"I believe we have a lot to discuss." She shrugged, revealing a little more of the pure creamy-white flesh he found so appealing.

He made a mental note to find some way of thanking Charlotte Spencer for her trouble. "Then let us not waste another moment." Sebastian offered his arm, though his gaze followed the line of her jaw, wandered down the elegant column of her neck. "Shall we?"

She placed her hand in the crook of his arm, and he had to suppress the urge to drag her to his eager body, to plunder her mouth like a man possessed. He stifled a groan.

They walked the short distance to the dining room in companionable silence. He kept a small staff and so Mrs. Cox and her niece were to serve dinner. They took their seats at opposite ends of the table, which suited Sebastian as the distance served to temper his racing pulse.

"I'm afraid Mrs. Cox's culinary expertise is rather limited," he said, straining his neck to see past the tall gilt fruit bowl. Where on earth had the woman found such a monstrosity? Sebastian stood, removed the elaborate display and placed it on the side table.

They passed pleasantries, like strangers seated next to one another at a dinner party.

"The soup is good," Sophie replied, dabbing the sides of her mouth with her napkin.

It all appeared rather amiable, yet he could feel the tension brimming beneath the surface. She was still annoyed with him. He could hardly blame her. But if they were going to work together, she would need to trust him. He had handled things badly, telling himself he'd acted out of a sense of responsibility. In truth, his only motivation had been self-preservation.

"I assume you went to inspect your brother's residence?" Sebastian said in a matter-of-fact tone, although he hoped he was wrong and she'd simply gone for a stroll. He walked over to the sideboard and picked up a bottle. "Would you like wine?" he asked. "If we wait for Mrs. Cox, I fear we shall both die of thirst. You may keep your glass at the table."

She looked at the deep-red liquid and then to the pristine white tablecloth.

"I'm not one for formality, as you know," he added.

Sophie nodded, and he filled her glass, careful not to spill any for his gaze was caught by a wayward curl caressing the side of her neck. He resisted the urge to touch it, to run it between his fingers and marvel at the softness.

She raised the glass to her lips and took a large sip. "I thought it best not to waste time," she admitted.

"And?" Sebastian asked, returning to his seat. He held his frustration at bay despite the urge to tell her she'd made a foolish mistake. "What did you discover?"

She held the glass in her hand, twirling it back and forth in a nervous ritual. "You're not angry with me?" she asked, revealing her surprise.

No, he was not angry—he was bloody furious.

"Should I be?"

She eyed him suspiciously. "You should know I will not tolerate your constant disregard for my feelings. Nor will I tolerate being manhandled by you out of some antiquated sense of duty."

His antiquated sense of duty was the only thing stopping him from dragging her off the chair, hiking her pretty dress up around her thighs and settling himself between them.

"I understand," he nodded, offering his most sincere smile. He was no John Edwin, but he could grace the stage with this performance. "You see, I have come to accept that we have the same goal," he continued. "One is not Oxford and the other Cambridge. You want to find your brother and return to Marchampton. You want to understand the reasons for Dampierre's interest in the necklace." He raised his glass in salute. "As do I."

She was staring at him as though he had grown a carrot for a nose.

"Now," he continued. "You were telling me you went to your brother's house."

"To his lodgings," she corrected a little stiffly. "He no longer owns a townhouse."

"Forgive me," he said with an inclination of the head. "I meant the house he had hired for the duration of his visit."

Her cheeks flushed. "James has not been seen there, officially, for over a week."

Sebastian arched a brow. "Officially?"

"The house came complete with a cook, a maid, and a butler. Although they've not seen James, the maid believes items belonging to him have been removed from the house without their knowledge."

There was a gentle knock at the door. Mrs. Cox and her niece entered carrying a selection of rather mouth-watering dishes, including venison pie, baked salmon and a roast chicken. Sebastian realised he had underestimated Mrs. Cox's talents in the kitchen.

He waited until they were alone again before pointing out Miss Beaufort's grave error.

"Of course, you must know that if your situation were a game of chess, you would have just placed yourself in *check*." If she insisted on acting independently, then she must accept responsibility for her mistakes. "I must say the pie is delicious."

She narrowed her gaze and wrinkled her nose. "What on earth are you talking about?"

He took a sip of wine. "Let me explain," he said, trying not to sound too condescending, too arrogant. "Let us suppose I am searching for someone who has disappeared. The first thing I would do is hire a man to watch the person's house, their last known address."

"What, for a week?" she scoffed.

"For as long as it takes." He paused to let her digest the information. "You understand that you would have been followed back to this address, and now this house will be under observation. You will be under observation."

She sat back in her chair and folded her arms across her chest as if contemplating his logic.

Sebastian groaned inwardly.

It was hard enough to remain focused on the task. Her face glowed, her cheeks rosy from the wine. Stray curls caressed her jaw and neck, giving the appearance of having been recently ravished. Now, she presented him with an ample display of her bosom.

"Assuming the person knows the location of James' residence, of course," she countered.

"You mean the one in Bloomsbury Square?" He could not help but find her look of utter amazement satisfying. "Like you, I've also had quite a busy afternoon. In fact, I still have another call to make tonight."

"Tonight? You're going out?"

"I need to pay a visit to Labelles." He pushed the last morsel of food onto his fork, popped it into his mouth and chewed slowly before putting down his cutlery. "In case you're wondering, it's a brothel catering to the higher end of the market."

Miss Beaufort stood, pushing back the chair as she threw her napkin down on the table. "While I appreciate your honesty, this is hardly an appropriate conversation to have during dinner."

"You surprise me. I had not taken you for a prude," he said, not bothering to disguise his amusement.

"I am not a prude," she retorted. "I have no interest in what

86

you desire or which one of the Covent Garden ladies will be servicing your needs tonight."

He stared at her face, all twisted in bitter resentment, a perfect picture of feminine jealousy and he couldn't help but laugh.

"What is so funny?"

"It's the look on your face. Besides, you're wrong about Labelles. It isn't in Covent Garden," he said, catching his breath. "It's in Marylebone." When he noticed she was not amused, he paused for a moment to regain his composure. "I need to visit Labelles to make some enquiries. That is all."

"What sort of enquiries?" she asked as she sat back down in her chair.

"Well, while you were checking your brother's house to see if he had packed his smalls," he said with a hint of sarcasm, "I called in at my club. While there, I discovered that James met with friends who dragged him off to Labelles. One of them, a Mr. Benjamin Fordham, remembered James being involved in an argument. Apparently, it had something to do with one of the girls, but they had all drunk copious amounts of wine and brandy, and Fordham's memory was rather hazy. The last time they saw James, he was going upstairs to one of the rooms."

"What, James went upstairs with one of those girls?" She shook her head. "I can hardly believe it."

Sebastian was going to say that's what some men do, but he did not believe it of James either. It took a certain type of man to lie with a prostitute. If James had come to London to raise the capital needed to develop his estate, then whatever steered him from the path would have been extremely important. Perhaps the Comte de Dampierre was also a patron of Labelles.

"I agree," he said, "which is why I must visit the premises."

"Very well," she said as though he needed her permission. "I'm coming with you."

This time, it was Sebastian who stood abruptly and threw his napkin on the table. "The hell you will." The words were out before he could reconsider and he pushed his hand through his hair in a bid to control his temper.

The corners of her mouth turned upwards into a feigned smile. It was the sort of smile that gave the impression she was about to move her queen against him, and in a few simple moves he would be in checkmate.

"If the house is being observed, as you suggested, then you cannot leave me here alone."

"You will not be alone," he retorted. "Haines will be here."

"Of course," she nodded. "Haines was also here this afternoon when I opened the front door and walked out onto the street."

Check

"A mistake he will not make again," Sebastian warned.

"Are you so certain? Do you know how helpful people can be when they know you are new to town? How do you think I found my way to Bloomsbury Square? I'm sure there are no end of dissolute rakes roaming the streets, only too willing to show a young buck the way to Labelles," she arched a brow, "in Marylebone."

Checkmate.

She lifted her glass to her lips and took a sip of wine before casting him a satisfied smile.

Sebastian sighed as he slumped back into his chair. "You are not a young buck, Miss Beaufort," he said with some resignation as his eyes drifted over her impressive cleavage. "What would your brother say if he knew I had allowed you to visit a house of ill repute?"

"Under the circumstances, he can hardly say a thing." She shrugged. "Besides, I'm not completely naive. I do know what goes on in those sorts of places." She stared him straight in the eye and lifted her chin. "I know what it is like to feel desire at the hands of a man," she purred. "I know how it feels to be so drunk with it, you can think of nothing else. As I'm sure you remember."

Sebastian almost choked on his wine at the last remark.

The thought that he had roused such a passion in her made him so hard he could not think straight. All he could feel was the blood rushing through his veins. All he could hear was his heart pumping in his chest. All he could see was her mussed up hair and heaving bosom.

God. How he wanted her. He wanted to bury himself inside her until nothing else mattered.

"Are you feeling well?" Her voice drifted over him, soft and musical to his ears and before he knew what was happening, she walked around the table to stand at his side. "Surely you're not shocked at such a declaration? I was merely stating a fact." Her hand moved towards the lock of hair over his brow and froze.

Sebastian stopped breathing. If she touched him, he would not be able to stop himself from reciprocating; he would take what he so desperately wanted, what he so desperately needed.

"Well, will you take me with you?" she said, her hand falling back to her side.

"Yes, Miss Beaufort. You may accompany me," he answered huskily. "As I said earlier, we are working towards the same goal." Besides, it would be a judicious move on his part, for he could not guarantee she would sit patiently and wait for him.

"I shall be ready in twenty minutes." She patted her hands together as she rushed towards the door.

"What about dessert?"

She glanced over her shoulder and shrugged. "We'll save it for later. I have always been partial to a midnight feast."

He cast his most sinful smile. "So have I."

CHAPTER 13

*L*abelles was far from the licentious haunt Sophie expected. On first appearance, the house looked like any other respectable Palladian-inspired townhouse, with its Venetian windows and Doric columns flanking the door-way. Business was most definitely thriving, she thought, as she stepped out of Dane's unmarked carriage wearing her breeches and tailcoat.

Dane looked up at Haines, who tried his best to hide his wary expression. "Wait for us near the corner of George Street and Seymour."

The coachman gave one of his inconspicuous nods and steered the carriage down the street and out of view.

"For a man who appears to be made of stone, Haines has a very soft heart," Sophie said with a hint of affection.

"What makes you say that?" Dane asked curiously, gazing over her shoulder into the darkness.

"Well, besides the fact he is extremely loyal and holds you in such high esteem—"

"Of course, he does," he interrupted. "He is in my employ."

Sophie sighed. "I was about to say, during the short time I have spent in his company, he has done nothing but defend you. One must have a soft heart to see past your transgressions."

She must have a soft heart, too, and an addled brain. Regardless of how Dane had behaved in the past, she found it impossible not to like him.

Dane placed his hand over his heart as though mortally wounded. "So, like the rest of Marchampton, you have cast me in the role of evil villain."

She put her hands on her hips. "Have you forgotten you scooped me up, dumped me in a carriage and left me without so much as a word?"

"No, I have not forgotten." His tone held a hint of regret and his eyes a spark of tenderness that touched her heart. "And for that, I am truly sorry."

Sophie took a step towards him and placed her hand on his arm, drawn by an inexplicable need to offer comfort. "I accept your apology."

Something had changed between them.

She could not fight the feelings that consumed her. She craved his company, his witty banter, the heated looks that made her stomach flip and her heart flutter. It became increasingly more difficult to believe he was the same man who had spent the last six years bedding women instead of tending to his estate.

Perhaps he had changed.

The sound of a carriage rattling by jolted her to her senses. It would not be wise for two gentlemen to be seen in such an intimate pose. And so she dropped her hand and stepped back to a more respectable distance.

He continued to stare at her, his hungry gaze searching her face and she became aware of the rapid rise and fall of his chest.

"The need to protect you outweighed all reasonable thought," he said softly.

She sighed. "I know."

"So, besides the fact Haines holds me in such high esteem, what else has he done to be worthy of your estimation?"

"I'm afraid when it comes to women, Haines is hopelessly heroic not to mention gallant."

Dane laughed. "Please tell me you are joking."

"I am not. Did he not tell you what happened at the coaching inn when we stopped to collect supper?"

His expression grew dark, and he frowned. "No, he did not."

Sophie noticed the way the muscles in his jaw stiffened. "Oh, don't be angry with him," she said, placing her hand on his sleeve again. "You see, he would not leave me alone for fear I would abscond and so sent Amy into the inn. Minutes ticked by before we heard the commotion, the raucous laughter, and loud jeering. Then we heard a woman scream."

Dane turned away, his hands clenched at his sides as he muttered a profanity. "You're going to tell me it was Amy." He swung back around to face her, his eyes filled with dread.

Sophie pursed her lips and nodded. "There'd been a boxing match in a field on the outskirts of town and a group of gentlemen had congregated in the courtyard. They were drinking and ..."

He closed his eyes and let out a deep sigh.

"I suppose it was meant to be a little harmless fun," she continued in an attempt to make it all sound less dramatic. "Without saying a word, Haines barged past them all, scooped Amy up in his arms and carried her back to the carriage."

"And you believe that is gallant and heroic?" His countenance suddenly appeared much improved and the corners of his mouth twitched in amusement.

"Of course."

Dane folded his arms across his chest. "Pray tell how it is any different to me scooping you up and placing you in the carriage?"

"It is entirely different. Amy was in danger of being ravished."

"As were you," he added with a wicked grin. "You were in danger of being thoroughly ravished by a reckless rogue."

Sophie swallowed. There was no mistaking the deep husky tone to his voice. How did he manage to make it sound so appealing?

"But you did not hear me scream," Sophie countered.

"No," he admitted. He took a step closer and whispered, "But I would like to rouse a whimper from those soft lips."

He was certainly skilled in the art of seduction, for she was suddenly consumed with the thought of touching him, of kissing him, of running her hands over his bare chest.

The sound of drunken laughter further down the street caught their attention, and he grasped her arm. "It is not wise to converse on the doorstep," he whispered. "Perhaps we may continue our conversation later, over dessert?"

Thank goodness he was holding her arm; her legs had almost buckled at his suggestive tone.

"Whatever happens in here," he continued, "whatever you see or hear, try your best not to look shocked. I shall introduce you as a young cousin. It will explain your remarkably clear complexion." A frown marred his brow. "Are you certain you want to do this?"

She gave his arm a reassuring pat. "I have an independent mind and a passionate spirit. What more do I need?"

"I have a feeling your independent mind may be put to the test." He stepped up to the green door, ignored the brass knocker and rapped gently three times.

The butler opened the door to greet them.

A butler!

Sophie examined his powdered wig, white stockings and black buckled shoes—a butler in a brothel! She was forced to hide her surprise, and they hadn't even crossed the threshold.

"The Marquess of Danesfield and Mr. Bertram Shandy," Dane announced.

The butler led them into the hall and told them to wait while he took Dane's calling card and exited through a door on the right.

"Where on earth did you dredge up a name like Bertram Shandy?" Sophie whispered.

"I did not dredge it up," he informed her. "Mr. Shandy is my second cousin. He is a pretentious prig and rather a fop. It will account for your feminine walk and accentuated gestures. Besides, I think you look like a Bertie."

Sophie did not have a chance to reply as the butler entered the hall and walked towards them.

"Madame Labelle will greet you momentarily," he nodded. "If you would care to make your way into the gallery room, you may take some refreshment." The butler escorted them to the last door on the left and then bowed.

"Are all brothels like this one?" Sophie whispered as they entered the room.

"Of course not. Madame Labelle caters to the elite, of which you are now a member."

They wandered over to a drinks cabinet and Dane poured them both a glass of port. "I suggest you sip it," he said, handing her the glass. "And best we stand here. If you sit down, there's no telling what may happen." When she gasped, he added, "I am only teasing."

Mindful that her gaze had not dared to leave Dane since entering the room, Sophie took a sip of port and lifted her head.

Like everything else about the house, the furnishings were elegant. She spotted a large gilt sofa covered in rich red brocade; the finest Persian rug adorned the floor, and Greek-inspired statues of naked women occupied the alcoves on the far wall.

There were various groups of people milling about the room and in one corner a lady played hostess, pouring tea for the three gentlemen seated opposite.

It was all disappointingly normal.

One wall was dedicated to an abundance of paintings and so, feeling a little more confident, she wandered over to take a closer look.

The first painting was of a woman standing before a window.

The sunlight pouring through penetrated the thin fabric of her dress, showing the curvaceous outline of her body. She looked beautiful, powerful, yet demure.

In the next painting, a man sat back against a rock. He was naked, bar a piece of red cloth draped across his manhood. A woman sat between his legs, her head resting in his lap, looking up at him as he smiled back. His expression suggested the promise of an intimate exchange.

Further along the wall were twelve miniatures, each one depicting an erotic scene. All the men were highly aroused, alarmingly so. Sophie angled her head to examine some of the poses and then turned to look at Dane, who was lounging against the wall, studying her.

He straightened, walked over and stood behind her as though showing some interest in the scenes, too. "I must say, you are playing your part extremely well. One would almost believe you're enjoying looking at these engravings."

"I am," she replied, for she liked the way he reacted when she spoke boldly. She walked back to the first painting, the one with the girl at the window, and he followed and stood behind her. "What do you think of when you look at this one?" she asked, wondering why she didn't feel shy or embarrassed. She almost chuckled when the next question popped into her head. "When you look at it, do you find it arousing?"

Sophie smiled when she heard his sharp intake of breath. Standing in such proximity, she could feel the tension in the air between them, could feel an intense attraction that went beyond anything she had ever felt before.

He bent his head and whispered in her ear, his tone low and husky. "I feel aroused when I look at you."

He straightened, but she could still smell his masculine scent. The smell was so potent it sent her blood racing until it pooled between her legs, leaving a throbbing ache screaming to be appeased.

"Lord Danesfield, how good of you to come." The gentle

purr of a woman's voice broke the spell, and they both turned to greet the mistress of the house. "Mr. Shandy, let me welcome you to Labelles."

Madame Labelle stood before them like any other respectable lady greeting her guests. She appeared younger than Sophie had imagined, yet her face had a world-weary countenance that betrayed her profession. Her golden hair, the shade of honey, was dressed in an elaborate coiffure. She wore an exquisite ethereal-blue silk gown trimmed around the bosom with pearl rosettes. It was designed to display the shoulders and a lot more besides.

"It has been a while, Lord Danesfield," she said, running her fingers seductively across her cleavage. She glanced down at the front of his breeches. "I see my paintings have provided a modicum of entertainment while you've been waiting."

Sophie suppressed a gasp. Dane had been here before!

The knowledge that this was not their first meeting caused a hard lump to form in her throat. Why had he not told her? Did he think her too naive to notice their familiarity? Even if Madame Labelle hadn't mentioned it, the connection was obvious to all.

"Tell me," Madame Labelle whispered softly. "Do you still prefer Antoinette?"

Sophie felt the blood charge through her veins.

"Yes, tell me, cousin," Sophie said through gritted teeth, affecting a deeper voice than was usual as she slapped Dane rather hard on the back. "Is it the thought of Antoinette that evokes such a premature stirring of one's loins?" Sophie took a step towards their hostess. "Let us hope, for Antoinette's sake, it is the only premature event of the evening."

Madame Labelle laughed, while Dane shifted uncomfortably. "Oh, my lord, why have you not brought Mr. Shandy to me before. He is a veritable hoot. Will you not kiss my hand, Mr. Shandy?"

Sophie took the hand offered and kissed it gently. "Delighted, madame," she said, offering her most gracious bow.

As she stepped back, she noticed Madame Labelle's curious gaze and her heart skipped a beat.

"Has anyone ever told you, Mr. Shandy, that you have the face of an angel?" Madame Labelle's fingers traced the low neckline of her gown. "I have always been rather partial to angels," she continued, letting her finger delve lower down the valley between her breasts.

Dane coughed into his fist. "Is Antoinette available?"

Sophie tried to suppress her anger. Why did he want to see Antoinette? Why was he so blatant about it?

Madame Labelle smiled. "I shall have her sent up to the green room in fifteen minutes. You do remember? It is on the first floor, the second room on the right. And you, Mr. Shandy," Madame Labelle continued, turning to Sophie. "You may tell me why you find my paintings so enthralling."

Sophie watched Dane stroll out of the door on his way to his assignation. It took all the self-control she possessed not to chase after him and kick him in the shin or slap his face. She wanted to believe he'd changed, wanted to believe she was the only woman he desired.

But this was not about her or Dane. This was about finding James and, by her calculations, she had less than a week in which to do it.

"Now, Mr. Shandy," Madame Labelle said as she threaded her arm through Sophie's and led her around the room. "Is there a particular type of lady you prefer?"

"I am afraid, when it comes to ladies, I have rather limited tastes."

Madame Labelle seemed delighted at her response. "It is exactly as I supposed," she said. "I understand completely. You must say no more."

Sophie was well and truly baffled.

"Perhaps we should discuss the matter in the privacy of my chamber, for I would not wish to make a scene."

What does one do when being propositioned by the madam of a brothel?

Sophie did the only thing she could do under the circumstances. She brought Madame Labelle's fingers to her lips and asked respectfully, "Is there a place where I may see to my *toilette*?"

Madame Labelle gave her a knowing smile. "Of course, the blue room on the first floor is free. It is at the top of the stairs. You may see to your needs there, and I shall await you in my private room, which is just across the hall."

Sophie raced up the stairs as she needed to speak to Dane and had no desire to see him the arms of another woman, even if he was paying for the pleasure.

She almost fainted when she barged into the room, only to be met with the bare behind of an elderly gentleman, whose grunts and groans roused an image of a pig in distress. It was only when she felt her face burn, that she knew she had entered the red room by mistake.

Moving along the landing to the next room, Sophie placed her ear to the door in the hope she was not too late. There were no sounds coming from the room, so she took a deep breath and opened the door.

Dane, who was still fully clothed and perusing a set of leather-bound books on a shelf, swung around to face her. "What the hell are you doing up here?" he whispered.

"I could ask you the same question."

"You know why I'm here." He crossed the room to stand before her. "I need to see Antoinette."

Good heavens. The man had no shame.

"Apparently there are a lot of things you need from Antoinette," she replied, articulating every word.

He chuckled. "Do not tell me you're jealous?"

"Of course not." She prodded him in the chest, each jab forcing him to step back. "Just downright foolish for believing … for hoping you were not the libertine everyone professes you to be. To think I even considered giving myself to you."

He raised a brow and his mouth curved into a salacious grin. "You did?"

All the old feelings came flooding back, all the miserable memories.

Why was she so surprised?

Despite all her flagrant breaches of etiquette, she was still the country girl at heart, and she would never be enough for him.

Perhaps he believed her protestations against conformity meant she condoned such libidinous conduct. Yes, she wanted to be free from the constraints forced upon ladies of her station. Yes, she wanted a liaison with him; she wanted to feel desire and pleasure at his hands.

"Are you so licentious that you could not wait?" she asked, her voice revealing disappointment and a hint of sadness.

He grasped her upper arms and drew her closer. "Sophie, I pay Antoinette for information, nothing more."

It took a moment for her to absorb his words. All her mind could assemble was how sweet her name sounded when spoken so softly from his lips.

"Information?"

"It is all a ruse. I do not have time to talk now, but I will explain later." His gaze fell to her lips. "Perhaps when you have heard what I have to say, you may still have an appetite for dessert." His eyes locked with hers as his hands moved to cup her face. He bent his head and took her mouth in a gentle kiss that held a wealth of promise.

The sound of someone tutting in mild reproof captured her attention, and she turned to see a woman standing at the door.

"You could not wait for Antoinette, no?"

Wearing nothing more than a thin chemise, long corset, and a scandalously short petticoat, Antoinette strolled into the room as though walking down the boulevard on a sunny Parisian day. She closed the door and turned to face them, her red curls

spilling over her shoulders and bouncing on the rather voluminous display of pale-white bosom.

"Oh, it's you, me lord," Antoinette said, her dialect now
characteristic of a wench from Whitechapel. "Well, I'd never
have taken you for a Molly," she continued, her eyes wide.

"Give us a moment, Antoinette." Dane pulled Sophie to the
corner of the room and took her hands in his. "You need to leave
us," he whispered. "She'll tell me nothing while you're here.
You must trust me."

"Do you think she knows what happened on the night James
came here?"

He nodded over Sophie's shoulder towards Antoinette. "At
the very least, she will be able to tell us about the girl. Wait for
me downstairs. I'll be along shortly."

"I can't," Sophie whispered. "Madame Labelle wishes a
private audience. I think she has taken a liking to me."

"I would expect nothing less, Mr. Shandy," Dane mocked.
"After all, you do have the face of an angel."

No doubt tired of waiting, Antoinette walked over to the bed,
sat down and smoothed her hands over her white stockings.

"That is the point," Sophie continued. "I suspect she has seen
through my disguise."

"I do not want to cause any trouble for Antoinette. If you
wish to be independent minded, then you must find a way to
extricate yourself from this situation." He leant down and
brushed his mouth against hers. "I trust you will be able to find
an explanation to satisfy Madam Labelle."

He obviously thought her capable, and knowing he trusted
her gave her confidence in her abilities.

Besides, tonight she was Mr. Shandy.

And Mr. Shandy knew how to let a lady down gently.

CHAPTER 14

"*P*ay me no heed, Mr. Shandy," Madame Labelle said, patting Sophie's knee as they sat next to one another on the plush red sofa. "And forgive me if I was a little presumptuous. Visitors expect a certain coarseness of character, and I often get carried away playing the role."

"Your honesty is refreshing, madame," Sophie replied.

Having spent the last twenty minutes conversing about the weather, poetry, and Madame Labelle's love of Greek-inspired furniture, Sophie had finally plucked up the courage to respond to her more pertinent questions.

"However," Sophie continued, "I believe I acted impulsively in coming here tonight." Sophie stood and paced the floor, her hands clasped behind her back in a gentlemanly fashion. "You see, I decided to accompany Dane purely as a matter of enquiry, you understand." Sophie thought it best to remain as vague as possible whilst trying to add a modicum of honesty. All in the hope, it would sound sincere.

"Please, say no more." Madame Labelle held her hand up in a gesture of reassurance. "I only sought to offer guidance regarding your ... well, what I believed was your preference for a certain type of lady. I did not mean I would be the one providing such enlightenment."

A little embarrassed, Sophie nodded. "No, of course."

"May I tell you something, Mr. Shandy?" She did not wait for a reply. "I have met with many people over the years, too many," she continued gazing at an imagined scene in the distance, her sorrowful expression made all the more solemn by the dim candlelight. "I'm sure it would not surprise you to hear they have not always been pleasant. Indeed, many were insolent, often debasing, and on occasion utterly vicious." She rubbed her wrist as though alleviating an imagined pain, as though she still bore the scar. "Yet tonight is the first time, in such a long time, I have been made to feel like a lady."

Sophie dismissed the vivid images conjured by such a declaration and when she spoke, she did so with a warmth of feeling that reflected her compassion. "You flatter me, madame."

Madame Labelle stood and walked gracefully over to Sophie, taking her by the hand in a gesture one expects from a friend or companion. "I did not choose this life. It chose me. Such is the fate of some women." She shrugged in resignation. "If you should ever find yourself in such a desperate position. If you should ever need assistance, Mr. Shandy, then please know you may call upon me here and I will welcome you." She leant forward, placed a kiss on Sophie's cheek and whispered, "You are the first lady who has been kind enough to treat me as an equal."

Sophie gasped. "I … well, I …"

"Do you think after all these years I cannot tell the difference?" Madame Labelle raised her hand. "Let us say no more. I thank you for your company, but now I believe it is time to bid you good night, Mr. Shandy."

Sophie stepped away and bowed. "Thank you for such stimulating conversation. Good night, madame," she said, before leaving the room.

It had been rather an enlightening evening.

A simple issue of birth was the only thing separating her fate from Madame Labelle's. Whether one was forced to marry for wealth and station or whether one had no choice but to be a madam of a brothel, it all amounted to the same thing—compliance within the constraints of a society where men held all the power.

Sophie considered herself lucky. There were no family members forcing her to take a husband to enrich the family's bloodline. She had no interest in money, no desire to wear the latest fashions. Indeed, she would happily spend every day in the same dress, tending her cottage garden—if she could make her own choices.

As Sophie stepped out into the hall, she was surprised to find Dane propped up against the wall, his arms folded across his chest.

"The butler informed me you were still with Madame Labelle," he said, his expression grave as he straightened and walked towards her. "We need to leave." He took her by the elbow and practically dragged her to the door.

"At least give me a moment to put on my hat," she said sharply, for her emotions were running high this evening.

They'd retrieved their hats and were walking down the street at a brisk rate before Dane spoke. "After what Antoinette has told me, it is not safe for you there."

Sophie was almost running to keep up with his long strides. She stopped directly under a street lamp. "I cannot keep up with you when you walk at such a pace," she complained, slightly breathless.

He hastened to her side, placed his hand on her elbow and directed her to a place further down the street, to where the light was more subdued. "Catch your breath here for a moment," he said, looking back over her shoulder. "Haines will be waiting just around the corner." He hardly gave her a moment before he cupped her elbow and began moving again. "Do not turn around," he whispered. "I believe we are being followed."

Sophie gasped. "Are you certain?"

It took every ounce of self-control she had not to turn around and gape.

"The two men who are walking some way behind us were outside my house when we left this evening. I believe their aim is to merely gather information, else they would have had another man waiting here on the corner."

"How did they know we would be coming to Labelles?"

"They must have followed my carriage. After visiting your brother's residence, they know you're looking for him. They obviously know he came here, so it is only logical we would do the same." He glanced down at her, his face in partial shadow as they passed between the street lamps. His eyes were dark, unyielding; his jaw was clenched in steely determination. He looked sinfully handsome and downright dangerous. "When we turn the corner, I want you to run to the carriage and don't stop, no matter what you see or hear."

"What about you?" she asked, feeling a sudden pain in her chest.

"Do not worry about me. I'll be right behind you."

They turned the corner and out of view. He released her elbow, propelling her forward, so she had no choice but to run towards the carriage.

Aware of the danger, Haines did not get down from his box seat to open the door but prepared himself for a hasty departure. Sophie opened the carriage door and without dropping down the steps, vaulted into the carriage. She flung herself back against the squab, the sound of her heartbeat thumping in her ears.

What if something happened to Dane?

What if she never saw him alive again?

The next minute passed so slowly it felt like a lifetime. Fear choked her, and she could hear her breathing coming short and fast as the carriage started rolling forward.

Were they leaving without him?

Her thoughts became wild and chaotic as her mind conjured

all sorts of morbid images: a handsome, blood-soaked body, warm brown eyes now cloudy, opaque.

The dull thud of footsteps pounding the pavement caught her attention, and she gripped the cushioned seat as the door swung on its hinges and Dane jumped in.

The carriage picked up speed, and he slammed the door, fell back into the seat opposite and placed his hand over his heart, tapping his chest as he struggled to control his breathing.

Her terrified gaze shot to his hand. Ruby-red rivulets of blood stained his fingers and trickled down from split knuckles. He caught her gaze and removed a handkerchief from his coat pocket, dabbed it on the torn skin and winced when he clenched his fist to admire the damage.

"Your hand," she panted. "What happened?"

"It's nothing," he replied dismissively. "I have a rule about fleeing a scene without giving my pursuers an idea of what to expect should we ever meet again." He flexed his fingers, and she heard a bone crack. "I believe I caught one of them a little too hard on the jaw."

He placed his hat on the seat next to him, threw the handkerchief inside and used his good hand to run his fingers through his thick hair. A damp lock fell over his brow. He was still slightly breathless, and his eyes sparkled with exhilaration.

It was possibly the most enthralling vision she had ever seen.

A rush of pure physical desire flooded her senses, making her catch her breath, making her skin tingle. All she could think about was the memory of his warm mouth moving against hers, a memory she was desperate to relive.

He glanced up at her through the shadows, evidently mistaking her heated look for one of anger. "It's just a graze. It will heal." He shrugged, his tone apologetic. "I was never in any—"

"When will we be home?" Sophie interrupted, trying her best not to stumble over the words. "I mean, how long will it take?"

He hesitated and then peered out of the window at their surroundings. "Five minutes, perhaps. Why?"

"Would you mind pulling down your blind?" she asked, her hands trembling as she unbuttoned her coat and shrugged it off her shoulders. She folded it into a neat package and placed it on the seat with her hat.

"Certainly, but you'll be cold without your coat." He leant forward and pulled down the blind, plunging them into semi-darkness.

She almost laughed aloud. Was he feigning naiveté? Or was she so unskilled in the art of seduction, he was missing the signs? Sophie leant forward and pulled down her blind, too.

"You cannot expect to sleep—"

"Hush," she murmured in a soft, languorous tone. "I do not want to sleep, Dane. I do not want to think or talk."

I want to live. I want to choose. I want to be free.

With all the courage she could muster, she reached across and placed her hands on his knees. The hard muscles flexed beneath her fingers and she heard his sharp intake of breath. Before rational thought took over, she slid across and tumbled into his lap. "I just want to feel," she whispered in his ear.

He was silent for a moment as he breathed deeply. "Then I am more than happy to oblige," he murmured as she wrapped her arms around his neck and brushed her mouth softly against his.

She expected him to take control, but he did not.

Instead, he let her move her mouth over his in a slow, sensual assault that left her aching for something more. Desperate to feel the warmth of his body, she pressed herself against him letting her tongue skim lightly across the seam of his lips. Moving her hands to grip his shoulders, she turned in his lap, lifting one leg over to straddle him. His low, guttural groan of appreciation spurred her on, and she claimed his mouth again, her tongue finding his in a desperate bid to stoke the flames of passion coursing through her body. She let her hands trail down over his broad chest, giddy at the feel of him, even through his clothes.

"You *do* want me?" she asked, doubt creeping in.

"I have never wanted anything more in my entire life." His deep drawl sent her pulse racing, and he placed his arm around her waist and shuffled them both to the edge of the seat. He felt hard beneath his breeches, and as he pulled her closer, he rubbed against her most intimate place. "Is that not proof enough?"

The carriage rocked back and forth as it raced along the uneven road, the movement causing her to rub against him again and again, until she felt so drunk with desire she threw her head back and whispered his name.

"You've had your three minutes," he panted. "Now it's my turn."

She lifted her head and gazed into sinful brown eyes. "That only leaves you with two minutes," she teased.

"You will be amazed at what I can achieve in such a short time."

He wasted no time at all.

Despite grazed knuckles, his nimble fingers undid the buttons on her waistcoat, and he pulled her shirt until it was free of her breeches. Placing a hand behind her neck, he brought her mouth to his. He kissed her gently at first as he moved his free hand up inside the front of her shirt, his palm cupping her breast, his thumb brushing gently over her nipple.

"Oh, Dane," she whispered against his mouth.

He reclined back in the seat, and she followed him, grabbing the lapels of his coat, clutching the material in her fists as he took her mouth in a frenzy of unadulterated passion.

His hands drifted down to her waist and pulled her against him, and she could feel the rigid length of his arousal.

"Just think what it will be like when we are naked … when I am pushing deep inside you," he said as his mouth worked its way across her jaw and down her neck.

Sophie couldn't breathe; she couldn't think.

She felt hot, molten fire pulsing between her thighs, spreading through her body, building in heat and intensity. She could feel him, hard and solid through his breeches. Her skin tingled, her body trembled, desperate for something more.

Using both hands, he grasped her hips and began moving her back and forth in rapid strokes. Instinctively, as she rubbed against him, she arched her back, thrusting herself forward, giving access for his tongue to trace her nipple in circular motions through the fine fabric of her shirt. Then her breath came in short, sharp pants as she cried out, as her body convulsed with pure pleasure.

She collapsed in his arms and could have stayed there forever, her head on his shoulder, his strong arms clutching her close against his chest. But the carriage slowed and despite her slight embarrassment, she straightened. She was frightened to look at him, frightened she had disappointed him. After all, he had brought her pleasure. And she had brought him none.

What if she wasn't enough for him?

What would a mistress do that she hadn't?

Feeling a surge of anger at her lack of confidence, she looked up to find him lying back against the seat, his eyes closed, his breathing still ragged. She felt another burst of desire and could not help but lean down and kiss him softly on the mouth. His eyes shot open, and he pulled her closer, deepening the kiss.

The carriage rumbled to a halt, forcing her to pull away, and she moved to the seat opposite and straightened her clothes.

"If I'd known it was going to be like this," she said with a coy smile, "I would have let you have the whole five minutes."

His mouth curved up into a wicked grin. "It's not even midnight. Perhaps you still have an appetite for dessert."

Nerves threatened to overwhelm her, and she trampled them down. "I have suddenly developed a very large appetite," she said, hardly recognising her own voice.

"Then you're in luck because I believe we have only just

sampled the first course." His smile suddenly faded. "But we need to discuss what I discovered at Labelles."

She had spent the last six years preparing for this moment: for a chance to make her own choices, for a chance to prove she was more than a match for any woman. They would deal with her brother's problem in the morning. A few hours would not make any difference.

"What did you discover?" she asked playfully. "That two gentlemen can desire one another?"

"Trust me, you are no gentleman. Your body is too soft, too deliciously round in all the right places."

She gave a feigned gasp. "How very bold of you, my lord."

"Oh, I'm no longer a lord. I'm a prince hoping to be ravaged by a tiger."

$\mathscr{H}$e was going to marry Sophie Beaufort.

There, he had said it. Well, perhaps not aloud and not directly to the lady herself, but he had formed the words, nonetheless.

He glanced at the lady in question as she sauntered up the stone steps, her hips swaying in the tight breeches as she carried her coat over her arm. In fact, he was so damn smitten the words may as well have been carved into his forehead.

Besides, he would not be able to bed her without placating his conscience. And by God, he would bury himself deep inside her even if he spent the rest of his life paying for the pleasure.

It would not be a sacrifice; he was going to have to marry, eventually. Why not Sophie Beaufort? He liked her, found her intriguing, interesting, and her passionate nature was more than a match for his own.

The memory of her examining Madame Labelle's erotic engravings, of her panting and writhing in his lap, caused another stab of lustful desire. Of course, he expected such feelings to fade once his insatiable thirst for her had been quenched.

Mrs. Cox rushed to greet them in the hall, straightening her apron and cap as though she had just woken from a nap. "Will you be wanting anything from the kitchen, my lord?" she asked, failing to suppress a yawn.

"Nothing for me, Mrs. Cox," he replied, presenting her with his usual charming smile. The feel of Miss Beaufort's soft thighs wrapped around him was the only thing *he* needed. "I believe I am in desperate need of my bed. What about you, Miss Beaufort? Can Mrs. Cox be of service or are you as eager as I to get to bed?"

Miss Beaufort smiled and raised her brow, showing amusement at his mischievous remarks. "If it is not too much trouble, I would love a glass of syllabub." She stepped closer and touched Mrs. Cox affectionately on the arm. "But would you mind if I took it up to my room? You see, like Lord Danesfield, I too can think of nothing other than tumbling into bed. Yet, the thought of tasting something sweet is just too tempting an offer to pass."

Good Lord.

For a woman of little experience, she was extremely skilled in the art of titillation, Sebastian thought. Had it not been for Mrs. Cox, he'd have said he would like to taste something sweet in his mouth, too, and it wouldn't be syllabub.

"I shall have Amy bring it right up," Mrs. Cox replied.

"There's no need. You may send Amy off to bed as I will not require her services tonight." She waved her hand over her gentleman's clothes. "I shall follow you to the kitchen and then you must get yourself off to bed, too."

Miss Beaufort was obviously determined to test his patience.

He watched them walk off down the hall before she stopped and looked over her shoulder. "Good night, Lord Danesfield," she said softly. Her gaze swept over him: a look that made him feel as though she had stripped him of his clothes and was pleased with what she saw.

"Good night, Miss Beaufort," he replied, refusing to allow the smallest spark of disappointment show.

He waited until she was out of sight before climbing the stairs to his chamber.

Once inside, he took the candle from the side table and lit the wall sconce. He removed his coat, waistcoat, and cravat and draped them over the back of the chair, which he casually dropped into to remove his boots.

Whilst visiting Labelles had proved to be fruitful and had given him plenty to consider, he could not seem to focus on anything other than his delectable guest.

No one had ever captured his interest to this degree.

Perhaps it had something to do with the fact that he couldn't predict her mood. She had shocked him when she'd thrown herself into his lap. So what the hell was she doing eating blasted syllabub when she should be in bed with him?

Perhaps he should go to her room and simply knock on the door. But what would he say?

He relaxed back in the chair and closed his eyes, indifferent to the fact he was creasing his clothes. But even in the darkness, she was still there, straddling his lap, thrusting soft mounds of creamy flesh at him as the tip of her tongue traced her lips.

Bloody hell!

He stood abruptly and dragged his hand down his face to quell his raging desire. Perhaps she just enjoyed teasing him. Perhaps she'd thought on the matter and decided he was not worth the effort. Or more to the point not worth her virtue.

How could he argue with that?

Pulling his shirt over his head, he stomped over to the wash-bowl and thrust his hands into the cool water, splashing it over his face and arms, yet it provided little relief. Perhaps he should secure a betrothal before seducing her, he thought, removing the rest of his clothes and climbing in between the cold sheets.

He laughed as he remembered something James Beaufort had said about trying to trap lightning in a bottle. He had a strange feeling securing a betrothal from Miss Beaufort would be even more difficult.

He was still awake when he heard the gentle tap on the door, but she did not wait for a response before entering. Feigning sleep, he watched her through half-closed eyes as she stepped inside and gently closed the door. She stood motionless for a moment, her back pressed against the jamb, her slow, deep breaths audible.

She came closer. Her gaze drifted over his bare chest and he took the opportunity to study her.

Her ebony hair hung in loose waves. Although it was much shorter than he preferred, there was something alluring about the way it danced on her shoulders. He had no idea what she was wearing for her body was shrouded in a red plaid blanket. Her gaze roamed back up towards his face, and she bit down on her lower lip.

Guilt gently pricked his conscience, but he was far too intrigued to open his eyes fully. It was then that the blanket slipped from her shoulders, sinking to the floor in a pool around her feet.

He had died and gone to heaven.

It was either that or he was lying in his bed at the complete mercy of an angel.

Like a scene to rival any of Madame Labelle's erotic paintings, she stood in a thin chemise. Every curve was visible, yet muted by the soft candlelight. He almost groaned in appreciation, but his mouth was dry. Every muscle in his body grew taut with anticipation. She stretched out her hand and let her fingers glide over the muscles in his chest. He stopped breathing. When they trailed down over the muscles in his abdomen to the sheet straddling his hips, his blood pumped through his veins at so rapid a rate he thought he may lose consciousness.

He had never been so hard in his life.

No other woman had ever aroused his passions to this degree. No other woman had ever seduced him, mind, body, and soul.

As her fingers skimmed the edge of the sheet, he could no longer restrain himself. "You could have at least woken me so I may participate," he said softly, his tone betraying his arousal. "Or are you simply hell-bent on pleasurable torture?"

She jumped back. Her hand shot up to her mouth to smother a gasp. When she eventually lowered it, he was greeted by the tips of two perfect nipples protruding through the fine fabric. He closed his eyes with a low, guttural groan.

"I wasn't sure ... I didn't know if ..."

One did not often find an innocent in the guise of a wicked temptress, one who sought to secure her own ravishment.

"I thought you'd changed your mind." He sighed.

"I ... I thought you might come to my room."

"It would be unwise for me to be seen entering your room."

Oblivious to the effect her undergarment was having on him, she placed her hands on her hips, drawing his attention to the dark shadow at the apex of her thighs. Unable to control his eager body, he threw back the sheets and jumped out of bed to stand in front of her.

Her eyes widened at the sight of his jutting manhood. "You're naked," she gasped.

"Obviously," he grinned. "Isn't that why you were peeking under the sheets?" He stepped closer and his hands settled on her waist. "As much as I find your chemise utterly enthralling," he said, grasping the material and bunching it at her hips. "I believe I would prefer to see it lying on the floor." In one swift movement, he lifted the item up over her head and threw it over his shoulder.

She stood before him, wearing nothing but the finery of her birth—and how fine it was, he thought, as he took a moment to appreciate her creamy-white skin, her soft, round breasts, the delicate flare of her hips. Noticing her flushed complexion he raised his hand and cupped her cheek.

"You are beyond beautiful, Sophie," he whispered. "But if you are not ready for this. If you do not wish ..."

He noticed her finger tremble when she placed it to his lips to silence him. "This is what I choose," she said. Standing on the tips of her toes, she kissed him on the mouth in a slow, deliberate exploration that alluded to something deeper than physical desire.

"You cannot possibly know how much I want you," he whispered, his body aching with need.

"Then perhaps you had better show me."

Powerless to resist such an enticing invitation, he crushed her to his chest, felt her shudder as his throbbing erection pressed against her stomach. Her hands came around to rest on his back. The tentative touch of her fingers on his skin sent a shiver through his body, and he took her mouth in a desperate frenzy. Mere seconds later their kiss became a frantic mix of panting, breathless moans, and urgent hands scrambling over bare skin in a bid to find any place that would bring relief to the craving that consumed them.

He could not get enough of her.

The need to mate with her, the need to thrust himself inside her, engulfed him almost to the point of no return. Somewhere in the depths of his mind he remembered she had never been with a man before. He did not want so hasty a coupling to dampen her passion for him. He wanted her to ache for him, to feel a hunger that could never be sated. So he drew upon years of skill and tore his lips from hers.

"We should take it a little slower," he panted.

She stared up at him, desire sparkling in her bright blue eyes.

"Come," he said, taking her hand and pulling her down onto the bed. "Let me show you how much I want you."

She went with him without saying a word. Her eyes locked with his in a look that spoke of longing, of lust and of something else—trust. The thought rocked him to his core. He would not disappoint her; she would never regret giving herself to him.

He lay on his side next to her, took a strand of ebony hair and let it fall gently through his fingers. As he leant over her and placed a soft, tender kiss on her swollen lips, they parted on a sigh. He planted kisses along her jaw and down her neck, cupped her breast and traced around the pretty pink nipples until they hardened beneath his touch. Moving down, he took one in his mouth, his tongue flicking over the peak and she arched instinctively to meet him, her hands coming up around his neck, her fingers grasping his hair in an attempt to press herself more fully against his mouth.

It took every ounce of strength he could muster, not to bury himself inside her, there and then.

To prolong the moment, he let his fingers glide over her stomach, delving lower until he reached the dark, silken curls between her thighs. As his tongue flicked back and forth over her nipple, his fingers, in slow rhythmical movements, massaged the soft, damp flesh of her womanhood.

"Dane ... I ..."

Writhing in his arms, she moaned and panted, then she grasped his hair and guided him back up to her mouth. Their mouths met with a burst of unbridled passion, hot and wet, tangled tongues and guttural groans. Try as he might he could not slacken the raging fever coursing through his veins. Whenever he inhaled, he could smell her womanly scent; stimulating his senses, surrounding him, drawing him deeper and deeper into an abyss.

"I need to taste you," he growled, breaking the kiss to move between her thighs.

"*Dane*," she gasped.

The sound of his name falling from her lips spurred him on. He did not give her a chance to protest, for his mouth found her with an urgency he could not control, and with the first circle and flick of his tongue, she was writhing beneath him once again.

God, she was so sweet.

When she thrust her hips up to meet him, he quickened his pace. He devoured her, matching every soft whimper with a gentle suck and flick until her breath became ragged and she dug her nails into his shoulders, shuddering as she found her release.

~

The whole world shattered into a million sparkling pieces. Everything she knew, everything she thought, everything she felt had just been obliterated in a moment of overwhelming bliss.

Somehow it still wasn't enough.

She wanted more from him.

She stared at the man who had brought her such pleasure, at the man she had chosen to be her one and only lover. The seductive grin playing at the corners of his mouth conveyed a confidence in his ability to please.

As though hearing her silent plea, he moved above her with panther-like grace: a slow, languorous prowl that made her pulse race and her inner muscles contract. Feeling the warmth radiate from his broad chest as he hovered over her, she raised her hands to caress the hard planes.

"You are magnificent," she breathed, conveying what was in her heart without thought or censor.

His low chuckle held a hint of embarrassment. "I was just thinking the same about you."

The heat in his eyes caused her heart to flutter. As she lowered her gaze, she noticed the thin scar running from his shoulder and across his chest, slicing through the dusting of dark hair. She traced the smooth line with the soft pad of her finger. His body shuddered in response. Her mind became flooded with various images: of a jilted lover exacting her revenge, of him being discovered in the arms of another gentleman's wife.

As though sensing her disquiet he moved to her side, took her hand and brought it to his lips, placing light kisses across the tops of her fingers.

"It is nothing," he whispered, taking the tip of her finger into his mouth, his tongue circling it before he pursed his lips and sucked gently, sending shivers sweeping through her body.

Suddenly, all thoughts became incoherent, disjointed, until all she could think about was the pleasure he gave her. With her free hand, she cupped the back of his neck and pulled him to lie on top of her, pouring every passionate emotion she had ever felt for him into a kiss that quickly became desperate and urgent.

With his knee, he coaxed her legs further apart. She felt the delicious weight of his hot body, felt the hard length of him nudge against her. He pulled away, the loss like an empty void opening in the pit of her stomach. But then he took her nipple into his mouth once more, simultaneously pressing against her until she became so desperate for the feel of him that she clutched his firm buttocks and thrust herself against him.

"I'm sorry," he panted, "but I simply cannot wait a moment longer."

"Please, please hurry," she begged, not really understanding what it was she wanted.

"Tell me you want me."

"I … I want you. It has always been you."

Needing no further inducement, he entered her. She shifted slightly to accustom herself to the intrusion. How she loved the feel of his body against hers: large, warm, commanding. Instinctively, on the next slow thrust, she wrapped her legs around him, relishing in his groan of appreciation as the movement caused him to slide deeper.

"Forgive me," he whispered, claiming her mouth with pure carnal lust.

She was so lost in the dizzying heights of her own desire it took a moment for her to feel the sharp pain as he gave one long, powerful thrust to bury himself completely. He stilled, as though not wanting to add to her discomfort. But the searing pain was soon forgotten, replaced with a stirring of deep emotion she did not expect.

She was joined with him in the most intimate, most sacred of acts. Spread beneath him in wanton abandon, with a man she swore she would never show her vulnerability to again. And yet, she was not sorry. As he moved, she closed her eyes: a moment to treasure the memory as her body hugged the thick length of him.

When she looked up, he was staring at her. And with each slow rhythmical thrust those sinful brown eyes caressed her, as though to see into her soul increased his sense of pleasure. He rolled his hips as he drove deeper, rode harder. The tension built within until she was so tightly strung her body cried out for release. Aching in anticipation, her frantic hands clutched at the taut muscles in his back, grabbed his buttocks and urged him on.

"My God, you're incredible," he groaned between breathless pants.

"*Dane*," she cried as an intense feeling of ecstasy rippled like warm waves through her body, leaving her shuddering and convulsing beneath him.

In the distance, she heard his roar of satisfaction, felt the warmth of his body as he collapsed on top of her. He rolled on to his back, wrapped his arm around her and pulled her closer, his heart pounding beneath her hand as she placed it on his chest.

"Is it... is it always like this?" she asked dreamily.

He wrapped his arms tightly around her and kissed the top of her head. "Never as good as this."

CHAPTER 16

*M*adame Labelle was relaxing in her hip bath in front of the fire when the clock chimed five.

She breathed a sigh of relief when the heaving and banging above stairs finally ceased, for they had been far more rowdy than usual. The young blood obviously had something to prove; else his friends were running a book on who could groan the loudest. Poor Beth would need considerably more for breakfast, she thought, as she scooped up a rose petal from the water and caressed it between her fingers.

For some reason, her thoughts were drawn to Mr. Shandy: a thornless flower of grace and beauty, whose strength was of the heart, not the fist. A woman to be admired and respected, a woman she could have been had her parents lived, and she'd remained in the pretty Sussex village. In some other life, where things were not tainted and corrupt, they may have even been friends.

The loud rap on the door did not startle her. Nothing could shock or surprise her anymore. Indeed, when she opened the door to discover that the Comte de Dampierre requested her presence in her private drawing room, the only thought she concealed was disdain.

With no time to change, she threw on her dowdy nightgown and covered it with a silk wrapper. Then she brushed her golden hair so it hung over her shoulder. As she placed the brush back on the table, her gaze fell to the small Bible: a fragment of her other life. Her father had always said it was not for us to question the hand of the Lord. The path to enlightenment reveals itself to all in due course.

Well, she was still waiting.

She placed her palm on top of the book and closed her eyes. "I'm sorry," she said softly, knowing it would take more than a heartfelt apology to absolve her of all her sins.

Making her way downstairs, she noticed Morgan standing guard outside the door. "Does he ever sleep?" she whispered, nodding towards the closed door.

She did not expect an answer, for the man was an animal, distant and detached from humanity, trained only to respond to his master's call. Yet she thought she glimpsed a flicker of compassion in those cold, blue eyes, a warning to tread carefully as this was not a social call.

Victor was alone. He had his back to the door; one hand braced against the mantel as he stared into the fire. A hazy mist from a half-smoked cheroot swirled ominously around his shoulders, drifting up towards the ceiling to make its escape.

"Ah! Marie." He turned to face her. "Have I disturbed you?"

"Not at all, Victor," she lied. He had been a constant disturbance since the fateful afternoon when he approached her outside the Servants' Registry Office. "You wish to speak to me."

Victor snorted. "Always the obedient servant," he mocked, throwing his cheroot into the fire. He sauntered over, grasped her chin between his finger and thumb and kissed her roughly on the mouth. "Though your lips, they always betray you," he sneered, pulling away with such force she stumbled.

"I am tired, Victor, that is all," she replied in an attempt to placate him.

"You are tired ... you, Marie. The one who has her every need provided for. The one who benefits most from our ... little enterprise." He waved his hand in the air to stress his point.

The one who benefits! I am a mother to whores, a liar, a deceiver.

"The one," he continued, "who would betray the hand that feeds her."

His words sent a shiver down her spine.

Betray!

If Victor believed her inconstant, she was as good as dead. Had he found the girl? Did he know she had aided her escape?

She struggled to maintain her composure as a wave of panic took hold and so she stepped forward and placed her hands on the lapels of his coat in the hope he wouldn't notice them shaking.

"Victor, what am I supposed to have done?" she asked. "What reason could I have for betraying you? Where would I be now without your support and guidance?"

I would be a wife, a mother, a woman with dignity.

"You would be nothing," he spat.

"Have I not always done what you've asked?" She looked him keenly in the eye. "And I will continue to do so."

He studied her with some suspicion. "We shall see," he replied, his voice laced with contempt, and he brushed her hands away from his coat as though they were the filthy hands of a chimney sweep. "Sit down," he barked, gesturing to a nearby chair.

He turned and yelled for Morgan, his tone crude and coarse like a butcher hawking meat at the market.

Morgan entered, took a few solid strides and stopped in the middle of the room. With his hands clasped behind his back, he stared at an imaginary place in the distance. His flat nose and protruding forehead gave him the look of a man who instilled confidence in his ability to get the job done.

"The men you posted at Beaufort's residence," Victor began,

pacing back and forth. "You will tell me again what they have discovered."

Morgan recounted the events in a tone lacking feeling or inflection. "The gentleman caller questioned the servants, then left. Hodges followed him back to a house in Red Lion Square."

Victor stopped his pacing and turned his attention to Marie. "Now, you will tell Marie who else lives in this house in Red Lion Square." His eyes were sharp, focused and resembled a hawk watching its prey, waiting for the smallest flicker of recognition so he could swoop in for the kill.

"The house is also occupied by the Marquess of Danesfield."

Victor bent down, so his eyes were level with hers. His hands gripped the arms of the chair, boxing her in. "And where do you think those gentlemen spent their evening, Marie?" he spat, the smell of cheap brandy and stale tobacco irritating her nostrils. "Where, Marie?" he shouted when she failed to answer.

"Why, they spent the evening here, Victor," she replied, her voice calm and steady. "As do many high-ranking gentlemen. Indeed, there are still a few lords sampling our wares as we speak."

Victor grabbed her by the arm and hauled her to her feet. "Do not mistake me for a fool," he muttered through clenched teeth. "Did you know this Dane is Beaufort's closest neighbour? Did you know these men were looking for him?"

"Victor, please. It is nothing more than a coincidence," she pleaded, struggling to free her arm.

"I do not believe in coincidence, Marie." He pulled her to his chest, forcing her to stand on the tips of her toes. "What did you tell him?" he bellowed. "What did you tell this Mr. Shandy while you were alone with him?"

He threw her back down into the chair, the force causing the front legs to rise clean off the floor.

"Nothing, Victor, I told him nothing," she cried. "This is absurd." She flinched as he lifted his hand to strike her. Behind him, Morgan stiffened, and his sudden cough caused Victor to turn around. "I did not know of any connection to Lord Beaufort. You must believe me," she whispered, using the distraction to plead her case.

"Then what the hell was he doing in here, Marie? What was he doing in your private room?" He bent down, grabbed her face and squashed her mouth together with his bony fingers, only releasing her when she tried to speak.

"I … I invited him, Victor, but it is not what you think. I invited him because he … because … Mr. Shandy is a woman."

Victor straightened abruptly and took a step back, his face frozen, immobile. Lost in contemplation, he played with the point of his beard, twirling it back and forth with his fingers. "You are sure of this?" he asked, seeming pleased by the prospect.

"I am certain, Victor," she replied, trying to quash the uneasy feeling whirling around in her stomach. "I was simply intrigued by him … by her." She had nothing to feel guilty about. Her confession had probably saved Mr. Shandy's life.

Victor folded his arms across his chest and tapped his lip with his finger. "Describe him to me, his hair, his eyes."

Marie found it an odd question, but she was in no position to challenge him. "His hair was black, perhaps too long for the current fashion, but it was tied back in a queue. And his eyes, well …" Marie thought for a moment. She had been touched by the sincerity of those angelic eyes. "They were the brightest blue."

Victor seemed delighted with her answer. "Antoinette," he mused, turning to Morgan. "Bring her to me." He waited for his man to leave and then turned his attention to Marie. "While you have been granted a … reprieve of sorts, it is only temporary." He removed his watch and checked the time before returning it to his pocket. "I do not trust you, Marie, and so I shall require some attestation of your loyalty."

Before Marie could answer, the door burst open, and Antoinette stumbled in pulling a wrapper over her shoulder. It was impossible to tell if she had been roused from sleep or from the arms of an amorous lord.

"Antoinette," Victor said with a sigh to suggest he found the whole affair rather tedious. "As much as I detest the idea of discussing business at such an ungodly hour, I want you to tell me what … services you performed for the Marquess of Danesfield."

Why on earth was Victor interested in Danesfield's licentious habits?

Antoinette licked her lips as though the sensation stimulated her memory. "Let's just say, he's quite keen on my vocal abilities," she replied.

Antoinette had chosen her words carefully, knowing Victor's distaste for vulgarity.

Victor's lips curved into a wry smile. "And the marquess, did he take a dip in the *cupidinous font*?" When Antoinette stared at him blankly, he rephrased his question. "Did you have relations of an intimate nature?"

Recognition dawned. "Not this time," Antoinette replied. "His lordship was concerned for his gentleman friend. He didn't want to leave him alone for too long."

"Did he say anything else?"

Antoinette cocked her head to the side and stared up at the ceiling. "Well, we got straight to it, if you know what I mean. But he did ask if there were any new girls."

"And how did you reply?"

Antoinette placed her hands on her hips. "I told him it's not nice to ask after other ladies, told him there was no one else in the whole of Labelles with a mouth sweeter than Antoinette's."

Victor's beady eyes studied Antoinette. "The marquess, he always asks for you … specifically?"

Overcome with a sense of dread, Marie rose from the chair under the guise of pouring herself a drink. "I'm sure he's had other girls," she remarked casually.

If Antoinette said anything to displease Victor, she would end up on one of his little trips, never to be seen again.

But Victor did not give her a chance to answer.

"Never mind," he said, waving her away. "That will be all for the moment."

Victor waited until Morgan had led Antoinette from the room before speaking. "Fate has brought your Mr. Shandy to our door." He took the glass of brandy Marie offered and sat down on the chaise. "Fate has punished us in order to reveal our reward."

Marie watched him over the rim of her glass. Although his coal-black eyes revealed no emotion, his general countenance suggested he was in good spirits. It was a bad sign. The coil of fear tightened in her stomach.

"And how are we to be rewarded, Victor?"

"Perhaps we should thank Lord Beaufort," he replied, taking a sip of brandy, "for meddling in our affairs."

Marie sat down opposite him, every muscle in her body tense. "I'm sure you will find a way to repay him, Victor."

"Do not worry your head, Marie. Beaufort will rue the day he interfered. Indeed, he will have to live with the knowledge that in rescuing one maiden he inadvertently led us to another."

Marie stopped breathing. "You speak of Mr. Shandy?" She struggled to hide the tremble in her voice.

"I speak of Miss Beaufort," he corrected with some annoyance. "Lord Beaufort's sister. I find the thought of her parading about town in a pair of breeches highly distasteful. And the marquess, he will pay for it dearly."

Fear gripped her in its talons. "You intend to use Miss Beaufort to replace Annabel?"

"No, Marie. Fate has another purpose for Miss Beaufort." He swirled the amber liquid around in the glass. "And you, you are going to help me achieve it."

CHAPTER 17

Sebastian woke to the sound of clinking glass. He propped himself up on his elbows and glanced instinctively towards the window.

Squinting in the darkness, he followed the sound to the figure sitting in the chair in the corner of the room. With his shoulders hunched and head drooped low, his body appeared larger than his head. When Sebastian slid his hand under the pillow in an attempt to locate his knife, the figure spoke.

"Oh, you're awake." The feminine voice, whilst cheerful, sounded a little apprehensive.

Sebastian narrowed his gaze. "Sophie?" He patted the other side of the bed to reassure himself it was empty. "What are you doing out of bed?"

The mere thought that she should be in his bed was enough to arouse him again.

"I did not want to wake you," she whispered tentatively. "You were sleeping so soundly."

"I do not normally sleep very well at all," he replied, both amazed and alarmed he had not heard her movements. "Is that why you're sitting in the dark?"

"No ... well, yes I suppose it is."

He could hear the nervous hitch in her voice and knew she was trying to place some distance between them. But why? Had she returned to her room, he could have believed she felt some regret over her decision to deepen their acquaintance. However, she had waited for him, albeit on the other side of the room and in the dark. Perhaps she was feeling a little shy after having been so intimate with him.

"I could have sworn I heard a clinking sound," he said to distract her while he climbed out of bed to open the curtains. Dawn was fast approaching, and its soft, muted rays cast a faint glow over the room.

"It was probably the noise of the spoon scraping against the glass," she replied.

When he turned towards her, he caught his breath. Wrapped in the tartan blanket and her hair in disarray, she sat huddled in the chair, eating Mrs. Cox's syllabub.

He had never seen a more appealing sight.

"It seemed a shame to waste it after Mrs. Cox had gone to all the trouble of whipping the cream." She looked up from the glass as she placed another spoonful into her mouth and froze. Her eyes grew wide as they perused his naked form before darting back down to the floor.

He bit back a chuckle for he found her reaction highly amusing. He liked seeing her like this, so shy and vulnerable. It was a side she so seldom revealed.

As if on cue, she muttered something under her breath, and he suppressed another grin when she straightened her back, lifted her head and looked him square in the eye. "Would you like some?" she asked with a newfound boldness.

Would he like some? He wanted everything she had to offer and more. "That all depends," he drawled, taking a step towards her, "on what it is you're offering."

With a coy smile, she dipped the spoon into the glass and scooped up a generous helping. "Here," she said, holding out the spoon.

Sebastian could not decide if it was the most innocent of gestures or a prerequisite to seduction. The lady certainly was an enigma. It was not until he had taken a step towards her that he discovered he had been wrong on both counts. With a flick of the spoon, she watched with delight as its contents flew through the air and landed on his chin.

There was a moment of silence. Neither knew what the other would do. Sophie pursed her lips in an attempt to suppress a grin while she waited for his reaction.

"When I catch you," he began, wiping his chin and sucking syllabub off his finger "I shall make you lick it all off." He watched her eyes widen with fear, with excitement. "You have until the count of three," he said, noting her hesitance. She obviously did not believe him. "One …"

"Don't be ridiculous."

"Two …"

"You can't," she began, but then must have decided that he could for she placed the glass on the table, wrapped the blanket tightly around her shoulders and bolted for the door.

"Three." He reached the door before she had a chance to open it, grabbed her round the waist and pulled her back against his bare chest. "You'll have to do better than that," he whispered in her ear.

"How about this?" She stamped on his toe.

"Ow!"

As he relaxed his grip, she dropped her weight, twisted her body and ducked underneath his arm. "I'll have you know, I can be a formidable adversary when I put my mind to it," she boasted, running to the far side of the bed.

"A point I would do well to remember." He feigned a limp to gain some ground. For dramatic effect, he grabbed the bedpost, using it for support.

The smile vanished from her lips. "Dane, I'm sorry," she said, looking down at his toe. "Have I hurt you?"

"I'll live."

Good. She was so concerned with his toe she'd forgotten all about his nakedness. The sooner she accepted him as a man and not some symbol of patriarchal dominance, the sooner he could get her to St George's.

Then she made the fatal mistake of taking a few steps towards him. Letting go of the post, he pretended to stumble and reached out for assistance. As she caught him, her blanket fell to the floor, and he noticed she was wearing nothing but a chemise.

"Now, I believe there is the matter of dessert to attend to." He collapsed onto the bed, taking her with him.

"What about your toe?" she exclaimed, but then a spark of recognition flashed in her pretty blue eyes. "Why, you monster," she cried, pounding his chest with her fist. "And to think I felt sorry for you."

Sebastian wrapped his arms around her. "In battle, one does what one must," he said, staring at her sweet mouth.

"Well, the joke is on you, for there is not one drop of syllabub left on your chin."

"When I mentioned dessert, it was not syllabub I had in mind," he said as his mouth found hers with a need he could not quite comprehend.

Breakfast was a far more formal affair than usual. The servants bustled around with renewed efficiency, bringing in plate after plate of ham, eggs, bacon, and an assortment of bread and jam. Everyone appeared deliriously happy. It was all rather ironic considering the fact his guest had taken to parading about town in gentleman's attire, had been rescued from footpads after visiting a brothel and had since been ravished by the master, twice!

He glanced across the table at Miss Beaufort, who had just taken a bite out of a piece of toast plastered in a ridiculous amount of strawberry jam. She looked up at him and smiled. It felt as though his heart had suddenly dropped into his stomach.

It was not the sort of smile he was used to. It was not the smile of a coquette, not delivered with skilled artifice. It was a smile of genuine affection, with a genuine degree of warmth to indicate she found pleasure in his company. Never before had he held any fanciful notions of chivalry. Yet he could not suppress the need to protect her, to care for her, to bury himself inside her and never let her go. Indeed, he had been so caught up in their game of seduction he had almost forgotten about James Beaufort.

"I believe it's time we discussed the matter of Antoinette," he said, silently acknowledging the sooner this whole business was concluded, the sooner he could arrange a special licence and make this thing between them official.

"You must have read my mind." She placed the teacup back on the saucer. "I must admit, I have been feeling a little guilty for ... well," she blushed, "for placing my own needs above those of my brother."

"We must be discreet," he began. But he knew she had misunderstood when her cheeks flushed deep crimson. "I mean, we must be judicious in our enquiries, not in our ..." he waved his hand back and forth between them rather than embarrass her further. "There was nothing we could have done last night. Besides, James is more than capable of taking care of himself."

She appeared to consider his comment. "You're right about James. But I still don't understand why he's involved with Dampierre."

Sebastian swallowed a piece of ham and placed his cutlery on his plate. "I suspect it has something to do with Annabel."

Sophie looked at him blankly.

"Annabel," he repeated, "the girl who accompanied James when he gave me the necklace." He reached across the table for the coffee pot.

"I thought you said you didn't know her," she replied,

shaking her head and holding up her hand when he offered to pour her a cup.

He smiled to himself for there was a hint of jealousy in her tone. "I don't," he reiterated. "When James stopped my carriage, he called out to her. Then last night, Antoinette told me that a girl by the name of Annabel had run away from Labelles."

"Annabel's a prostitute?"

"Well, this is where it all gets rather interesting." He paused while Mrs. Cox removed some plates and took them out to the kitchen. "Antoinette said that Annabel was a servant, not a prostitute. She said the girl had been at Labelles for a little over a week. Apparently, she was not supposed to leave her room but had somehow ended up serving drinks downstairs."

A deep frown marred her brow. "Do you think James helped her to run away?"

"Most definitely," he nodded, although why he would risk his life for a servant girl was another matter.

"How very heroic of him." She sighed, clasping her hands to her bosom. "He can be extremely gallant when he has a mind to."

"Indeed," Sebastian replied with a hint of sarcasm. He was so gallant he had left his sister to fend for herself in his absence. "There was talk that a gentleman had offered Madame Labelle a rather large sum of money in exchange for the girl."

"It could not have been James. He does not have that sort of money. Not when—" She paused briefly and then sighed. "He did not offer money, did he? You think he offered our mother's necklace."

"I'm afraid it is the only thing that makes sense," Sebastian said. She looked down into her lap, and Sebastian stretched across the table and lifted her chin. "He must have felt it was necessary," he said softly in an attempt to soothe her. The way he felt at the moment, he would give everything he owned just to see her smile.

"It is not the money," she said slowly. "James will find

another way to secure the funds he needs." She sighed once more. "My mother adored the necklace. But some things are more important than jewels, more important than money."

He sat back in his chair. He wanted to tell her she was naive. He knew what it was like to watch those he was responsible for suffer from cold, illness, and hunger. In such circumstances, nothing was more important than money.

Lost in thought, she nibbled on a piece of cold toast. "The Comte de Dampierre, do you know where he fits into this?"

Sebastian shook his head. "No, Antoinette refused to discuss it. She said she had not told me anything I could not have found out from someone else. But she would say nothing against Madame Labelle or anyone else associated with her. She said she has no intention of ending up as Haymarket ware."

"Perhaps he is a patron. Now I come to think of it, Dampierre did say that James had offered to exchange the necklace for something of value. If James offered the necklace in exchange for Annabel, then that means Dampierre is somehow involved with Madame Labelle." She shook her head. "No, I don't know why, but Madame Labelle does not seem the sort of woman to become entangled with a man like Dampierre."

Now she did sound extremely naïve. He had suspected the connection but was waiting for proof. "I have asked Dudley Spencer to look into it. I must call round today and see if he has made any progress."

"Will Mrs. Spencer be at home? I should like to make her acquaintance."

He glanced across at her, admiring the way the simple ivory dress hugged her figure. "It would mean dressing as Mr. Shandy." He sighed, somewhat disgruntled she would be changing into gentlemen's attire.

"Why so glum? You have always seemed so fond of my breeches."

An image of her at Rockingham Pool flashed through his mind. He was just thinking of offering to help her squeeze into the said garment when Mrs. Cox entered and spoilt his little daydream.

"There's a letter been delivered for you, miss." Mrs. Cox stepped around the table to hand it to Sophie.

"For me?" With some hesitation, she took the letter. "It is addressed to Miss Beaufort. Do you think it might be from James?" She hugged it to her chest, oblivious to the threat such a letter posed.

"Might I suggest you open it," Sebastian replied with some trepidation. Whoever sent the letter was aware of her identity and that she was staying in a house with an unmarried gentleman.

Sophie tore open the seal, and her gaze drifted down to the bottom of the page. "It's from Madame Labelle." She looked up with a puzzled expression and Sebastian resisted the urge to rip it from her hand. She continued reading and then glanced up at him. "She insists I meet with her this afternoon. She insists it is a matter of life or death."

CHAPTER 18

*S*ophie noticed Dudley Spencer glance at his wife, Charlotte, who looked up from pouring tea and acknowledged his raised brow with a sly smirk.

The tension in the air was palpable.

Dane raked his fingers through his hair. "Please, Dudley. Would you explain to Miss Beaufort that it would be nothing short of madness to meet with this woman?"

Mr. Spencer sat back in the chair and steepled his fingers. "But were you not the one who escorted Miss Beaufort to Labelles? You obviously had no problem leaving her alone with the woman," he replied, challenging his friend to defy his reasoning.

"Thank you, Mr. Spencer," Sophie said triumphantly, grateful someone could see there was an element of logic to her decision.

As Dudley Spencer had found no current record of the Comte de Dampierre, the previous comte having passed away without issue over three hundred years ago, then Madame Labelle was the only person who could shed any light on the matter.

Indeed, Dudley had discovered that Labelles was owned by

an investment company. The company also held the deeds to an assortment of warehouses in Wapping and a trade ship called *Le Pionnier*.

Dane shifted uncomfortably in the chair. "That is entirely different," he said with an air of arrogance. "For one, Madame Labelle was not aware of her connection to Beaufort. And at the time, she was in the guise of Mr. Shandy."

Mr. Spencer glanced in Sophie's direction, his gaze drifting slowly over her attire with some amusement. "Indeed." He paused for a moment and turned his attention back to Dane. "What is it you are afraid of?" he challenged, cutting straight to the point.

The words seemed to strike Dane like a whip. "You more than anyone should know the answer to that." He glanced across at Charlotte. "I fear Miss Beaufort would be placing herself at risk. One girl has already been held against her will and Madame Labelle had knowledge of it."

"While I understand your sentiment," Dudley replied, glancing once more at Sophie's attire. "I believe Miss Beaufort is more than capable of taking care of herself. Besides, it may be her only chance of discovering what happened to her brother."

"And tell me, would you afford your wife the same courtesy?" Dane said fiercely.

Mr. Spencer smiled and said with assured ease, "But Miss Beaufort is not your wife."

A look passed between the two gentlemen, suggesting the conversation was at an end. Mr. Spencer had been deliberately provoking, and Sophie could not help but wonder if the physical connection that existed between herself and Dane was apparent to others.

"More tea?" Charlotte asked, offering some distraction from the hard stare Dane directed at his friend.

Sophie obliged, grateful to have something else on which to focus. For although she had no intention of ever becoming Dane's wife, Dudley's remark stirred vivid memories of their passionate liaison, memories that caused her pulse to race and her breath to quicken. Now she knew why gentlemen found it necessary to loosen their cravats when emotions ran high. As she sat there sipping tea, she tried in vain to think of something, anything other than the deep sense of longing the memory evoked.

She gazed across at Charlotte, the perfect image of domestic respectability. Expecting her first child at Christmas, she was radiant, charming, and graceful. Most importantly, she was in love with her husband. Sophie had noticed the discreet glances she secretively stole. She noticed the way he looked back with a profound tenderness, as though she was the most precious thing in the world to him.

"I believe I need some air," Charlotte said with a smile, holding the arms of the chair to stand. While both gentlemen also stood, Mr. Spencer offered his assistance by placing his hand at the small of her back and guiding her to her feet. "Would you care to join me, Miss Beaufort? Or am I supposed to call you Mr. Shandy?"

Sophie placed her cup on the table and stood. "I would love nothing more."

As she turned to leave, Dane touched her lightly on the elbow and bent down, so his mouth brushed against her ear. "I would prefer if you would walk in the garden and not out in the square," he whispered.

"Of course," she consented with a small nod of the head. Had he asked her the same question a few days ago, she would have told him to go to the devil. Indeed, had his request involved hindering her progress in finding James, she would have said exactly that. In agreeing to this request, she hoped he would understand she was not opposed to everything he suggested.

As Sophie stepped out into the hall, Charlotte's maid came scuttling down the stairs carrying a fur-trimmed shawl, which she placed around Charlotte's shoulders.

"We shall not be too long," Charlotte began. "I believe they have some making up to do." She laughed as she gestured to the drawing room where the low, rumbling tones suggested the gentlemen were already deep in conversation.

Sophie could not help but be intrigued by their relationship. "Are they always so ... so direct with one another?"

Charlotte glanced affectionately towards the closed door. "Perhaps not in company, but the freedom with which they speak stems from a bond forged during their travels abroad. It was a dangerous time." Her eyes widened to add intrigue to her words. "Who best to turn to for advice than a man you know would die for you." She slipped her arm through Sophie's and led her out into the garden.

The rectangular shaped garden was what one expected from a townhouse in a more affluent area. It was formal in design, with three flowerbeds placed along the central axis, all edged in neatly trimmed box and smaller beds lining the outer walls. The design would be even more spectacular when viewed from an upper window, Sophie thought, as they stepped out onto the gravel path that wound around the central beds in a figure of eight.

"You do not mind if I take your arm?" Charlotte asked. "I have been prone to bouts of dizziness and Dudley is such a worrier."

"I am more than happy to be of assistance," Sophie said a little too formally. She stopped abruptly. "Oh dear, I fear I sound more like Mr. Shandy every day. Of course, I don't mind," she rephrased with a grin.

Charlotte was silent for a moment and then took a deep breath. "May we be candid with one another, Miss Beaufort?"

"Please, you must call me Sophie," she replied, eager to further their acquaintance. It was the least she could do after all the wonderful clothes she had been given.

"Sophie," Charlotte corrected. "It must be wonderful to be able to discuss anything and know you may trust the answer you receive." Charlotte gave Sophie's arm a little squeeze. "I do not see why the gentlemen should be the only ones afforded such a luxury."

"I agree. You may be candid with me, Mrs. Spencer."

"You are doing your Mr. Shandy thing again," Charlotte said with a chuckle, "and please call me Charlotte."

Sophie chuckled, too. "If the gentlemen have forged their friendship through danger, then perhaps we shall forge ours through laughter."

She doubted there was anything dangerous about spending years on a grand tour in the company of loose women. If Dudley Spencer had spent time abroad with Dane, then perhaps he did not want Charlotte to know he'd assisted the marquess in pursuit of pleasure while his estate went to rot.

As they reached the bottom of the garden, they sat down on a stone bench with armrests in the shape of swans.

"I believe Sebastian is in love with you," Charlotte announced in a rather matter-of-fact tone.

"What?" Sophie jumped to her feet so fast anyone would have thought she'd just sat on a bee. When she agreed to talk candidly, this was not the sort of topic she had in mind.

"Please, sit down," Charlotte said in a calm tone as she patted the seat next to her. "I did not mean to frighten you. I just wondered if you knew and now it is obvious you do not."

Sophie sat back down on the bench and sighed. "There are many ways to make one laugh, Charlotte, without resorting to the ridiculous."

"There is nothing ridiculous about love." Charlotte took Sophie's hand in hers, perhaps to prevent her from jumping up again. "And you certainly love him." She gripped Sophie's hand a little tighter. "There it is said." She turned away and looked around the garden as though that was the end of the matter.

"Now I know you are being ridiculous," Sophie protested. "I do not even like him that much." Well, that was a lie. She liked him a great deal and could not deny she was attracted to him in a physical sense. However, while she had changed her opinion of him over the last few days, she could not forgive him for the way he had shirked his responsibilities.

"Oh, look, over there on the bird bath." Charlotte pointed to two robins balancing precariously on the edge. "I have heard it said that robins are symbolic of new beginnings." With a sparkle in her eyes, she placed her hands over her stomach. "Well, I suppose a baby is a new beginning and falling in love always heralds a new beginning. Do you think our little robins are also in love?"

"I am not in love with him and I do not—"

"I do not believe you," Charlotte interrupted with a wave of her hand. "One doth protest far too much."

"I will not deny he holds a certain fascination." Sophie was determined to be as candid as possible in order to prove her point. "But I could not possibly love a man who whored his way around Europe while his tenants were left to rot in squalor." Sophie regretted the words as soon as they had left her lips. She did not want to cast aspersions on Dudley Spencer's character or cause Charlotte any distress, particularly in her fragile condition.

"Who told you that?" Charlotte appeared highly irritated.

"Told me what?" She did not have the heart to repeat it again.

"Who told you Sebastian whored his way around Europe? Because they most certainly are not talking about the man who is sitting in there." Her cheeks flushed as she stabbed her finger towards the house.

"Forgive me. The last thing I wanted to do was cause you any distress. In the village, it's common knowledge the marquess used money from his estate to fund a rather unconventional *Grand Tour*. The tenants have been suffering for years as a consequence."

Charlotte stared at her with a look of utter disbelief. "My dear," she began in a much more composed manner. "Are you telling me you believed these lies, you believed Sebastian was capable of such selfishness, such cruelty and yet you still consented to be his mistress?" Charlotte suddenly clapped her hands in joy. "Oh, you are definitely in love with him."

Sophie did not know which charge to dispute first. The fact Charlotte believed the villagers of Marchampton were liars or the fact she believed Sophie was Dane's mistress.

"You're letting your emotions run away with you," Sophie said respectfully, as though they had been friends for years and could say anything to one another. "I know we agreed to be honest, but perhaps it is best to restrict our topics to things of a less personal nature." Sophie could feel the heat rising to her face and bowed her head as realisation dawned.

She was, essentially, Dane's mistress.

To respectable society, her loss of innocence also meant the loss of her reputation and as such, she would be deemed unsuitable company for any lady, including Charlotte Spencer. But that was not what saddened her.

Suddenly, the tears fell.

"Oh, please to do not cry." Charlotte took both of Sophie's hands in hers. "It is my fault for pushing you on the matter. I should have respected your privacy. It is just that Sebastian is so very dear to me and—"

"Forgive me, I am just being silly." Sophie sniffed as she dabbed the corner of her eye with the pad of her finger. "I don't even know why I'm crying. It is not like me at all."

"You have had a lot to contend with these past few days and …" Charlotte paused and lowered her head to look into Sophie's eyes. "When a woman gives herself to a man for the first time, it can be an overwhelming experience. But it is of no consequence, you will marry him, and all will be well." She looked back over her shoulder and then turned to Sophie and whispered. "When I married Dudley, I was already carrying his child. Look how well that has turned out."

Sophie was surprised by her confession, but there was a huge distinction between them. No one could mistake Dudley Spencer's love for his wife. Dane, on the other hand, had said quite openly it was his duty to marry. Not once had he mentioned love as a deciding factor. Regardless of whatever it was she felt for him. She could never marry a man who did not love her above all else.

"I'm sorry, Charlotte, but I can never marry. I am too tempestuous, too irresponsible, and too stubborn to be someone's wife or mother." And what gentleman would want a wife like that, she added silently, certainly not a peer in need of an unblemished bloodline. "The truth is I like being Mr. Shandy on occasion. I like riding out with the wind in my hair and swimming in the lake in just my chemise."

Charlotte smiled. "And you do not believe Sebastian would accept you doing such things? The fact you are sitting here in gentleman's clothes is a testament to his unconventionality."

"I did not give him much choice in the matter," she snorted, remembering how angry he had been as he rode along Keepers Lane to find her sitting astride Argo in a pair of gentleman's breeches. "I do not think he is as unconventional as he would have us believe. Besides, if Westlands is to thrive, he needs a more refined lady at his side. One who can inspire confidence in his tenants, one who will overlook his indiscretions."

Charlotte looked puzzled. "I should think the years he has devoted to recouping the estates losses would inspire confidence in itself. Do the tenants know that if it wasn't for Sebastian they would all be destitute?" Charlotte folded her arms across her chest in exasperation. "In his youth, I do not doubt he had his fair share of admirers. But during the last six years, he has devoted himself entirely to his estate. He has not had time to sleep let alone whore his way around Europe."

Sophie did not want to dampen the woman's admiration further. "Charlotte, please calm down. You must think of the baby." Sophie placed a hand on Charlotte's shoulder. "I understand he is a very dear friend to you …"

Charlotte grasped the hand at her shoulder tightly. "You do not understand. I could never repay Sebastian or Dudley for what they have done for me. Although at least with Dudley, I can show him how much I care." Charlotte looked away into the distance, her green eyes full of pain. "One day I will tell you the story," she whispered, "but, for now, it is enough for you to know that Sebastian is a selfless man, a man who risked his life rescuing me from a hell-hole in France. I shall never forget the moment I looked up from my straw bed and saw his face, bloody and bruised, yet he still had a smile for me."

Sophie was momentarily speechless.

Images flooded her mind: Charlotte lying on the floor in some rat-infested dungeon, her face smudged with dirt, her clothes ragged. Sebastian dressed in nothing but a pair of tight, buckskin breeches, carrying the helpless woman to safety as she clung on to his muscular, bronzed shoulders.

A war raged within, as an array of emotions scrambled for supremacy: jealousy, fear, and pride—each one challenging the other for the right to breach the walls of her heart. But as the images faded, and the dust settled, she was left with one formidable emotion—love.

She loved him.

She had always loved him.

Charlotte had been correct in her observation.

Fear clawed at her heart. If it was so obvious to Charlotte then perhaps it was obvious to Dane.

Oh, what had she done?

She had tasted the forbidden fruit; she had felt his lips on hers, had felt what it was like to be held in his arms. Now the memory of him would be all the more painful. She should leave. She should go home to Marchampton, move into the cottage and pretend he had never come back.

"Sophie, are you well?" Charlotte's voice broke her reverie. "You look rather pale. Let us return to the house. I think we are both in need of a distraction."

Sophie helped Charlotte to her feet and slipped her arm through hers. They had entered the garden as strangers, and would leave as trusted confidantes. Sophie would have liked nothing more than to remain friends. But she could not bear to hear stories about Dane, and Charlotte spoke about him with such affection it would probably break her heart. Perhaps when she had settled into the cottage, she would write to her.

"I am so glad we have had the chance to speak privately." Charlotte turned and smiled warmly at her. "If my experiences have taught me anything these past few years, it is that life is like the weather—unpredictable. When it is dark and miserable, we must have hope. But when it is warm and sunny, we must rejoice. We must embrace it and trust that its memory will sustain us when the rain comes again."

"How philosophical of you," Sophie replied, feeling a little better than she had a few moments before.

"Well, Dudley did not just marry me for my money," she giggled. "Now, let us go inside, treat ourselves to a slice of cake and see if we can find a way for you to meet your Madame Labelle."

CHAPTER 19

*A*fter some gentle persuasion and Dudley Spencer's promise to help devise a plan, they all agreed that the meeting with Madame Labelle should go ahead.

The discussion lasted no more than twenty minutes, but it had been the most awkward twenty minutes of Sophie's life. She had barely acknowledged Dane throughout the whole exchange, believing that if she appeared aloof, she would be able to disguise her true feelings.

She had never stopped loving him.

The thought left her feeling exposed and vulnerable, and her stomach did little flips every time she thought of it. The carriage ride home had been just as challenging. Dane had mistaken her silence for anxiety and so spent the rest of the journey trying to convince her he would risk his life to protect her—which only made her heart race all the more.

The opportunity to spend time upstairs with Amy had been a welcome relief.

With her arms folded firmly across her chest, Sophie stood with her back to the bedroom window as she examined Dane's maid. "I know the coat is a little on the large side. But if you would just straighten your back, it would not look so bad."

Amy offered a weak smile, revealing her reluctance to participate in their charade. "I don't know how you do it, miss." She shrugged her shoulders as though she had an itch she couldn't scratch. "I can hardly breathe with this thing wrapped around my neck." She tugged at the ends of the neatly tied cravat, and Sophie rushed over, patted her hands away and pushed the ends down inside the waistcoat.

"The more you think about it, the worse it will be." Sophie placed her hand on Amy's arm to offer some comfort. Sophie had worn breeches many times whilst roaming around in the countryside, but had also struggled with the feeling of being slowly suffocated by a cravat.

Amy turned her head and sniffed the shoulder of the coat. "Does this thing smell musty to you?" she asked, her nose wrinkled to the size of a button.

Sophie bowed her head and inhaled before jerking back sharply. It smelt like a wet dog. "It's just a little damp," she reassured, wondering where Dane had found it. "Let me find something to mask the smell." Sophie wandered over to the dressing table, removed a few dried lavender stalks from the vase and crushed the heads in her hands. "There that should do the trick," she said, smoothing her hands over the coat in the hope the scent would linger long enough to placate Amy. "Now, do you remember what it is you must do?"

Amy nodded. "I'm to wait in the square until Haines brings your madame."

Sophie nodded. "You must sit with her for at least ten minutes and then—"

"But what am I supposed to say to her," Amy blurted, forgetting it was rude to interrupt and in other houses, maids had been dismissed for far less.

Sophie's mouth curved into a mischievous grin. "You are going to have the mistress of a brothel at your disposal. I am sure you will think of something." She had a few questions she would not mind asking herself.

Amy went a little red in the face. "I don't expect she'd know much about affairs of the heart, what with her being in a different sort of business. Besides, Mrs. Cox says you can always tell when a gentleman's interested in a lady."

Sophie struggled with the idea of Mrs. Cox being so knowledgeable when it came to gentlemen. "Really?" she mused, her interest piqued. "And how does one know when a gentleman is interested?"

"Well, Mrs. Cox says that men like order. They usually have a routine, and the Devil himself couldn't change it even if he had a mind to. She says you can always tell if a gentleman is interested as they start doing things they wouldn't normally do."

"I see," Sophie said with a teasing smile. "You mean like Haines suddenly eating his meals in the kitchen instead of taking them out to the mews."

Amy blushed again. "Well, I suppose. Or like his lordship letting you stay here without a chaperone. Mrs. Cox said that ladies don't usually stay overnight. His lordship always escorts them home in the early hours." She stopped abruptly and put her fingers over her lips. No doubt aware that her tongue had run away with itself and such comments were not to be repeated outside the kitchen.

There was an uncomfortable silence as Sophie tried desperately to maintain a passive expression. It was no business of hers who Dane entertained. So why did she feel so angry, so disappointed, so humiliated? When she had questioned his need for two townhouses in London, he'd told her he used the one in Red Lion Square for business. It had not occurred to her that business meant clandestine meetings with his mistresses.

"You should not be discussing his lordship's affairs," Sophie said, her tone far too severe. "Or mine for that matter." She took a deep breath to settle her pounding heart and began fussing with Amy's cravat in a bid to focus on anything other than the women who'd shared Dane's bed. "Now," she continued, taking a step back to study her protégé. "Do you have your pocket watch?"

Amy fiddled around in her pocket, casting Sophie a satisfied smile when she managed to pull the watch out without dropping it.

"Wait with Madame Labelle for ten minutes. Then direct her to the carriage and Haines will transport her to Leicester Square," Sophie instructed. "I shall be waiting near the gate at the east entrance."

"What shall I do once she's gone?" Amy asked as she chewed on her fingernail like a girl half her age.

"You must wait for Haines to return and he will bring you home." There was no need for the girl to worry. Haines would not want to leave her alone for too long. The man would probably thrust his bare hand in a brazier to ensure her safety. Sophie reached for Amy's hands and held them in hers. "Are you ready?"

Amy took a deep breath. "Yes, miss," she nodded, still looking rather sheepish.

Dane and Haines were waiting at the bottom of the stairs when Sophie and Amy sauntered down, dressed like two young dandies about town. Dane paced back and forth, his hands clasped behind his back, whilst Haines stood in the corner like a disgruntled bear.

On hearing the soft patter of footsteps, they both looked up and although Sophie tried her utmost to avoid Dane's gaze, her eyes were drawn to his by a compulsion she could not control.

The more time she spent in his company, the more she was able to determine his mood. Even with his mask firmly in place, she was aware of every unconscious movement, the restless flexing of his fingers, the straightening of his cravat, the conceited curl of his lips she'd so often mistaken for vanity, but which she now knew he used to disguise the true nature of his feelings. Just when she felt she was beginning to understand the man, she discovered yet another reason to question his character.

In truth, he posed the perfect contradiction.

He had assumed responsibility for her, put his plans aside to assist her, and even risked his life to save Charlotte. Then, like the flip of a coin, he revealed another side of himself. The side that cavorted with women, the side capable of showing complete disregard for his people and his estate. It was all rather perplexing. How could she despise him yet at the same time love him with an overwhelming passion?

When they reached the bottom stair, Sophie guided Amy forward. "May I present Mr. Shandy's counterpart, Mr. Dunstable," she announced, choosing to sound jovial. Both men looked as though someone had just died.

Amy sniggered at the introduction, but Haines and Dane assumed a restrained silence. Haines struggled to raise his gaze from the floor. While Dane held his jaw so rigid, he looked as though he was about to murder someone with his bare hands.

"Miss Beaufort," Dane said, "may I have a moment." Moving to slip his hand around her back, he drew her further along the hall, away from prying eyes and ears. The warmth radiating from his palm made her legs tremble, and her heart skip a beat. "I believe it would be best if *I* were to meet with Madame Labelle," he whispered. "I am sure she would have no objection and—"

"She has not asked to meet with you," Sophie interrupted, feeling a little annoyed at the way he tried to control every situation. She would not be manipulated like one of his mistresses. "She specifically asked to meet with me. The sooner we verify what happened to James at Labelles, the closer we shall be to finding out where he's gone." And the sooner I can go home and try to forget about you, she added silently. "Besides, I need to confirm she has a connection to Dampierre. And I doubt she would talk to you about such things."

"And you believe she will talk to Mr. Shandy," he sneered. "If Dampierre is a partner in the investment company that owns Labelles, then he owns her, too. Her loyalties lie with him. Don't be fooled by her friendly overtures. She has been schooled in the art of deception." He leant forward and said somewhat brutally,

"It is simple. Dampierre wants the necklace as compensation for the girl, and he will use you to get it."

He had a way of making her feel like a fool, just like he had six years ago. Sophie took a step back, straightened her coat and said defiantly, "Well, we will know for certain when I meet with Madame Labelle."

Some thirty minutes later, Sophie entered the square on the east side and sauntered up and down the gravel path. She had already tipped her hat to two young ladies, who had blushed and sniggered at each other as she passed. She had even stopped to admire a baby, being pushed in a perambulator by his nurse. Which was probably not something a young gentleman was prone to do, but the baby had been so adorable Sophie had found it impossible to resist.

She wondered what Dane was thinking as he watched her from the window of number eight: a rather grand townhouse owned by a merchant who was apparently indebted to the Marquess of Danesfield and who had seemed most pleased to have a gentleman of such prominence use his home.

Distracted by the baby, she had not noticed Dane's unmarked carriage draw up alongside the square. Nor had she noticed its passenger alight until the tip of a vibrant green ostrich feather almost tickled her nose.

"What a beautiful baby," Madame Labelle said as she linked arms with Sophie and stared into the perambulator.

After complimenting the nurse, who still seemed slightly shocked that such respected personage should disregard propriety and converse with her in public, they moved along the path as though they had just nipped out for a leisurely stroll.

Sophie turned to Madame Labelle. Dressed in a poison-green muslin dress, coupled with a black-cherry Spencer and matching pillar-box hat, she was so exquisitely dressed she could have passed for the daughter of a duke.

"Did you have an interesting time with Amy?" Sophie said, wondering if the maid had plucked up the courage to ask any questions.

"Was that her name? What a darling. She was so shy I could hardly get a word out of her." She paused and inhaled deeply. "I'm pleased to say, your coat smells so much better. I could not decide if her coat smelt of dog with a hint of lavender or the other way around."

Sophie offered her a weak smile. "I'm sorry you were obliged to sit with Amy, but you know the danger I am placing myself in just by meeting with you today."

Madame Labelle raised a brow. "I take it you are not referring to your scrupulous reputation, Mr. Shandy."

"No," Sophie replied rather bluntly, for as much as she liked Madame Labelle there was no doubt she was involved in these iniquitous events. "I am referring to your connection to the Comte de Dampierre."

It was as though the mere mention of Dampierre caused Madame Labelle to turn to stone. Her body became stiff and rigid; her carefree countenance replaced with a cold, stern disposition. She stopped and turned to face Sophie, the vivacious sparkle in her eyes now diminished to a spiritless stare.

"You must not trifle with him," she pleaded. "You do not know what he is capable of."

Sophie could hardly believe she was talking to the same woman, for her eyes were alight with pure terror. What had Dampierre done to her to reduce her to such a state? Sophie had witnessed his attempts at intimidation: the ice-cold stare and the razor-sharp blade.

"If he is as fearsome as you say, then why are you still at Labelles? What is he to you, your partner … your lover?"

"He is neither," Madame Labelle whispered as she looked

away, her face flushed with shame. "He owns Labelles, and he owns me."

There was a moment of silence while Sophie contemplated the significance of her words. To be at the mercy of a man like that, well, it did not bear thinking about.

"Have you not thought of running away?" Sophie implored.

Madame Labelle smirked. "Run away? There is not a place I could go in this world where Victor would not find me." She glanced at Sophie as though she were a small child who could not possibly understand the world she lived in. "And what would I do? Work in a tavern, let myself be mauled by the dirty hands of men who felt it was their right to do so."

"Well, Dampierre has not found Annabel. Perhaps there is a chance for you, too," Sophie replied confidently. It was the first time she had mentioned Annabel, and Madame Labelle smiled as though genuinely impressed with the extent of her knowledge.

"My dear, Mr. Shandy," Madame Labelle said, her tone conveying a hint of cynicism. "Annabel has the assistance of Lord Beaufort. Else she would have found herself dragged back to Wapping by her hair and deposited on the first ship out of here."

Sophie's eyes widened. "Was that to be her fate?" No wonder James had offered the girl assistance. She knew it had to be something important for him to offer her mother's necklace. "Is Dampierre still looking for Annabel?"

Madame Labelle snorted. "She has been alone with your brother for more than a week. I doubt the buyer would still have confidence in her purity. Besides, Victor would not take the chance. He has a reputation to uphold," she said sarcastically. "He does not deal in soiled goods."

Sophie was shocked. "You mean, Annabel was to be sold?"

The thought that Dampierre traded in women disgusted her, and she wondered if that was what he meant when he said he would take her on a journey. Would he take her to a foreign land and sell her to the highest bidder?

Thankfully, he was too late. She had given her virtue away freely. To a man who made her head spin and her heart flutter. Even if there had been other mistresses in the past, Dane made her feel special, protected and cherished.

Madame Labelle held up her gloved hand but then paused to wait for a lady and her maid to pass. "I have said far too much already. It is Victor who insisted I meet with you today, and you must do exactly as he asks, for all our sakes."

Sophie's body shook: an ice-cold tremor shooting down her spine. She glanced over her shoulder, expecting to see Dampierre's beady eyes bearing down on her, his sharp stick thrust in her back. Relieved to find no one there, she turned and glanced discreetly towards the window, to where Dane stood keeping watch. She could just make out his muscular frame propped against the wall, his arms folded firmly across his chest as he studied her from the first-floor window. The sight of him warmed her body and soul. He was strong and commanding, and she felt safe in the knowledge he was there.

"He will not rest until he gets what he wants," Madame Labelle continued, as though anxious to stress the point that the Comte de Dampierre was not the sort of man one crossed.

Sophie paused. A part of her was reluctant to ask the next question for fear of the answer. "And what does he want?"

"Victor wants the necklace," she answered bluntly. "He believes it reparation for the injustice caused." The words were said without feeling or emotion. Perhaps because it was her intention to make it clear they were Dampierre's words and not her own. "He said you would know the one to which he refers."

"He wants the ruby necklace. The one my brother offered in exchange for Annabel."

Once again, Madame Labelle appeared surprised that she was so well informed. "He will not rest until he gets it. Though why he is so obsessed with the thing is beyond me. He has never even seen it."

Sophie frowned, the comment rousing her curiosity. "You

mean he was not at Labelles on the night in question … on the night Annabel escaped?"

"No, he was not," she replied a little nervously. "But I can say no more on the matter." She shook her head involuntarily as if reaffirming the need to remain silent on the subject. "You must bring the necklace to him or …" she stopped abruptly and took a deep breath. "Or he will find some other way to recoup his losses." Madame Labelle opened her reticule and fumbled about inside. "Here, you must take this." She removed an ivory card and handed it to Sophie.

"What is it?" Sophie flipped the card over to find an invitation to Lord Delmont's masquerade. Dampierre had friends in high places. "But I have never even met Lord Delmont."

"Neither has Victor," she snorted. "Let us just say, Victor has something belonging to Lord Delmont, and Delmont will do anything to see it returned." She glanced at the invitation in Sophie's hand. "Victor likes drama. He likes to complicate things," she continued with a hint of disdain. "He insists you attend and has even provided you with a costume." She glanced across at Dane's carriage, which had just pulled up alongside the square. "It is in a box in your carriage. Victor assures me this is all he asks of you."

"Why would he want me to attend a masquerade?" Sophie asked in astonishment.

Madame Labelle linked her arm with Sophie, forcing her to walk slowly back to the gate. "You are to wear the costume and your necklace. At some point during the evening, he will reveal himself to you so you may hand it over in relative safety." She stopped and looked Sophie directly in the eye. "Before you say anything, he knows your marquess has it with him here in London. He dropped a red velvet pouch outside Labelles during a fight. The men recalled seeing it, despite the fact their eyes looked like juicy fat plums."

"He is not *my* marquess," Sophie snapped a little defensively.

Why did everyone assume she had a formed an attachment to him?

That seemed to bother her more than the fact she would be expected to meet with Dampierre—and alone at a masquerade, to boot. She had always wanted to go to a masquerade where one did not need to worry about silly things like etiquette and reputation. Perhaps Dane could accompany her. She would like to dance with him, to twirl around happily in his arms with not a care in the world. To dance just once, just one delicious memory to keep her warm on those cold winter nights. Her stomach fluttered with excitement.

Suddenly, as though being chided by a strict governess, the voice of reason scolded her for being a slave to her own fancy.

"Lord Danesfield will never allow me to walk into a masquerade unaccompanied," she continued, shaking her head.

Madame Labelle smiled. "Victor anticipated your response, which is why he has agreed that Danesfield can go with you," she paused and raised a brow. "But he must secure his own invitation. I am sure, for a man of such great standing, it will not be a problem." There was a hint of contempt in her voice, which was probably to be expected after years spent servicing the needs of the aristocracy.

As they reached the east gate, Sophie turned to bid her farewell. "I doubt we will ever have cause to meet again," she said earnestly, "but should you ever need assistance, then please seek me out at Brampton Hall."

Sophie was not sure what had prompted her to make such a declaration, particularly as the woman was potentially involved in Dampierre's barbaric schemes. There was something about Madame Labelle that roused her compassion, roused her sympathy. In truth, if Sophie's dalliance with Dane became public knowledge, then she too would have to deal with the same level of contempt shown to the madame.

Madame Labelle wiped a tear from her eye and reached out to grasp Sophie's hands.

"My dear, Miss Beaufort," she whispered softly. "I had thought it safer to see you only as Mr. Shandy, for no woman of quality could possibly be so warm and kind to someone like me." She glanced up at the window to where Dane stood. "He does not deserve you."

As Sophie followed Madame Labelle's gaze to the window, her eyes widened in surprise. Dane was staring back at them, his arms stretched against the window frame as though he was ready to raise the sash and leap out. He looked powerful, masculine and roguishly handsome. The warmth she felt in the pit of her stomach suddenly ignited into a roaring flame.

"How did you know he was there?" she gasped, feeling breathless as she struggled to contain the fire that engulfed her entire body. She could almost smell his musky scent, almost feel his hot lips against hers; feel the weight of his hard body pressing down on her.

Madame Labelle smiled. "You have looked up at that window a hundred times or more. Now, unless you have a twitch …" Madame Labelle laughed and drew her into an embrace. "What a wonderful dream it must be, to have someone who thinks only of you. But love is such a fragile thing, is it not?" She pulled away, but her hands remained on Sophie's arms. "Promise me something," she whispered, her eyes swimming with emotion. "Do not let him break you. Do not let him douse that fiery passion. For a woman, life can be precarious. It can be ripped from our hands in an instant, so you must make every single moment count." She gave Sophie's arm a gentle rub and then she dropped her hands and straightened her back. "Goodbye, Mr. Shandy," she said with a curt nod.

"Goodbye, madame. And take care."

Madame Labelle stepped closer and whispered, "Goodbye my darling, Miss Beaufort."

Sophie watched as Madame Labelle sauntered across the street with an aristocratic swagger so opposed to her status and climb into Dane's unmarked carriage. When it had rumbled out of the square, Sophie's eyes flew up to the window. But Dane was no longer there, and she was suddenly overcome with a feeling of disappointment, a feeling of emptiness, of loneliness and a desperate feeling of longing.

Lost in contemplation, she had not noticed him cross the road and enter the square. Suddenly, he was standing in front of her, so large and so strikingly handsome that she threw her arms around his neck in relief.

He placed his hands on top of hers and lowered them gently to her side. "Have you forgotten you're wearing your Mr. Shandy guise," he said in a husky drawl. "It would do nothing for my reputation to be seen hugging a gentleman in Leicester Square."

"Oh, Dane," she cried, thinking she must make the most of her the time she had left with him. "I want to go home."

"And you will," he reassured, concern etched on his beautiful face, "as soon as this business is concluded. What did Madame Labelle want?"

Sophie stared into his warm brown eyes, her heart pounding so quickly she could hardly breathe. "We will talk about Madame Labelle later, for you misunderstand my plea." Her voice brimmed with desire. "I mean I want to go to your home. I want to go now. I need you."

CHAPTER 20

*I*t had been torture watching Sophie converse with Madame Labelle, knowing he could do nothing other than wait and hope that nothing untoward happened to her.

Not since the day he'd walked into the old convent in Saint-Francois a Beauvais, with bread that was highly sought after during such turbulent times, had he felt so utterly useless. It was there he had found Charlotte, looking clean but gaunt, her hair cut short and her dress gaping around her shoulders where her bones protruded. He had tried to slip her a larger piece of bread, but the loss of liberty unites neither minds nor hearts, and an argument broke out, resulting in the inmates forfeiting all food for the entire day.

He had not slept that night or the next three nights after. Not until she was safely back on English soil. With Charlotte, it had started out as just another assignment and ended as something deeply personal.

Now, he was able to comprehend the gut-wrenching torment Dudley must have felt. The need to protect those one cared for was overwhelming, completely consuming.

The relief he felt when Sophie flung herself at him, throwing her arms around his neck—it was beyond heavenly, and he was suddenly overcome with a primitive urge to calm, comfort and claim. It had taken every ounce of control he possessed not to throw her down on the ground and pleasure her until his head stopped throbbing, until his muscles relaxed and he had banished the fear clawing away at his heart.

Then she had asked to go home.

Not to Marchampton, thankfully, but home with him.

The word sounded so sweet coming from those soft, sumptuous lips, his soul had soared. Then she looked up at him with those dazzling blue eyes, a look that promised a host of sensual pleasures and told him she needed him.

It was his undoing.

"You are overset," he said, swallowing hard, trying not to stumble over the words as he attempted to rein in his raging desire. "Was it something Madame Labelle said?" He knew the answer but needed to focus on something other than the look of longing piercing his soul.

She shook her head as she bit down on her lower lip. He had never seen her look so … so adorable, so utterly ravishing. The thought caused a throbbing ache in his groin and one of equal measure in his heart.

"You're not listening to me," she cried, lifting her hands as though about to caress his chest, before thrusting them down by her side in frustration. She stepped closer. "Do you need me to spell it out?" Her breath felt like a soft breeze against his ear.

Closing his eyes, he inhaled her sweet scent. The undertones of roses and her own unique fragrance clung to her skin, stoking his need for her to that of a delirious fever.

He offered her a salacious grin, his impatience to lower her down onto the grass and drive himself home was evident in his voice. "No," he growled, "I do not."

Grabbing her by the sleeve of her coat, for he could hardly take her hand, he turned abruptly and strode out of the gate and down the road towards Cranbourn Street, heading left into Bear

Street and towards the waiting hackney whose driver had been paid handsomely for his service.

Oblivious to every other person on the street, he kept a firm hold, forcing her into a trot just to keep up with him. He ignored the disgruntled looks of those he'd barged into in his eagerness to be alone with the woman who roused his passion to the point of insanity. It had been mere hours since their last coupling, yet he felt famished, deprived, ravenous to the brink of starvation.

"Red Lion Square," he barked to the driver, opening the cab door and almost pushing Sophie inside. "If you're quick," he continued, his impatience clearly evident, "then I'll double your fare."

He needed her now.

He needed her like he needed air to breathe. But as desperate as he was, he refused to pleasure her in a hackney.

Climbing in, he slammed the door and lowered the blind in the hope a passionate kiss would suffice, would be enough to keep the fire stoked during their short journey. Yet in such a simple plan, he had failed to account for the fiery nature of the other occupant. He barely had time to catch his breath before she shoved him back in the seat and straddled him in such a delightfully wicked fashion he could not help but groan in satisfaction.

"I'm sorry," she whispered, placing kisses along his jaw, behind his ear, as her hand fluttered across the fall of his breeches. "I do not know what has come over me."

He did not know either, and quite frankly he didn't care.

After a mild tussle with his conscience, all thoughts of decency and decorum flew out of the window. Her warm hand brushing against his bulging manhood played a pivotal role in his decision.

"Good God," he panted. It was madness, like sweet torture. The need to be inside her was unbearable. He swallowed hard, trying to hold on to the last thread of restraint that lingered somewhere in a lonely cobwebbed corner of his mind. "Sophie, we cannot … we do not have time."

He could not take his future wife in a hackney!

"But I thought … you said …" she began between breathless kisses, "that a lot … can be achieved in just a few minutes."

He was not fully aware of what happened next.

Drunk with desire, they tugged at each other's clothes, their lips still locked as they moaned with pleasure. He could hear his heart beating loudly in his ears, could feel the blood pumping around his body as they jostled against each other with the motion of the carriage.

He wasn't entirely sure how he had managed to push her breeches to her knees or free himself from his own restrictions. But the sight of her beautiful, round derriere as she lowered herself onto him with a slow, seductive wiggle, would be ingrained in his memory for the rest of his life.

Lost in a whirlwind of reckless passion they rode each other to completion. The blissful wave of pleasure slackened his craving, but only momentarily. On their return home they had rushed upstairs to indulge in a slower, more languorous form of amusement that had lasted well into the evening.

Still, it was not enough for him.

Raising himself up on his elbow, he gazed down in awe at her luscious form sprawled naked in his bed. With a white sheet draped over her body and tangled around her legs, she was the image of a Greek goddess.

Absorbed in the deep rhythmical rise and fall of her chest, he took pleasure in the sound that suggested pure contentment. He could live the rest of his life like this. Touching her, tasting her, to the point he could well and truly lose his mind. She murmured softly as she drifted in and out of sleep and the sound stirred something deep inside him, something he struggled to define.

It seemed hard to believe she was the same girl who had taunted and tormented him to distraction. Now, she was tormenting him in an entirely different way. He reached out and let his fingers trace the line of her outer thigh, trailing up over her hip before laying the palm of his hand on her stomach. The thought of her swollen with his child caused another deep stirring, and he was somewhat shocked to find that the idea pleased him. He was going to have to broach the subject of marriage, and soon, as they could not continue in the same reckless manner.

Perhaps now she was relaxed and sated, it would be a good time to discuss the matter.

"Wake up, sleepy," he whispered, leaning down to place a kiss on her parted lips. "You have not eaten since breakfast and by the rumbles emanating from your stomach it is clearly not happy."

Roused by his voice, she pushed her arms above her head and stretched. The low humming sound that escaped from her lips caused a familiar tightening in his abdomen, which proceeded to travel to his groin.

"What time is it?" she yawned, fluttering her eyelashes as she became accustomed to her surroundings.

He glanced over towards the mantel, but in the subdued candlelight could not quite read the hands of the clock. "I have no idea. At a guess, I would say it's nearly nine."

It was a calculated guess for he had heard the church bell chime eight, had heard Mrs. Cox's hesitant tread as she hovered outside the door. No doubt she was wondering why no one had gone down for dinner. She had paced back and forth and then returned with a tray which she'd left outside the door.

Sophie shot up, but then remembered she was naked. Grasping the sheet, she wrapped it around her chest. "But Haines … Mrs. Cox … they'll know." She took a deep breath but did not finish the sentence. "Why didn't you wake me?" she snapped.

"You looked exhausted. I thought you needed the rest." He winked and flashed her one of his devilish grins as he swung his legs off the edge of the bed and bent down to pick up the breeches lying in a crumpled heap on the floor. "You know, you do say the most wicked things when you're sleeping," he continued enjoying the way her face had taken on the resemblance of a beetroot. "I didn't know you held me in such high regard."

Sophie looked horrified. "What … what did I say?"

Opening the door to retrieve the silver tray, Sebastian glanced over his shoulder. "It's not something I feel I could repeat in the presence of a lady," he teased closing the door with his foot. "But I believe you're more than satisfied with my performance."

"I am?" She narrowed her gaze as she studied him, before reaching for a pillow and hurling it at his head. "Oh, you fibber. I never said anything of the sort."

"Well, no, not exactly," he replied, steadying the tray as he avoided the flying object with a timely twist of the hip. "But you did do an awful lot of mumbling. You cannot blame a man for concocting his own interpretation."

He placed the tray on the bed in front of her and noticed her frown as she glanced at the two plates positioned side by side.

"Two plates!" she groaned. "They're obviously aware I'm in here." Her distress was evident in her tone. "No doubt they are accustomed to your dissipated habits, but that does not—"

"Mrs. Cox is aware I do not always follow custom, yes," he interjected before she became overly dramatic. He lifted the cover off the plate, picked up a slice of cold ham and took a bite.

Sophie stared at him, slightly aghast and then pulled the sheet tightly across her body as she said with an element of hauteur, "Do not think for a moment I have anything in common with the other women you have entertained here."

He tilted his head and considered her, slightly baffled by her train of thought. "Why would you think I've had other women in here?" He had intended discussing marriage, not his business ventures. Besides, the women he had sheltered had never been in his private chambers. They had kept to their own quarters and been spirited away as soon as a convenient moment arose.

"Amy said you never let your mistresses stay overnight. She said you always escort them home in the early hours."

Sebastian tried not to laugh, for he was truly flattered by her display of jealousy.

"Sophie, I do not have a mistress. You are the only woman who has had the pleasure of being in that bed."

He waved his hand casually in the direction of the bed, which was a ridiculous gesture when he came to think of it, for there was nothing casual, nothing temporary, about the way he felt about her. Indeed, she was the only woman he would lay with from here on in.

"I thought you knew better than to listen to servants' gossip," he continued.

"Are you saying you've never had one of your mistresses at this house? That Amy is mistaken in her belief you've escorted women home in the middle of the night?"

He was going to say she had misunderstood, and a jealous ear hears only what it chooses, but thought better of it. He glanced around the room for his shirt and located it on the chair.

"I am saying, you are not aware of all the facts," he replied, shrugging into the crumpled linen. If they were going to have a serious conversation, he would not be distracted by pretty blue eyes roaming over his bare chest. "Perhaps it is time I told you how I have been occupying myself these last few years."

He dropped into the chair, stretched his legs out in front of him and crossed them at the ankles with languid grace.

"You do not have to explain yourself to me, my lord," she huffed.

"My lord?" he sneered jerking his head back. "What happened to *Oh, Dane, please, Dane*." He smiled to himself as her face flushed a pretty shade of pink. "Surely, after all that has passed between us, you must feel a little curious. Surely, you must be eager to learn more about the character of the man you have taken to your bed."

He had said the words purely to shock, but there was a

glimpse of some unnamed emotion in her eyes. Was it pain or resentment? He certainly did not mean to cheapen their union or imply she was only concerned with the more base of needs.

"Perhaps it is best I don't know." She turned her head away from him to stare at an invisible object on the wall.

He sat up straight and narrowed his gaze as he contemplated her reply. "Ah, I see, Miss Beaufort," he began, mimicking her use of formal address. Although he took no pleasure in it, for it placed an element of distance between them that he found unnerving. "You believe I'm guilty of the type of licentious pursuits the villagers of Marchampton love to gossip about. What is it that disturbs you? That I squandered my inheritance or that I spent it on women with loose morals?" he mocked. "I had credited you with more sense than to take notice of such tittle-tattle but, obviously, I was mistaken."

She turned sharply and her eyes locked with his. "I know what I have seen," she challenged. "John Hodges' daughter nearly died from the cold, damp conditions they were forced to endure. Where were you when the rain came pouring in through their roof? Where were you when their daughter needed medicine, and they could not afford to pay?"

He swallowed deeply in the hope it would ease the pain of regret. Why did she have to mention Mary Hodges? He had been forced to make a choice. If he had stayed at Westlands, the lives of all his tenants would have been at risk. Not a day had gone by when he had not thanked the lord for Mary's recovery.

"It is not what you think," he replied solemnly.

"Well, please feel free to enlighten me," she said in the tone of a stern governess but did not wait for an answer. "If you were not carousing around the Continent with a courtesan, what were you doing?"

He stood, walked over to the bed and leant against the wooden post. "I was working," he answered humbly.

There was a moment of silence where she simply stared at

him, a frown marring her brow. He could almost hear her repeating his words for fear she had misheard.

"Working? What do you mean?"

"May I sit?" He gestured to the end of the bed.

"It is your bed. You may do as you please."

He ignored the sharp edge to her tone. Perhaps it was her way of preparing herself for whatever unpleasant revelation she believed he was about to make.

He perched himself on the end of the bed. "You should eat something," he said in response to the deep growl rumbling from her stomach. He nodded towards the plate. "Eat and I will tell you."

With a sigh, she removed the plate cover and studied the selection of cold meats. Casting a wary glance at the sheet tucked under her arms, she asked, "Would you mind buttering my bread roll?"

"Of course not."

Picking up a knife, he cut and buttered her roll then gave it to her and watched her take a bite. There was something comfortable, something intimate, in so informal a gesture and he longed to hold on to it, to nurture it into something deeper, something more profound.

"You must understand I would never have left Westlands if there had been any other alternative. It is something I deeply regret."

That was not entirely true.

He was sorry his tenants were forced to endure the effects of his father's cavalier attitude towards money. But the experience of working alongside Dudley, of righting some of society's wrongs, well, it had been life changing.

"Tell me, honestly," he continued, "what was your opinion of my father?"

She narrowed her gaze as though intrigued by the question. "I believed him to be a good man, a family man, a man who was diligent in the running of his estate." She paused, bit down on her lip and then took a deep breath. "He looked after his tenants, and they respected him for it."

"Unlike me," he snorted.

"Well ..." She shrugged.

"My father had been dead a mere five days when I discovered there were sizeable debts written against the estate. The creditors were quick to bang on the door to demand their money. My father's man of business, a Mr. William Farrow, had kept them at bay by promising a rather inflated rate of interest which, unfortunately, was well documented." He sighed. "Unlike the small amounts Mr. Farrow had embezzled." He shook his head as he remembered the crippling feeling of disbelief, of desperation. "I have spent the last six years paying for it."

Sophie looked aghast. "I do not know what to say. What had your father done with all the money?"

Sebastian shrugged. "He spent it on everything and anything. He had a weakness for horse racing, for diamond-encrusted pocket watches, for widows with expensive tastes, on anything to dull the pain, anything to fill the hole left by my mother."

Sebastian could not be angry with his father. Angry at himself, yes, for not noticing the torment his father was going through. If only he had known, then they could have consoled each other. Perhaps things would have been different.

But then he would not be sitting in his private chamber with Sophie.

"I see." Her eyes were awash with sympathy. "And so you were not on the Continent living in lavish surroundings while your tenants struggled to survive." There was a hint of shame in her tone.

"No, I was working with Dudley. After selling off all that was not nailed down, there was still a deficit. I dismissed Mr. Farrow and employed Dudley Spencer. Which turned into more of a partnership and then a friendship, but that is an extremely long story which I will save for another time."

"But why did you not say something?" she said with a sigh

of exasperation. "You let all but a handful of servants go and so everyone thought you had no interest in Westlands when really you were trying desperately to save it."

He looked down into his lap. "I could not bear for others to think badly of my father," he began, his voice reflecting his anguish. "He was weak. It was not his fault."

Sophie leant forward and placed her hand on his. It was smaller and softer, yet it gave him strength. "But you let others think the worst of you," she said. There was a moment of silence and then she chuckled. "I cannot imagine you working as a man of business. How on earth did you keep it a secret?"

He shook his head. "You misunderstand. The work with Dudley, well, it was of a sensitive nature."

She absorbed his words and then with wide eyes asked, "You're not working for the government?"

"No, I am not working for the government. But with our connections in Society—" He stopped abruptly and then added, "You do know Dudley is the illegitimate son of the Duke of Morton?"

"Is he really? Then why is he working as a man of business?"

"There was some disagreement over whom he should wed. Dudley would prefer to make his own living than to bow down to the demands of a father who has little regard for his personal welfare. Besides, we have done extremely well helping those members of the *ton* who found themselves in a pickle. Dudley still takes on the odd job here and there. But nothing that would take him away from home."

She appeared highly amused. "And what possible pickles do the elite of Society find themselves in?"

He shifted further onto the bed, making himself more comfortable. "We were hired by Lord ... well, by a certain person who shall remain nameless, to track down his runaway daughter. We found her on the way to Gretna, and she was brought back here until we could sneak her home without anyone noticing." He gave her a smug grin. "Which happened to be in the middle of the night," he added. "The gentleman put it about that his daughter had been ill with a fever and the rogue in question did not dare to contradict for fear of being shipped off to Calcutta in a crate."

"How fascinating," she said, her eyes wide with delight. "Oh, do tell me more, I …" She stopped abruptly. "Do you mean the ladies you escorted home in the middle of the night were clients?"

He turned his hand over so he could hold hers. "Sophie, the only women who have been in this house, are the ones associated with our business. I am not saying I have always been a saint in such matters. But the stories you have heard from the gossips in Marchampton or Amy or Mrs. Cox, well, they are simply not true."

"You mean you're not a reckless rogue?"

"Only where you're concerned."

She looked down into her lap. "You must think me naïve and rather foolish."

"Not at all. I find your jealousy rather endearing," he replied, attempting to lighten the mood.

"Jealousy!" she exclaimed lifting her head to meet his gaze, but then seeing his teasing expression she grinned. "If you believe I'm jealous, then conceit must surely be your middle name."

He brought her hand to his lips and kissed it softly. "While we are in the mood for disclosing secrets, isn't there something you need to tell me?"

"I am not sure what you mean," she answered looking a little wary.

Intrigued by her guarded response, Sebastian wondered what other secrets she was hiding.

"Do not look so frightened," he said. "I am talking about the reason Madame Labelle insisted on meeting with you. I was

169

convinced Dampierre would make some move to kidnap you and ransom you for the necklace."

"Would you have paid?" she replied coyly with an exaggerated flutter of her eyelashes.

Sebastian shrugged. "That all depends on how grateful you would have been." His hungry gaze roamed over her bare shoulders. "Are you going to tell me what was so important that Madame Labelle insisted on meeting with you in public? Did she remember something about James?"

"Well, not exactly." She paused and breathed deeply. "You were right. The Comte de Dampierre owns Labelles, amongst other things. Dampierre insists I attend Lord Delmont's masquerade. I'm to wear the necklace, and he has even provided me with a costume. Madame Labelle has left it in your carriage. That reminds me, I must check to see if Amy has hung it up to air."

Sebastian stared at her, his expression hard and unforgiving. "You're not going," he said sharply. It was not a question. It was an order he was determined she would follow.

"I told Madame Labelle that's what you would say," she replied with a weak smile. "Particularly, once you knew Dampierre would also be in attendance and expects me to hand over the necklace."

"You're not going," he repeated, stressing the words with patriarchal authority, as she appeared completely unconcerned that she would be placing herself in danger. Thank the Lord, she didn't know where he'd put the necklace. It would not surprise him to wake and find them both missing.

"Dampierre has agreed you may accompany me," she added pressing her case.

He stood abruptly and walked over to the window, just to place some distance between them, for he had been an arm's reach away from shaking her to her senses.

She opened her mouth to speak, but he interjected. "Do you know what a crush it will be? I would struggle to find you even if your face wasn't covered. At a blasted masquerade, it will be nigh on impossible." He pushed his hands through his hair in frustration. "Why on earth have you waited until now to tell me?"

Sophie blushed. "I ... I was thinking of something else at the time if you remember. I did not wish to spoil the moment." She shook her head. "And because I knew you would act like this." She gestured to his pacing with an element of censure. "Can you not see there is some logic in accepting the offer?"

He sighed. "Not when I find it difficult to believe he only wants the necklace. What if he is simply looking for a replacement for Annabel?" The thought of losing her, of her ending up in such a situation, well, he could not bear to contemplate it. "What do you expect me to say when you seem content with serving yourself up as the prized pig?"

"I beg your pardon."

He stopped pacing. "It is just a turn of phrase. You know what I meant by it." He dropped into the chair and took a deep breath. "Did Madame Labelle mention Dampierre's interest in Annabel?"

Sophie swallowed. "Not at all. Madame Labelle simply assured me that Victor ... that Dampierre wants some form of recompense and is, therefore, willing to accept the necklace." She looked him keenly in the eye and said with earnest. "What choice do we have? I cannot return to Marchampton until the matter is closed. Dampierre could call on me at any time. You cannot camp on the doorstep. You cannot always be there to offer your protection."

I can and I will once you accept a proposal of marriage.

He stood and walked over to her, took her hand in his. "There is something I have been meaning to ask you," he began but was interrupted by a discreet tap on the door. He tried to ignore it, tried to focus on asking the question that plagued him, but Sophie kept glancing towards the door and the person knocking was persistent.

"Are you going to answer it?" she asked with a nervous edge to her voice.

Reluctantly, Sebastian dropped her hand and walked over to the door. He opened it just wide enough to peer out, using his body to prevent the caller from looking inside.

"What is it?" he asked with some impatience.

Haines was standing at the door, looking like a boy who had just put a hole in his best breeches. "Forgive me, my lord, I didn't mean to disturb you. There's someone waiting to see you downstairs."

"Who is it?" There were only a few people who knew he owned the house, let alone he was in residence.

Haines did not reply, but raised his brows and jerked his head in the direction of the stairs.

"Very well," Sebastian grumbled. "I'll be right down."

Haines perused Sebastian's crumpled attire. "I think you'll need to smarten yourself up a bit for this one."

CHAPTER 21

*A*fter donning a clean shirt and cravat, Sebastian shrugged into his waistcoat and hastily fastened the buttons. If the caller expected to be received formally, then he was gravely mistaken. He would rather be damned than wear a coat, in his own house and at such an ungodly hour. Besides, until he knew the identity of his late night visitor, there was always a chance he would have to get his hands dirty. Should the need arise, he would prefer not to be encumbered by excessive clothing.

With some reluctance, he advised Sophie to return to her room, the distraction downstairs offering the perfect opportunity to do so unnoticed. Finally, after a minor disagreement where he had reinforced the need for sleep, and she had managed to bribe him into agreeing to discuss the masquerade, he made his way downstairs.

Haines, who was waiting for him in the hall with one hand resting on the newel post, looked up. "I've put them in the drawing room, my lord," he said, straightening. "Mrs. Cox is making tea, but maybe you'll want something stronger."

Sebastian gave him a quizzical look. "Them?" he asked a

little surprised. He glanced at Haines' empty hands. "Is there no card?"

Haines shook his head. "No, my lord. But I believe the gentleman knows you, or else I'd not have let them in."

"I confess it has been a long time since you've behaved so mysteriously," Sebastian continued, thoroughly intrigued. "I do hope I'm not going to be disappointed."

Indeed, he had been dragged from the comfort of his bedchamber, from soft lips and a warm embrace. It had better be for something bloody important.

The first thing he noticed as he strode into the room was that the only source of light came from a pair of silver-gilt candelabras, each standing on the side tables flanking the marble fireplace. The soft glow cast a modicum of illumination over one of his guests.

The lady sat bolt upright in the chair, although there was nothing stately about her posture. On the contrary, she gripped the arms as though she was ready to flee at a moment's notice.

He had seen her pert nose and rosy pink lips before. But now, in place of the broad-rimmed riding hat, were honey-gold tresses swept back in a simple style one would consider both practical and easy to manage. Gone were the breeches and coat, replaced by a dull, mauve dress with not a single adornment: no little pearl buttons, no lace edging on the sleeves or collar. She reminded Sebastian of a governess, albeit an extremely pretty one. The type employed by the more unscrupulous of gentlemen for their own particular needs rather than that of their children.

Appearing somewhat uneasy by his assessing gaze, she turned her head towards the window, to the tall figure lurking in the shadows.

"I hope we have not disturbed you, Dane," the faceless man drawled, his deep voice dripping with sarcasm. "Please tell me you have managed to get some sleep since we last met."

James Beaufort stepped into the light. His coat was creased, and there were dark circles under his eyes.

"I wouldn't worry about me. You look as though you haven't slept for days."

Beaufort gave a weak smile. "More like a week."

"I can tell just by looking at your clothes," Sebastian said, gesturing to Beaufort's crumpled attire. Thankfully, the gentleman carried it off with graceful poise and an air of self-assurance that made one overlook such imperfections.

Beaufort's gaze drifted over him. "You're hardly one to talk. Your hair looks as though you've just tumbled a serving wench in a haystack."

Sebastian forced a smile but groaned inwardly. "Since you thrust the ruby necklace in my hand, I've had a rather exhausting week."

He was not complaining. It had also been the most exciting, the most enthralling week of his life.

James Beaufort had no idea his sister had followed him to London, and as much as Sebastian wanted to punch him squarely on the chin for leaving such a wild woman alone without a chaperone, the matter of Sophie Beaufort needed to be handled with some delicacy.

James stepped forward and threw his arms around his friend. "It's been a long time, Dane," he said, patting Sebastian on the back. "You've not changed at all. I see you still have that mischievous smile the ladies always loved." James raised a brow. "Although you really should do something about those bloodshot eyes, they are not very becoming." He leant closer and whispered. "Perhaps the answer lies with who, rather than what, has been keeping you awake at night."

Bloody hell!

James turned to the lady and held out his hand. She rose from the chair, placed her gloveless hand in his and James brought it to his lips, kissing it with a level of tenderness and devotion. Indeed, there was not a single bit of creamy-white skin left untouched.

Feeling a little uncomfortable at such an exaggerated display of sentiment, Sebastian cleared his throat.

"Forgive me," James said, looking up reluctantly. He straightened his back before making his announcement. "My dear, may I present Sebastian Ashcroft, Marquess of Danesfield, and my oldest friend. Dane, I would like you to meet my wife, Lady Annabel Beaufort."

His wife!

A lifetime of aristocratic breeding prevented Sebastian from gaping in shock. Neither did he display any visible signs of anger or irritation. While he had been safeguarding James' sister from extortion, kidnapping and quite possibly murder, he had been planning a blasted wedding. Instead, he simply bowed and offered his felicitations.

Sebastian gestured towards the sofa and waited for the couple to sit before dropping into the chair by the hearth. The urgency to marry certainly explained their reason for remaining in London and now that the introductions were over, he intended to get some answers regarding the whole affair.

He decided to start with how the hell they knew where to find him.

"I must confess, I'm curious as to how you knew to come here," Sebastian said. He was equally curious as to how James had known he was leaving London in the first place. "Surely, when you stopped my carriage, you knew I was heading back to Westlands."

Before James could answer there was a tap at the door and Mrs. Cox came in with the tea tray. She placed it on the table in front of the sofa. "Would you like me to pour, my lord?"

"No, we shall see to it ourselves," Sebastian replied abruptly, for he was impatient for answers and feared the woman might mention his female guest. "Thank you, Mrs. Cox," he added by way of an apology.

"Please, allow me." Annabel Beaufort did not wait for

anyone to contradict and expedited the task with ardent domesticity.

"I didn't know you'd returned to London until today. I was surprised to see you back so soon. Monty said you were not planning to return for some time," James took a sip of his tea before returning his cup to the tray.

Back so soon? Was he being deliberately obtuse?

"Not as surprised as I am."

"The boy I hired to watch my lodgings told me that a gentleman had called looking for me. Naturally," James said, "the boy followed the gentleman to this address, and he happened to be watching the house this afternoon when you and your friend returned."

James spoke in such a matter-of-fact tone that Sebastian had to grip the arm of the chair for fear of lashing out.

"I had little choice in the matter," Sebastian said bluntly. "The Comte de Dampierre called looking for your necklace." At present, it was best not to divulge all the details, but he was overcome with the sudden urge to see his friend squirm.

"How in blazes did he know you had it?" James asked, his expression darkening.

"It appears he is quite cunning, particularly when he has been betrayed."

The sound of a china cup clattering against a saucer caught Sebastian's attention. He glanced at Annabel Beaufort, whose pallor was ashen and whose countenance was suddenly altered to that of a startled rabbit. James retrieved the cup and saucer and placed it on the tray before taking her trembling hands in his.

Suppressing a pang of guilt for his tactless approach, Sebastian thought it best to reveal what he knew of Annabel's situation. The sooner he understood the facts, the sooner he could determine Dampierre's motives.

"I have spoken to Antoinette and Madame Labelle, and they have explained the predicament you found yourself in," he said softly, his tone conveying his compassion.

James shot up from his seat. "Predicament!" he yelled. "The villain tricked an innocent woman into thinking she would be earning an honest living as a governess, only to hold her captive in a brothel. I would hardly call it a predicament."

Annabel stood and held on to her husband's arm. "Please sit down, James," she said softly, attempting to soothe him. "Lord Danesfield did not mean anything by it."

Sebastian could see the pain etched in every contour of his friend's face, the fear in the depths of his eyes. Annabel had been but a roll-of-the-dice away from living a very different life. It was a feeling Sebastian knew well.

James raised his hand and caressed his wife's face. "I am only grateful I was there to help," he said as he stared into her eyes. He allowed her to lower him back down onto the sofa and then he turned to Sebastian. "Can you imagine how terrified she must have been, to have her worst nightmare become a reality? I cannot bear to think of what would have happened had I not been there."

Sebastian silently cursed. In helping Annabel, James had left Sophie for the wolves. Indeed, he could not bear to think of what could have happened to her had she gone off to search for her brother without enlisting his help.

"You could have gone to the authorities," he snapped.

James appeared horrified by the idea. "What and cause a scandal? It would have achieved nothing other than tarnish the reputation of an innocent woman. Besides, what evidence is there?"

"I do not wish to sound callous," Sebastian challenged, offering Annabel an apologetic smile before turning to James. "But there must be others who have found themselves in the same situation. You have a duty to report it."

James pushed his fingers through his hair and sighed.

"I have been saying the same thing," Annabel agreed, casting James a sidelong glance. "But he will not listen. We must do something. We cannot creep about in the hope the comte will grow tired of looking for me."

"But things are different now," James said softly. "You are my wife. I will not let him hurt you."

Sebastian shook his head. "You're naïve to think Dampierre will simply walk away and forget the incident ever occurred. He has a reputation to uphold."

"What as a blackguard?" James scoffed.

"Those of the criminal class cannot afford to show weakness," Sebastian informed him. "A ruined reputation is rather more serious than being snubbed at a ball. It becomes a matter of life or death."

James narrowed his gaze. "Where was it you said you have been these last few years?"

"You do not want to know," Sebastian answered cryptically. "What I can tell you, speaking from experience, is that Dampierre will not stop until he feels his reputation has been restored."

"And how am I to do that?"

"You took something of his," he paused and inclined his head respectfully. "Forgive me. I am talking about how Dampierre thinks, not what I believe." Having clarified his point, Sebastian continued. "You took something and must give something back in return. It must be something he deems of greater value if you're to placate his injured pride."

James folded his arms across his chest stubbornly. "You mean I should give him the necklace."

"I know it is not what we planned," Annabel declared, placing her hand on her husband's arm. "But we must do whatever we can to be rid of him."

Sebastian was not entirely sure if the necklace would placate Dampierre. Had James and Annabel been the only ones aware of his devious scheme to use innocent girls, then they could have easily been dealt with. It was not difficult to make a murder look like an accident. The murder of four or five people was a different affair. Therefore, the matter would need to be brought to a swift conclusion. Hence, Dampierre's desire to meet at the masquerade.

"As I see it, we have three options," Sebastian said. He hesitated. He was not sure whether it was something he should mention in the presence of a lady.

"I'm listening," James said impatiently.

"You can make a statement with the appropriate authorities. Or, you can give Dampierre the necklace."

"I'm not giving him the necklace."

"What is the third option?" Annabel asked.

Sebastian took a deep breath. "Or you can kill him."

In that moment of stunned silence, Sebastian heard the patter of feet coming from the room above. James looked up and then cast him a devilish grin.

Sebastian swallowed, as his instincts told him his world was about to come crashing down around him.

CHAPTER 22

$\mathcal{H}$aving thrown on Dane's crumpled shirt, Sophie gathered her clothes and crept back across the landing to her room.

Once inside, she walked to the armoire and hung up her garments, hoping the creases would drop out. Then she climbed into bed. There was no point trying to sleep. Her mind was like a restless sea, bombarded with one thought after another until she found herself swept away on a wave of emotion.

She had been so wrong about Dane.

Her foolish pride had cast him in the role of villain, in the role of rake and rogue. The village gossip had been music to her ears for it had allowed her to place the blame at his door rather than her own. Now she came to think of it, he had done nothing to warrant her censure. So he had teased her and made light of a young girl's infatuation. It had all been in jest—but it had broken her heart.

With a deep sigh, she lay there and looked up at the canopy, wrapping her arms around her chest and hugging his shirt tighter to her body. It smelt of him: a musky masculine scent tinged with a hint of bergamot and some other wonderful fragrance she could not identify. The smell warmed her to her core, and she closed her eyes and pictured him. She pictured his hair falling over his brow, his lips curved into a wicked smile, his eyes: warm, brown pools of liquid chocolate caressing her soul.

Would she be able to recall the image when she was at home and alone in her cottage? Oh, she hoped so, for it was to sustain her for many years to come.

Pushing aside the feeling of despair that crept into her heart when she thought of losing him, of living her life without him, she tried to focus on what was real and true.

She loved him.

Even if he had never spoken of his father's misfortunes and of his battle to save his estate, she would have loved him all the same. She could not stop herself.

To men like Dane, duty would always be a priority when it came to marriage. He had said so himself on the journey from Marchampton. He was a peer of the realm and had a responsibility to secure his bloodline, to care for his estates, to make sacrifices for the greater good.

He had already proved his worth in that regard.

Men like Dane did not marry for love; they did not marry silly girls who believed themselves as strong as men—girls who gave their bodies freely without thought of the consequences. They married sensible, demure ladies who would be fitting mothers for their offspring and whose attributes were boasted about in the grandest ballrooms and salons.

They were men who made sacrifices for the sake of their titles.

Well, she would make a sacrifice, too. When the time came, she would let him go. She choked back a sob, ignored the gut-wrenching emptiness that consumed her. He needed a wife with a large dowry, large enough to secure his birthright for future generations. But in the meantime, in the few days she had left, well, she would love the man with all her heart. She would worship him body and soul. She would seize every single moment and treasure it as though it were the last.

She was still lying there staring up at nothing when someone tapped on the door.

"Come in," Sophie mumbled weakly.

Amy popped her head around before walking into the room. "Sorry, I was just coming in to light the fire." Amy bobbed a curtsy. "I thought you'd be downstairs, what with your brother visiting."

Her brother?

It took a moment for the words to penetrate her addled mind. "James is here, in this house?" She shot up, her tone a combination of shock and relief.

Amy looked a little confused. "Well, I think so. That's what Mrs. Cox said."

Sophie threw back the coverlet and jumped out of bed, ignoring the fact Amy was examining her choice of nightwear with some amusement.

"Would you mind handing me the wrapper?" Sophie pointed to the chair and in a matter of seconds she was rushing out of the door.

"But, miss, you can't … not like that …"

The maid's voice trailed off into the distance as Sophie made her way downstairs, grabbing the rail for support as she almost tripped in her eagerness to be reunited with James. She had not even had time to put a brush through her hair.

Dane would feel the sharp edge of her tongue for not informing her sooner.

After securing the ties of her wrapper, Sophie listened at the drawing room door and upon hearing her brother's voice charged into the room.

Three heads turned to face her, but only two pairs of eyes appeared shocked by her presence.

"Sophie!" James' eyes grew wide in disbelief. He stood and rushed over to her. "What are you doing here?" he asked, his expression a mix of confusion and delight. He picked up a short black ringlet and let it fall through his fingers. "What on earth have you done to your hair?"

Sophie was so relieved to see him she could not speak. He looked healthy and happy, and she had never been more pleased to see anyone in her entire life. She flung her arms around his neck and hugged him, much to the astonishment of the lady sitting on the sofa.

He returned her affection with a warm embrace, but when he kissed her on the cheek, she felt him stiffen. He reached for her hands, as they were still clasped around his neck, and pulled them down before stepping back to examine her. He was silent for a moment as his blue eyes flitted from her lips to her hair, to her wrapper and then back to her lips.

He lifted a ringlet and held it to his nose. "You smell of him," he said, his words heavy with disdain.

Sophie glanced over her brother's shoulder towards Dane. He stood there, his body hard and rigid, as though preparing for a sudden impact.

"His smell is all over you, on your skin, in your hair." James spun around to face Dane. "What the hell have you done to her?"

He did not wait for a reply but charged across the room, muttering something through clenched teeth before his fist landed with the force of a hammer on Dane's jaw.

"No!" Sophie screamed as she watched Dane stumble back into the chair. James punched him once more and then lifted him up by the scruff of his shirt and dragged him onto the floor.

Dane took another punch to the face and another to the stomach, causing him to draw his legs up to his chest and roll on to his side. Still, he made no protest.

Why was he not fighting back? Sophie could not understand it. He was more than capable of fending off the attack even if he did not wish to throw a punch himself.

"Get up," James spat.

"Stop this," Sophie cried, dropping to her knees and

throwing herself across Dane to prevent her brother from delivering another blow. She had never seen him so enraged.

"Get off him," James growled as he grabbed Sophie by the arm to pull her away.

Dane raised his head off the floor, his eyes hard and unforgiving. "You may hit me all you want," he spluttered, wiping blood from the corner of his mouth. "But you will take your damn hands off her."

Annabel stepped forward and grabbed her husband's arm. "What's the matter with you? You have not even given him a chance to explain. What if things are not what they seem?"

"Look at them," he scoffed as he pointed to the floor. "It is obvious for all to see. Why do you think he let me hit him? He knows what he's done."

Sophie got to her feet. With her back to her brother, she bent down to help Dane stand. She hadn't noticed her wrapper had come undone, and when she took Dane's arm and turned to face her brother, he was staring at the crumpled shirt, staring at her bare legs.

Dane reached across and drew the edges of the wrapper together.

"I am going to bloody well kill you," James said, enunciating every word, his eyes a penetrating ice-cold blue.

Dane stepped in front of Sophie, perhaps to shield her, perhaps by way of accepting the challenge. "My God, you're a walking monument to hypocrisy, and yet you have the audacity to judge me," Dane retorted. "Tell me, where were you when Dampierre came knocking on your sister's door? When he threatened her, when she rode to London on that beast of a horse all in the hope of saving you," he hissed. "I'll tell you where you were, getting bloody married!"

Sophie gasped. She moved to stand at Dane's side and stared at her brother. "You're married?"

James' face turned ashen as he shuffled uncomfortably, ignoring her question. "Dampierre came to Brampton Hall?"

"You left her. You left her for weeks without as much as a word." Dane stepped forward and poked his finger in his friend's chest. "And then you have the gall to come here and wave your fists about." He looked at James as though he was the worst kind of scoundrel. "You may be the hero of one woman's story," he added, sarcasm dripping from every word. "But you failed in your duty to protect the only woman who should have mattered to you."

James looked taken aback. "Duty?" he faltered. "You dare speak to me of duty?"

"She came to me," Dane shouted, stabbing a finger at his own chest. "She came to me, and I was duty bound to accept."

James took a step forward, stood toe to toe with his friend, their noses almost touching. "That does not give you the right to—"

"Stop it," Sophie yelled again, for she could not bear to listen to all this talk of duty and responsibility. Why could Dane not have said that he wanted to help her? That he was driven by some unexplainable desire. She turned to Annabel. "You're married?"

"Forgive me. I have not had the chance to introduce you formally," James interceded.

Annabel's smile lit up her entire face. "We were married yesterday, by special licence," she nodded.

It was a look of genuine happiness, and Sophie felt a small stab of jealousy, which she instantly dismissed. In truth, she was delighted for them. To see her brother alive and well and married, words could not describe the joy she felt. "How wonderful," she said, clasping her hands to her chest.

"Does anyone mind if I sit?" Dane asked with a deep sigh, throwing himself down on the sofa.

James scowled. "I have not finished with you."

"Nor I with you," Dane replied with a smirk and a raised brow but then winced and dabbed the cheekbone under his left eye.

"Perhaps we should all sit," Annabel suggested. "Sophie you sit here with me," she continued, casting James a mollifying glance as she took the seat next to Dane, leaving Sophie to squash in beside her.

James looked at the three of them, shook his head and then sat in the chair.

Whether the uncomfortable silence caused James to consider the fact that he was indeed a hypocrite, or whether he was desperate to prove a point to Dane, Sophie could not decide. Even so, James found it necessary to offer some explanation for his recent attachment.

"Sophie," James began, looking down his nose at Dane before turning his attention to her. "I want you to know, our marriage is, well, what I'm trying to say is that Annabel and I love one another." He stressed the word love and flicked Dane another irritated glare. "And although—"

"You mean you're *the* Annabel?" Sophie rudely interrupted, turning to face her sister-in-law with some surprise. "The one who escaped from Labelles?"

Annabel's face flushed. She glanced down into her lap and fumbled with her fingers. "Please do not think ill of me. I did not go there of my own volition." She looked up into Sophie's eyes. "You see, I was hired by the Comte de Dampierre to act as governess to his three children. Only, he did not have any children and instead I found myself a prisoner in his house." She swallowed deeply. "Had it not been for James, I am sure I would have been forced to"—she paused and shook her head—"I'm sure you know what sort of house it is."

Sophie did not have the heart to tell her she was wrong. Her fate would have been far worse than she could ever have imagined. She would have been sold and transported abroad to some godforsaken place, where the price was high for girls with fair skin and innocent eyes.

Of course, she had not told Dane that little bit of information because he would overreact and then they would argue, and she did not want to waste time doing that. There were far more plea-surable ways to spend time in his company.

Shuddering at the thought of what it must have been like to be lured away by the Comte de Dampierre, Sophie said, "You must have been terrified." She placed her hands over Annabel's and gave them a reassuring pat. "Well, you are safe now and must not worry about it anymore," she continued with some optimism, aware that Dane's expression could best be described as deeply cynical.

Annabel looked up at Sophie, her eyes also filled with doubt. "But we have just heard that Dampierre wants the necklace and I know James will refuse to give it to him."

"I'll be damned before I'll give that reprobate anything," James declared with an air of superiority.

"Then why offer it in the first place?" Dane complained. "What did you expect?"

"It wasn't me," James blurted sounding like a naughty schoolboy. "It was Monty. You know how he gets. I'd made the mistake of telling him my reasons for coming to town. He thought it was all some sort of joke, thought I was in my cups when I offered Madame Labelle five hundred pounds for Annabel." With pursed lips, he gave his wife an apologetic nod of the head.

Annabel cast him a reassuring smile. "Monty was not aware I had passed a note to James explaining my dilemma and begging for his help."

Dane cleared his throat. "Perhaps Dampierre is not as clever as he would have us believe." When they all looked at him with rather mystified expressions, he clarified, "To allow you access to paper and ink."

Annabel sat up straight, her eyes wide. "Oh, it was Madame Labelle who gave me the paper and urged me to write the note. She said my escape must appear credible. That is why she could not take the necklace."

Sophie and Dane both sat forward with wide-eyed expressions and directed their question to Annabel. "Madame Labelle helped you escape?" they said in unison.

Annabel nodded. "I climbed out of the bedchamber window. Madame Labelle helped me to tie the sheets, and James was waiting for me at the bottom." She glanced over to her husband with a look of pride and adoration.

Dane was still gaping, but Sophie was not surprised. Deep down, she knew Madame Labelle was an honourable woman who, where possible, would see justice done. In this instance, she had risked her neck, quite literally, to save an innocent girl and Sophie felt a sudden urge to do something, anything to rid her of Dampierre for good.

"Did you know about this?" Dane asked as he met her gaze.

Sophie shook her head. "No, of course not!"

He seemed to take no comfort from her answer. "You mean to tell me, during the thirty minutes you paraded about in Leicester Square, she never even mentioned it, never even hinted at the possibility?"

"No," Sophie replied bluntly.

James appeared aghast. "You met with Madame Labelle, in a public place, for all to see?"

"I did not meet with her," Sophie replied with an air of hauteur. "Mr. Shandy did." She offered him a satisfied smile as though that should be explanation enough.

James held his chin in his hand. "I'm confused."

"Now you see what I have been forced to put up with," Dane snorted. "Perhaps it is I who should be punching you."

Sophie folded her arms across her chest. "I am still here." She sighed, wondering why he made it sound as though he'd had no choice in the matter. It was not as if she'd forced him to follow her. "Trust me. It has been just as much of a hardship for me."

It had not been a hardship at all.

On the contrary, she had loved every single minute of it. She sat back on the sofa and studied Dane's profile. The sight of him almost caused her to sigh. It was not right that a man should be so handsome, or be allowed to sit in drawing rooms and cause no end of distraction with his firm jaw and wicked mouth. Even the swelling below his eye and the cut to his lip made him appear all the more striking, all the more dangerous, all the more lovable.

How on earth was she going to live without him?

Why such an unsolicited thought should choose to pop into her head, she didn't know. But rather than dampen her desire, it merely served to inflame it. He was here, in the room, right now. If she stretched out her hand, she could touch him. He was not lost to her, not yet.

She was suddenly overcome with the need to feel his mouth on hers, to feel the warmth of his body pressing against her, reassuring her. Desire grew. The feeling claimed her, spread rapidly through her body, robbing her of all rational thought.

Completely oblivious to her predicament, Dane said to the group, "Perhaps we should return to the question of the necklace."

But she could not focus on anything as she was consumed by an overwhelming need for him, a need so intense it was painful. "If you will excuse me," Sophie whispered as she stood. "I shall be back in a moment." If she could just get some air, she thought, angry at herself for being such a slave to her emotions. She was going to have to learn how to deal with these exaggerated feelings.

But then she would have a lifetime alone to do so.

CHAPTER 23

Sophie was in the dining room, pacing back and forth and wringing her hands when Sebastian walked in.

"Why are you in here?" he asked, his tone laced with concern. "You're not angry because of what I said, about being forced to put up with you?" He closed the door and stepped further into the room. "Because you know I didn't mean it. I only said it to annoy your brother. Surely, you know I would change nothing about our time together."

She could not look at him as his words had a ring of finality. "No, no, it's fine. Please, I'll be along in a minute."

She could hardly tell him she was so consumed with love for him, so aroused by the sight of him she could barely breathe let alone think clearly. She could not comprehend where the feelings had come from. One minute they were talking about the necklace, the next ... well. Perhaps this is what happened when those with an overly passionate nature fell in love. She had felt the same way after her meeting with Madame Labelle.

Perhaps it was because their journey was coming to an end.

Now her brother had arrived they could not continue as before. Sebastian's swollen eye was proof of that. They could not lie together. She would never feel the warmth of his skin. Never feel whole again.

He walked over to her and put his hand on her shoulder.

"Don't," she cried, and he turned her around to face him. The heat radiating from his hand caused her body to tremble, the connection stimulating every nerve.

"Are you going to tell me what's wrong?" His warm brown eyes soothed her, caressed her, drawing her in until she felt giddy.

Pulling away, she barged past him and strode towards the door, in search of a distraction. Her body ached for him, her heart cried out for him. He must never discover the depth of her love; she must never say the words.

"We … we should return to the drawing room." Her voice sounded weak, fractured.

Then he was behind her, surrounding her, pressing himself into her, his hands braced against the door. "Stay," was the only word he said. But it hit her like a tempest, almost knocking her off her feet.

As she whirled around to protest, to plead, he was looking down at her, and she could feel his breath like a soft whisper against her cheek. Helplessly, she watched as his lips came down on hers and then she was lost.

She tore frantically at his clothes in a bid to be close to him, devoured his mouth with a need more powerful than anything she'd ever felt before.

This would be the last time.

This would be the last time she would feel his touch.

She should have whispered to slow down, so she could sear the moment to memory. But the need to feel him inside her obliterated every other thought.

"*My God*," he whispered in her ear as he secured her thighs around his waist and thrust home. "This … this is madness."

Everything became a beautiful blur. A primal urge to race for completion consumed them and in no time she was biting his shoulder to stifle the sound of her release.

When he lowered her to her feet, he simply stared into her eyes. The rapid rise and fall of his chest proved to be such an intoxicating sound.

"Life will never be dull with you around," he panted.

And she felt her heart shatter in two.

After racing to her room to throw on one of Charlotte's dresses, Sophie breezed into the drawing room as though nothing had happened. "Lord Danesfield has gone to sort out more refreshment," she said to reassure them as to the reason behind their absence. Deferring to his title made their relationship sound more formal. "It appears Mrs. Cox has been waylaid performing other duties."

"Are you feeling better?" James asked, his eyes searching hers with some scepticism. Observing her more modest attire, he did not pass further comment.

Sophie considered the question.

Being in Dane's arms had eased all of her woes, for the moment. But she would have to find some other way of bolstering her strength in his absence. Of course, she could not say that to her brother and so smiled and said, "Yes, thank you. I just needed some air. All this talk of Dampierre left me feeling a little overwrought."

Some minutes later, Dane strode in carrying another tea tray. "Sorry for the delay," he said, placing the tray on the low table, before putting the first tray outside the door to be collected without further disturbance.

"Miss Beaufort is feeling much better now she has had some air," Annabel informed him.

He studied Sophie, a subtle smile playing on his lips, and then said with genuine emotion, "That is good news. I hope you found my words of reassurance somewhat helpful and know I am here to support you whenever the need arises."

Sophie tried her best not to blush as an image of Dane holding her against the dining room door, her legs wrapped tightly around him as he thrust deeply inside her, flashed through her mind. "It was extremely helpful, thank you," she beamed, taking it upon herself to pour the tea.

James eyed Dane with some suspicion. "In your eagerness to carry the tea tray, you seem to have lost a button."

Sebastian glanced down at his waistcoat but gave not the slightest indication the remark revealed anything other than what it ought. He placed his hand on his chest and stared down at the floor, a frown marring his brow. "No doubt Mrs. Cox will come across it." He moved to the hearth and poked the fire before directing his attention to James. "Now, while your room is being prepared, perhaps we should continue our discussion."

In an attempt to disguise the utter disappointment at not having Dane to herself, at not being able to leave her room and go to him for fear of being discovered, Sophie assumed the same confused expression as her brother and Annabel.

"Oh, you cannot leave," Dane continued as though guessing their thoughts. "Dampierre has had a man watching this house for the last few days. He will have seen you enter."

James thumped the arm of the chair with his fist and muttered something incoherent. "If I had known that—"

"What, you would not have bothered knocking?" Dane interrupted with a smug grin. "I am afraid it is a little late. Perhaps it's time to discuss our options. But I should warn you there is really only one logical solution to the problem."

"I cannot give him the necklace," James announced with a steely look in his eye.

Dane smiled. "I do not want you to give him the necklace. Considering the fact I am prepared to purchase it for double its market value then that is clearly no longer an option."

James frowned and pursed his lips. "Why would you do that?"

Dane did not reply immediately. "I was forced to part with all but one of my family's heirlooms and so the necklace would be a welcome addition. Besides, I find it extremely pleasing to the eye."

Sophie felt a sudden stab of resentment, for she knew what such a declaration truly meant. At some point in the future, she would be forced to see her necklace draped around his wife's neck.

James' lips curved into the beginnings of a smile, but he did not fully commit. "Then I shall look forward to hearing what you think it is worth," he countered.

What! Sophie screamed silently.

Why had neither of them stopped to consider how she might feel about it? It was one thing to give it to Dampierre in exchange for Annabel's freedom—Sophie could live with that. But to sell it to Dane so he could start some new tradition with his new wife ... well, she would have to do something about that. Perhaps she could steal it and persuade Dampierre to accept the trade.

As she struggled to contain her emotions, she noted her brother's countenance had suddenly altered, his expression dark and brooding.

Dane's mouth twitched at the corners. "I believe you have just realised there is only one option open to us," he said confidently, his eyes fixed firmly on James. "And so the question we must answer now is which one of us will kill the Comte de Dampierre?"

CHAPTER 24

*T*hree pairs of wide eyes stared at Sebastian in disbelief.

"There is no other way," he said, his tone merciless. "Even if you were to speak up and make a complaint, we cannot be sure those in office are trustworthy."

He watched as James sank his head into his hands, knowing the truth in Sebastian's words and knowing he was the one duty-bound to perform the wicked task. Sebastian would not let him do it, of course. He would find a way to extricate him from his obligation and carry out the task himself.

"But that's not the only reason," Sebastian continued. "As you rightly said, you cannot allow your wife to be drawn into a scandal. Equally, we cannot stand aside and allow such a fate to befall another innocent woman."

There was a moment of silence while they all appeared to consider his words.

"But, but you know what it will mean if we are caught," James stammered.

"We will not hang if that's what you're implying," Sebastian countered.

Sebastian's words were met with a sharp intake of breath. He looked to the sofa, to Annabel, who was sitting with her hand plastered to her mouth, and to Sophie, who appeared to be listening intently and did not seem the least bit alarmed by his callous words.

Sophie would make an excellent marchioness, he thought. They would have strong sons and spirited daughters. The more, the merrier. He doubted he would be able to keep his hands off her once he had her all to himself.

"Besides, we will all have an alibi," Sebastian added with a look of smug satisfaction. "Dampierre has been kind enough to provide us with the perfect opportunity."

As his gaze met Sophie's, she was looking back at him with some fascination. "You mean we are to attend the masquerade ball after all?" Her speech was slow and deliberate, almost seductive, stimulating the fine hairs on his nape and he was forced to divert his thoughts away from a more intimate direction and refocus on the task at hand.

"I have never been to a masquerade," Annabel added dreamily. Obviously, it had not occurred to her that the whole reason for attending was to commit murder.

"Believe me, they are over-rated," Sebastian replied with a lack of enthusiasm. "There is nothing remotely exciting about dancing with someone who has the hands of a temptress, only to discover that at midnight they have the face of a duck."

He walked over to the side table, poured himself a brandy, lifted an empty glass and gestured to James, who nodded.

Taking the drink, James drained the glass and handed it back to Sebastian. "If you're serious about this, then I cannot allow the ladies to attend." James shook his head and ignored Annabel's disgruntled sigh.

It was as though Sebastian had just received another blow to the stomach, a fatal wound to his masculine pride. In his opinion, Sophie was his responsibility. The thought of any other man, even her brother, laying claim to her, controlling her ...

The woman in question rose from her seat, and walked

over to the hearth to stand at his side. She folded her arms across her chest. The simple act of defiance caused his heart to swell.

"I'm afraid I must attend," she began, her words short and clipped. "Dampierre has given specific instructions, and he will know if I am not there. I believe I can distract him sufficiently to get the deed done."

"It is not your choice to make," James replied arrogantly.

Sebastian was suddenly relieved he was only a spectator in this bout. But he knew who he would put his money on.

Moving her hands to her hips, Sophie arched a brow. "I have entertained the Comte de Dampierre in your study," she said fiercely. "I have stared into his lifeless eyes, felt his cold, clammy hands on my skin. I have felt the tip of his sword against my throat."

Sebastian stiffened. "You did not tell me about that," he whispered through clenched teeth. He wondered what else she had omitted to tell him.

"So," she continued haughtily. "I think I have earned the right to decide what is best. It is my choice and mine alone."

As James shot to his feet, the chair close to tipping over with the force, Sebastian could not decide if his tortured expression was due to anger or shame.

Stepping forward, Sebastian placed a hand on his friends arm. "Before you say anything more, there is something I wish to discuss with you. Shall we step outside?"

Sebastian stepped in between them and James tilted his head to glare at his sister before allowing Sebastian to steer him from the room.

As soon as they stepped out into the hall and closed the drawing room door, James whirled around to confront him.

"If you are going to berate me for the way I have treated my sister then do not bother," James admonished with an element of vehemence, which Sebastian suspected was not entirely aimed at him and stemmed from a feeling of guilt. "Nothing you could say could make me feel worse than I do at this moment," he added, shoving his hand through his hair.

In response, Sebastian simply said, "Good."

"How the hell was I to know Dampierre would travel all the way to Brampton Hall?"

"She could have been killed," Sebastian replied with a low growl. The thought caused a searing pain in his chest. "She could have been the one locked in the room of that brothel." Although knowing Sophie, she would have rallied all the girls together and found a way to take down Dampierre.

"Do you think I don't know that." James paced back and forth. "But you saw for yourself, she is so damn stubborn."

Sebastian grabbed him by the elbow and pulled him further down the hall. "She is not safe until we dispose of Dampierre."

James appeared distressed. "It is one thing to unwittingly place someone you care for in danger, but to do so knowingly— you cannot ask that of me."

In any other circumstance, Sebastian would have agreed with him. The thought of placing Sophie in any danger felt like a knife to his heart. But he truly believed that while Dampierre was alive, both ladies were in grave danger.

"Do you not think I feel the same? I want to marry her, James."

James scoffed. "After the way you have behaved, I would not be satisfied with anything less. I still have an overwhelming desire to rip you limb from limb. But as you rightly said that would make me a hypocrite. Perhaps I should be grateful to you for taking her off my hands. I'm sure by now you know what it is you're letting yourself in for."

Sebastian considered his words. As a young girl, Sophie had been bothersome, annoying, and persistent in her methods to engage his attention. As a woman, he found her captivating, bewitching, utterly enthralling. She was constantly in his thoughts, in his dreams. From the moment she had tumbled from her horse and into his arms, he had not been able to keep his hands off her. Indeed, he appeared to be in a constant state of arousal.

"I'm in love with her," he blurted almost choking on the words, as it suddenly occurred to him that a life without her was not worth living.

James patted him on the shoulder, his mouth curved into a smile that suggested a level of empathy. "Once you are married, perhaps we should start a new club. One for men who are hopelessly in love with their wives."

Sebastian scoffed. "Somehow, I have the feeling it may take more than a declaration to secure your sister's hand."

"How you choose to go about it is your affair, but I would see her wed," he arched a brow, "and soon."

Sebastian nodded in acquiesce. "Now, as to this matter of the masquerade," he stopped abruptly, noting the disapproving look on James' face. "Please, just listen to what I have to say," he appealed. "Ask yourself this. If you could go back to that night at Labelles, walk away and erase it from your memory, would you do so? Knowing the danger you have placed us all in … would you … would you change it?"

James looked down at the floor as he considered the question. He glanced up at Sebastian, and with a deep sigh whispered, "No. I would not change a damn thing."

Sebastian placed a firm hand on his friend's shoulder. "Then let us retire to the drawing room so I may tell you my plan."

The following evening they were back in the drawing room, waiting for Sophie to dress for the masquerade. This time, James sat next to Annabel on the sofa, his arm draped around her shoulder, relating stories of Sophie's childhood infatuation with Sebastian.

"She used to hide behind the curtain, just to hear his voice," James chuckled. "You knew when she was there, for there was always one large eye peeking through the gap. But now look at him," James continued, waving a hand in Sebastian's direction. "It appears the roles are reversed, and it is my poor friend who paces the floor, pining like a puppy."

"I am not pining. I am simply eager to see what costume Dampierre wishes her to wear," he countered, although he could not deny that his mouth was dry with anticipation. A whole day had passed since he had last held her in his arms and both his mind and his body seemed to be persecuting him for the fact. "The design will reveal much in terms of Dampierre's intentions, and I must impress the memory into my mind. So I may find her if we are separated in the crush," he added, pleased he could find a plausible reason to explain the desperate longing that consumed him and was obviously apparent to others.

"I hope you're not expecting her to be able to find you," James mocked, scanning his attire. "Half the guests will be wearing the same black tricorn and domino."

Sebastian sighed. That was the idea. He needed to be able to move about unnoticed. He wondered if Dampierre had considered that fact when he had chosen Sophie's costume. Sophie had refused to let him see it, even when he had explained the practicality of his request.

"I believe you'll look rather dangerous with your mask on." Annabel blushed. "If I were wearing jewels, I might throw them at you for fear of my life."

Sebastian shook his head at their joviality. Had they forgotten the purpose of the evening? Perhaps it was their way of dealing with anxiety, for James had been agitated when Sebastian had told him he must stay at home with Annabel. If they were discovered at the masquerade and their story revealed, then their guilt would be assumed.

"Speaking of jewels," James said in a more serious tone, "I presume Sophie is wearing the necklace?"

"It is necessary in order to fool ..."

As the drawing room door opened, all conversation ceased.

In walked what could only be described as an ethereal vision from a bygone era. James and Sebastian stood, their mouths hanging open in awe. Sebastian hardly recognised her.

Against the white powdered wig woven with gold thread, her face was as pale as porcelain, enhancing the fullness of her rosy pink lips. The gown of red and gold taffeta was heavily boned. The deep, plunging neckline pushed up her breasts so they appeared as soft creamy-white mounds, so deliciously tempting he could not take his eyes off them.

"Well, how do I look?" she asked, her eyes alight with excitement as she gave a little twirl and held the mask to her face.

Sebastian was afraid to speak for fear his voice would expose the depth of his arousal. Dampierre was not a stupid man. Sophie would be like a bright beacon in the crowd.

"You look so beautiful." Annabel clapped her hands in delight. "You look as though you should live in the palace of Versailles, with courtiers waving fans and bowing at your feet."

Sophie met Sebastian's gaze, and she smiled. "Would you mind fastening this for me?" she asked, holding out the necklace.

As she walked over to him, he held out his hand, hoping she would not notice the slight tremble in his fingers. She turned around, her long, elegant neck just inches from his lips, and as he leant forward to drape the necklace around her throat, his mouth brushed against her ear.

"You have no idea how much I want you," he whispered, as he imagined his hand wandering lower, dipping down into the front of her bodice to skim the soft flesh, to take the peak between his fingers and rub until she begged for relief. Her hand came up to her throat to hold the necklace in place, and he took pleasure in the knowledge her fingers were shaking, too.

With the clasp fastened, she moved to walk away, but he pulled her to his side, the fall of her gown disguising the hard length straining against his breeches.

James stood, walked over to his sister and kissed her on the cheek. "You look wonderful." His gaze drifted over her gown before settling on the ruby necklace. "I remember our mother wearing this," he said, his tone soft and tender, "but it looks spectacular on you. It seems to glisten more brightly, and the rubies appear to be a richer shade of red. It is as though it was made for you."

Sophie reached up and placed her hand on her brother's cheek. "Thank you," she muttered softly. There was a moment when she stared into her brother's eyes as if she was considering how best to say goodbye, should she fail to return. "I am so pleased you're safe and happy," she said, her voice brimming with emotion. "And do not worry. Dane will look after me."

As Sophie moved to hug Annabel, Sebastian knew he was still not in any state one would call respectable. Perhaps because he had been having visions of her wearing the necklace. Only there were no clothes in his vision. He whipped his domino around him in such an exaggerated fashion it would have received a round of applause had he been on stage.

James walked over and gripped his shoulder. "Have a care," he said, his face solemn as he stepped back. "Although you will not look half as dangerous if you continue to swirl your cape in such a fashion. You'll have all the dandies lining up for an encore."

CHAPTER 25

*L*ord Delmont's mansion in Portman Square was a hive of activity, as carriage after carriage barged and jostled their way for a coveted place in the queue.

Sophie stared at the scene in wonder.

A warm, orange light blazed forth from every window, illuminating the parade of exotic guests: an oriental princess, a Greek goddess, a butterfly with life-size wings, who had all chosen to walk into the square rather than suffer any further delay.

"Lord Delmont is renowned for his extravagance," Dane said with exasperation as he glanced out of the carriage window. "He is always seeking new and novel ways to amuse his guests, and so I fear it will be rather a crush."

He spoke with a jaded view of such events, Sophie noted, as though he took no pleasure from the normal pursuits sought by other members of the aristocracy.

"With no formal announcements made, we will struggle to locate Dampierre," he continued as he stared across at her, his gaze scanning her costume before settling on the ruby necklace. "Yet, he will know the exact moment we enter."

Sophie liked the way he looked at her. The slow predatory

gaze roamed over her from head to toe, warming her body and soul, even on a chilly night such as this. When his eyes lingered on the necklace, she felt triumphant. It did not matter who wore it now. She felt confident he would always associate it with her.

A part of her wanted to thank Dampierre. His costume had provided the means for her to show another side of herself: a more refined and sophisticated side. But, amongst all the excitement, she had almost forgotten the true purpose of the evening.

They were going to kill a man.

The thought weighed heavily upon her. Did anyone truly deserve to die in such a manner? Would their lives be forever tainted, forever defined by this one evil act?

"We … we must be on our guard," she said. It was her fault Dane was involved. But if he did not rid them of Dampierre, they would be forever plagued by fear, and so she had to do everything in her power to help him. "We cannot afford to be distracted from our purpose."

"Are you nervous?" he asked, and she noticed the faint tremor in his voice. "Do you fear seeing Dampierre again?"

"No," she replied softly. Indeed, during the last few days, she had learnt much about Dampierre. The depth of his depravity made it easier. She could not rouse emotion for a man capable of such wickedness. "I do not worry about myself," she said upon reflection.

He gave her an empathetic smile as though he knew the feeling well.

"Tell me," she continued, "have you ever killed a man?" There was a tremble in her voice she could not disguise. She was afraid of the answer, of what it might reveal. Would it change her view of him?

He lowered his head, his gaze locked on some invisible point on the floor. "Yes," he answered solemnly, as though the word was a thick, iron chain around his neck. He looked up at her, searching her face. "In France, I was with Dudley and a few others … we were ambushed. It was a case of kill or be killed."

There was something cold and clinical about his reply and she wondered if he'd spent sleepless nights justifying it to himself. "I'm not proud of it." He shrugged. "But when there is a chance someone you care for may get hurt, you must do whatever is necessary."

And he was going to kill another man tonight ... for her.

It was not guilt she felt. It was fear. What if something should go wrong? What if something should happen to Dane?

Racked by the sudden urge to declare her love, she shifted uncomfortably in her seat. If life were simpler, she would stand on the roof of the carriage and shout out for all to hear. But she must never say the words, as she suspected, in light of their intimate relations, he would feel duty bound to offer for her.

"I understand," she whispered, straining to hold the words at bay. Yet she felt she should say something to express her feelings. "Because I would kill ... I would kill for you."

He moved across the carriage, pushing aside the voluminous amounts of fabric to sit next to her, taking her hand in his. "And I would fight the whole world to save you," he replied tenderly. Tilting her chin, he brushed his lips lightly across hers, then took her in his arms and kissed her deeply.

It differed from other kisses they'd shared. The tendency for lasciviousness often overwhelmed them. But this kiss ... this kiss reached out to her heart, sang to her soul.

"Should anything go wrong," he panted as he broke away from her. "I want you to go to Dudley." His hand moved down from her shoulder to rest on her stomach. "And if you are carrying my child," he said, his voice tinged with sorrow as though he was already grieving the loss. "Dudley will take care of you ... of you both."

Sophie felt a lump form in her throat as she had not even considered the possibility. Fear and panic gripped her. She covered his hand with her own in the hope of seeking comfort. But it only served to make the feeling worse, the gesture binding them together in some inexplicable way—his hand, her hand, and some wonderful, imaginary child all together as one.

"Will you do that for me?" he urged. "Will you promise me?"

What had she ever done to deserve such torture? If they were different people, if he were without title and responsibility then she would plead with him, beg him to forget Dampierre. She would beg him to run as far away as possible, with her, to care for her, to love her.

But their lives were not destined to be so.

Taking a deep breath, and with a newfound resolve, she lifted her hand to caress his cheek and whispered, "I promise." Then she turned to stare out into the night, hoping she could hold back the tears.

If Sophie thought the house had looked bright from the outside, it was positively dazzling on the inside. She counted five, three-tiered chandeliers, the illumination in the room increased by the reflection from the huge gilt-framed mirrors. As Sebastian had predicted, Delmont had spared no expense, as jugglers, a conjurer and a knight riding his hobbyhorse proved exciting entertainment for the raucous crowd.

As they pushed their way through the eager throng, Sophie could not fail to notice that the guests were rather more flirtatious, more amorous in their address than was customary. It seemed the punishment for wandering hands was nothing more than a playful slap and a giggle.

"We should find a quiet alcove where we can talk privately," Dane grumbled. He placed her hand in the crook of his arm and steered her away. "Delmont always serves supper after the unmasking," he continued, as they passed a gentleman balancing grapes along the neckline of a lady's gown as she attempted to flick them into his mouth. "He prefers his guests to be ravenous."

Sophie smiled. With his black mask firmly in place, Dane looked rather ominous. His dark eyes were more intense, more compelling, the bow of his lips more prominent, and she found could not take her eyes off him.

"There is something about a masquerade," she purred, feeling a small shiver run through her body. "Something in the air that lends itself to decadence." Coming to a stop just a few paces from the twirling dancers, she turned to face him. Emboldened by the atmosphere, she pushed her hand up inside his domino, up along the hard planes of his muscular chest. "I think I would like to dance."

It was not a request. Before he could object—how could they be on their guard if they were dancing—she led him out onto the floor.

They danced the cotillion, a dance she'd had the pleasure of performing on numerous occasions at Brampton Hall. Unlike Lord Delmont's party, their guests had not been as suggestive in their movements. Indeed, as the gentlemen circled the ladies, a deliberate effort was made to press against them. Sophie felt one particular gentleman brush so closely against her back she almost stumbled forward and was shocked to find his bare hands caressing her waist as he steadied her.

As the dance ended her gaze shot to Dane. She could sense the tension emanating from him, hear his teeth grinding together as he clenched his jaw.

"Do you see why I didn't want you to attend?" he scolded as they came together and he pulled her arm through his. "Now you know that I was not referring to the jugglers when I said Lord Delmont caters for all his guests' pleasures."

"Oh, don't be angry," Sophie giggled in an attempt to lighten the mood. "There was no harm done. Besides, I had you to protect me."

Her tone was deliberately seductive, but rather than soothe

him her words seemed to irritate him even more and he pulled her over to a large potted fern in the corner.

"This is not blasted Marchampton," he said. "You cannot simply ride off on your ridiculous horse in the hope I will follow. Or scoot off in your breeches as though they somehow make you immune to danger."

Sophie was shocked at his response. "You are being irrational."

Ignoring her comment, he raked his fingers through his hair in frustration. "I cannot work like this. I cannot work while you're with me." He waved a hand in the air at nothing in particular. "One minute I am so aroused I can barely keep my hands off you. My mind feels like it is disengaged from my body, as though it is floating about in some euphoric pool. The next, I am so damn annoyed I want to scream at you and shake you, for you seem to find Dampierre and this whole blasted thing amusing."

Amusing? Amusing!

She was desperately in love with him—may even be carrying his child—and she was going to have to step aside so he could marry another woman, someone worthy of his title. Why would she give a fig about Dampierre? Nothing could be worse than having your heart ripped apart piece by piece. Dampierre could go to hell, and she would take great pleasure in telling him so.

"Excuse me," she said coldly, stepping away from him. "I shall give you the space you need to work. Besides, I feel I am in need of some air."

He caught up with her on the terrace. "You cannot go off on your own."

He was right, of course. She was behaving like a spoilt child. They were not at the masquerade to have fun.

Their attention was caught by a flurry of figures pushing their way onto the terrace, all eager to be the first in line to witness the firework display. Sophie was not prepared for the deluge of rowdy guests pouring out of the ballroom. Swept along in a wave of excitement, she lost sight of Dane and found herself carried across the lawn towards the viewing area.

Amongst the shrieks and squeals, she thought she heard him calling out to her, but as she turned to look over her shoulder, she was pushed, jostled and shunted further into the crowd.

With the first loud bang, everyone looked up to the array of glittering lights illuminating the night sky. Once again she tried to move but was crushed between a Turkish prince and a shepherdess. The next bang sounded even louder, and the crowd jerked together in response.

As a hand closed over her elbow, she felt all the tension leave her body and almost sagged to the ground in relief. "Thank goodness you've found me," she gasped. She could not turn around, but took comfort from the fact that Dane was standing directly behind her.

"I was not expecting such a warm welcome."

It was not Dane.

While this man spoke with a similar air of authority and a sensuous undertone, it lacked the richness, lacked the depth of character and warmth of feeling that was unmistakable in Dane's tone.

"I believe you have mistaken me for someone else," she replied as calmly as she could, believing it was just another one of Lord Delmont's overzealous guests. "Now, if you would kindly remove your hand."

"Is that any way to speak to your host, to the man who has excelled in affording you every pleasure, in giving you what you desire?"

There was another loud bang, followed by a stream of twinkling lights falling from the sky. The crowd surged forward as they clapped and jeered to show their appreciation.

"Then you have failed in your task, Lord Delmont. What I desire, is to be returned to the arm of my chaperone."

Lord Delmont breathed deeply. "Your tongue is like the lash of a whip. Perhaps that's what others find so appealing."

As the crowd moved again, Sophie took the opportunity to turn around only to find herself practically pressed against the chest of her host. He was much taller than she expected and she looked up to see a mop of golden hair spilling over a black mask and a pair of ice-blue eyes lacking any emotion. "Excuse me," she said, edging to the left. "I fear I am in need of more stimulating company."

Before she could move any further, he swept his arm around her back and anchored her to his body. "Imagine my shock," he said with some amusement, his breath tickling her cheek, his eyes fixed on the bodice of her gown, "to find I have only had but a glimpse of those delicate treasures, yet I am still highly aroused."

She struggled against him but could not slacken his grip. She thought of shouting out for Dane, but she doubted he would hear her. Besides, she did not want to draw attention to his identity. "You do not frighten me, Lord Delmont. Indeed, I find your manner rather crass for my tastes."

Lord Delmont threw his head back and laughed, but no one paid him the slightest attention. "You find me vulgar. How amusing." He studied her for a moment. "Now, as much as I am enjoying our little game, I fear there is a matter of business to attend to. If you would care to follow me, I believe your uncle is waiting."

Sophie raised a brow. "Would he happen to be my uncle from France?" she asked, trying to dismiss the deep sense of foreboding. Things were not going to plan, but that was not surprising. If she left with Lord Delmont, then Dane would not need to kill Dampierre, and she would be forced to give him the necklace. She considered her position. If she went with Lord Delmont, Dane would be safe. And she would never be subjected to the torture of seeing another woman wearing her necklace.

"I believe it is. And he seems most eager to be reunited." Lord Delmont swallowed deeply, his eyes wandering over her body as though she was a ripe peach and he had not eaten for weeks.

"Then I do not wish to disappoint him," she remarked with icy composure.

"I doubt you would disappoint any man," Delmont drawled as he pushed his way through the throng, guiding her towards a cluster of trees running along the bottom of the garden. "I am most bereft that I will not get to experience you personally. But you see money has always been my first love, and I'm afraid my purse has suffered a fatal blow and is in desperate need of resuscitation."

Delmont led her to a small wooden door leading out into the mews where an unmarked carriage was waiting. As they approached, the door of the carriage swung open, and the Comte de Dampierre climbed out. Gripping his cane firmly in his right hand, he turned to greet them.

With wide eyes, Dampierre placed his left hand over his heart and exclaimed, "Let me congratulate you, Miss Beaufort, for you look exquisite, just as I expected." He bowed his head respectfully and then removed his gold pocket watch, flicked open the case and studied it under the carriage lamp. "Soon it will be midnight," he said, placing the watch back into the pocket of his waistcoat. "I am pleased to see you are true to your word. I do so appreciate honesty in all things."

Sophie should have felt terrified. But she looked upon the comte with a degree of superiority, and when she gave a half-hearted curtsy, she hoped her disdain was evident. "As I explained to Lord Delmont, I do not wish to disappoint."

Dampierre stroked his beard, twirling the end into a point as his beady black eyes perused her hair, her costume, her necklace. "No," he mused. "I do not believe you will."

Lord Delmont cleared his throat. "Forgive me. I do not wish to interrupt this little *tete-a-tete,* but I must return to my guests."

Dampierre's expression changed. He appeared affronted, as

though a lowly servant had dared to insult him. "Then be gone," he replied coldly with a flick of the wrist.

Lord Delmont straightened. Standing a good head and shoulders above Dampierre, he said through gritted teeth, "I will have my marker."

"Ah, yes, your marker," Dampierre repeated slowly. "May I suggest, in future, you do not risk that which you cannot afford to lose? There are those who would seek to profit from such an oversight."

Lord Delmont stepped forward, only to find the sharp end of a sword prodding his chest.

"To underestimate one's opponent is a dangerous game," Dampierre challenged. "A lesson you recently discovered at the faro table I believe." With the sword firmly in place, he called out, "Marie, would you be so kind as to give Lord Delmont his marker."

Sophie's gaze shot to the carriage door as Madame Labelle climbed down. She glanced briefly at Sophie, but her expression was somewhat vacant, unreadable. Perhaps she did not want Dampierre to know of their friendship.

Madame Labelle raised her hand from beneath her blue cloak. "Your marker, Lord Delmont," she said, with an inclination of the head.

Lord Delmont practically snatched it out of her hand, even though the movement caused the point of the sword to dig a little deeper into his chest. He scanned the document, perhaps checking its authenticity. Once satisfied, he bowed to Dampierre, turned on his heels and left without so much as a word or a backward glance.

Dampierre replaced the sword in its sheath and once again used it as a cane. "My apologies, Miss Beaufort. I did not intend for you to witness such vulgarity. Now that it is dispensed with, may I suggest we get to the matter of my reward ... or recompense if you prefer."

Sophie placed her palm over the chain of rubies. "And when

you have what you want, will it be the end of the matter?" she asked dubiously.

"Yes. It will be the end of the matter," Dampierre nodded as he repeated her words. "We shall discuss it in the privacy of my carriage." Noticing Sophie's wary expression, he added, "Marie, she will accompany us."

While Dampierre addressed her in both a polite and a cordial manner, Sophie knew it to be a well-crafted facade. He was a man driven by a lust for power. Coupled with his complete lack of compassion, he was a very dangerous man indeed. Even with all her boldness and bravado, Sophie knew she would be a fool to climb into his carriage and as such inadvertently took a few steps back.

Dampierre's mouth twitched. "You *will* get into the carriage, Miss Beaufort," he insisted in a menacing tone.

Sophie noticed Marie's wide eyes and discreet shake of the head. Was it a silent warning to obey or to bolt?

Then Dampierre played his trump card. Drawing his sword, he thrust it out to the right, missing Marie's cheek by a whisker. "I would hate Marie to have an accident. Scars … they can look so unsightly on a woman."

Against all logic, against the voice screaming for her to flee, Sophie acceded to his wishes. Casting Marie a reassuring smile, she walked past Dampierre and climbed into the carriage.

Once they were all seated, with Marie deciding to sit next to Sophie, Dampierre sighed with satisfaction and said, "There … a much more refined approach, do you not think?"

After banging the roof of the carriage with his cane, it lurched forward, tearing out of the North Mews at breakneck speed.

"Victor," Marie cried in disbelief.

"Where are you taking me?" Sophie clung to the edge of the seat. Once they were out of the mews, it would be nigh on impossible for Dane to find her. She reached around her neck in an attempt to remove the necklace. "Here. Take it and let me out."

Dampierre laughed: a high-pitched cackle that chilled her to her bones. "You think your pitiful necklace is worth the same as a man's freedom?" he asked, his expression darkening. "Well, it is not."

Sophie struggled to catch her breath. If he didn't want the necklace, then what did he want?

Madame Labelle appeared aghast. Her gaze swept from Dampierre to Sophie and back again. "But, Victor," she pleaded. "You said once you had the necklace you would be satisfied. You said it would be a fitting reward—"

"Be quiet, Marie," he scolded. "I said Miss Beaufort would provide me with a fitting reward." He turned his attention to Sophie. "Do you know what your brother's interference has cost me?" He did not wait for an answer. "It has cost me my freedom. I cannot stay in this country of yours," he said with an indolent wave of the hand. "I shall forever be looking over my shoulder. And I cannot tolerate such a thing." He leant forward and gripped Sophie's knee with his bony fingers. "But you, madame, you shall atone for the sins of your brother."

Sophie brushed his hand away. "I will do no such thing."

"Oh, you will," he replied firmly. "I do not need your permission. In truth, I prefer it that way."

"No!" Madame Labelle yelled. "Miss Beaufort does not deserve to pay for the crimes of her family." She choked back a sob, a look of torment etched on her face.

Dampierre banged his cane on the floor of the carriage. "And I did not deserve to pay for the crimes of mine," he bellowed, saliva dripping from the corner of his mouth. "These people they think they are superior, think they can dismiss me as though I am nothing." He paused to regain his composure and then said with some impatience, "We will be married, and she will bear my sons, and they will never have to bow and scrape. Their mother will be a lady, not some back alley whore, and I will show them all I am something."

While Sophie sat in stone-cold silence, her face a mask of indifference, fear clawing at her soul, Madame Labelle brought her hands to her face and wept.

CHAPTER 26

$\mathcal{L}$ ord Delmont was in his study, standing in front of the fire when Sebastian came charging through the door.

"Where the hell is she?" Sebastian marched over to Lord Delmont, who was marginally taller and considerably broader than Sebastian, and punched him squarely in the face. Delmont reeled, raising his hand as a shield. Before he could even attempt to fight back, Sebastian grabbed him by the ends of what was a perfectly starched cravat and pulled him down so that they were eye level. "I shall give you until the count of three," he snarled.

Sebastian was so enraged, so damn scared he could barely think straight. He had stood and watched two hundred or more guests pile out onto the terrace and in the time it had taken to draw breath, Sophie was gone.

No doubt Delmont had been watching them, waiting for an opportunity to pounce.

"Do not dare tell me you know nothing about it," Sebastian continued, wrapping his hand around the ends of the cravat to tighten his grip. He didn't care if he strangled the man. "Was it your idea to lure me away with a decoy?"

Sebastian had pushed and shoved his way to a corner of the

terrace, the elevated position giving the ideal opportunity to scan the crowd. Some guests had used the distraction to sneak off into a quiet corner, as Delmont was renowned for having the largest and most secluded garden in the row.

Then he'd noticed Sophie, albeit it was only her elaborate wig and the back of her red dress. She'd stepped away from the crush and escaped through a topiary arch, out of sight. He had spent almost fifteen minutes weaving in and out of sculptured animals and giant cones before crossing the gravel path to another section of equally monstrous shrubbery. When he had eventually caught up with her he discovered, to his dismay, that the woman was not Sophie, but Antoinette.

"I had no choice," she'd cried. "I had to do it."

But Sebastian had not waited to hear her explanation. Trying to suppress the feeling of panic, he raced through the maze of shrubs and trees, past the more amorous couples, until he was back out onto the lawn. He'd charged through the middle of the crowd, pulling and pushing people aside, ignoring their cries and complaints, searching ... searching, but to no avail.

Just when he thought fate had conspired against him, he'd spotted Delmont. Minus his mask, Delmont strode across the lawn, and Sebastian had followed him back into the house.

"Well, was the decoy your idea?" Sebastian repeated. When Delmont did not answer, Sebastian firmed his grip and with his left hand delivered Delmont a low blow to the stomach.

Delmont spluttered and tried to catch his breath. He stumbled forward, his arms flailing as he attempted to free himself. Mustering every ounce of strength he had, Sebastian refused to let go.

His future, his whole life was in this man's hands.

"If you do not tell me what I need to know, I promise you, I will make it my life's mission to ruin you, to torture you until you beg for mercy. Do you know the penalty for kidnapping the wife of a marquess?" Sebastian clenched his jaw and gritted his teeth, to stop him from pounding the life out of the man before he had a chance to speak.

Delmont raised his head to meet Sebastian's cold stare. "What … what do you mean?" he gasped, his eyes suddenly fearful.

"The lady you have spirited away is my wife and the mother to my unborn child." It was not a lie. As far as Sebastian was concerned, both were inevitable.

Delmont shook his head, his eyes glazed as he stared at nothing in particular. "Your wife … your wife," he muttered like a man deranged. "I thought she was a … well, I did not know she was … she was your wife." Delmont struggled for breath and Sebastian released the cravat and stepped back, wiping his face with the palm of his hand in a bid to calm his erratic heartbeat.

Delmont took a few deep breaths. "I swear to you … I swear I did not know," he gulped, rubbing his fingers around his throat in a soothing motion. "Dampierre had my marker. I would have lost everything."

Sebastian had dealt with men like this before, men whose lives were governed by the throw of the dice. There was always an underlying reason why they felt it necessary to fritter away their inheritance. Sebastian wondered as to Delmont's story.

"From where I stand you have lost the only thing that should matter," Sebastian said pitifully. "You have lost your honour. You are no gentleman."

Delmont hung his head and then said with a sigh, "I … I escorted her to the mews and left her there, with Dampierre and the woman."

Sebastian muttered an obscenity, raked his hand through his hair and shuffled restlessly. "Were they on foot, in a carriage, a hackney?"

"They were in an unmarked carriage," Delmont said with a grimace.

"Bloody hell!" Sebastian punched the air. Delmont flinched.

"You will pay for this," he warned as he turned on his heels and strode towards the door.

He needed his carriage, and he needed it now.

Sebastian was already striding down the hallway when he heard Delmont call out.

"Wait, let me come with you." Delmont hastened after Sebastian. "Perhaps I can be of some assistance."

Sebastian stopped, but he did not turn around. For some unfathomable reason, he pitied the man. Perhaps because he knew what it was like to be considered a wastrel. People often made assumptions regarding character, but tonight Delmont had lived up to his reckless reputation.

Had it not been Delmont, then Dampierre would have used some other fool to do his bidding. A part of him wondered if the Delmont he had heard so much about was indeed the full measure of the man. Well, he would give him one chance to prove himself. Besides, out of the two of them, Delmont was the only one who could identify Dampierre. Perhaps he would prove useful.

Turning to look over his shoulder, Sebastian said, "Very well, but if you so much as breathe in the wrong direction, I will kill you."

It occurred to Sebastian, as he sat in his carriage, that he was missing something, some vital clue as to Dampierre's motive. Why kidnap an innocent woman and then keep her locked in a brothel for days? Why not put her to work if that was the intention? All the other girls at Labelles were prostitutes; Dampierre only needed to say that Annabel, having failed as a governess, had decided to choose a different profession. Neither story could be proved, nor would any of the girls speak out against him.

"What do you know of Dampierre?" Sebastian looked across to Delmont, who had been silently studying him. He could almost hear the grinding of cogs as Delmont attempted to assess his character. "Have you ever had any dealings with him before?"

Delmont shook his head and scraped a golden lock from his brow. "No. I hadn't even heard of him until a few days ago when I met him outside my club. I'd lost my marker to Wainscot and well ..." He shrugged. "Dampierre had something Wainscot wanted, and so the story goes."

Sebastian narrowed his gaze. "Do you always play so deep?"

"I'm afraid that pleasure and pain are very much the same to me," he answered cryptically. "Look," he said in a more serious tone, "do not ask me why I do what I do, or why I am sitting here with you. I can hardly believe it myself. But I find that my conscience has been kicked from its comfy bed, and so I feel I must make amends in some way."

Sebastian appreciated his honesty and was equally frank. "I hope, for your sake, no harm befalls her." He paused for a moment to let Delmont feel the full force of his words. "Let me ask you a question," he continued in a more reasonable manner. "Why would a man like Dampierre, kidnap a respectable young woman, force her to live in his brothel but not make her work?"

"Dampierre owns a brothel?" Delmont said, somewhat unsurprised. He considered Sebastian's question. "Is the woman innocent, untouched, I mean?"

"I believe so, yes." Well, perhaps before she met Beaufort.

"But not his relative?" Delmont queried.

Sebastian shook his head. "No, not a relative. The woman had no living relatives to speak of."

A flash of recognition lit Delmont's face. "Some men, as I am sure you are aware, gain a great deal of pleasure from the fact a woman is untouched by man. Perhaps Dampierre ran out of virgins and so sought other means in which to restock his harem." Delmont stared at Sebastian as though waiting for a reaction, in case he had offended with his flippant remark. "There was once a plantation owner in the West Indies," Delmont continued filling the silence, "who paid two thousand guineas for a pure English virgin, although it was her father who sold her out and shipped her off. I have never seen the fascination myself. I expect it to be a rather clumsy affair and so have always avoided inexperienced entanglements."

After a moment's reflection, Sebastian sat bolt upright and Delmont, as if anticipating another blow, covered his head with his hands.

"You are a genius, Delmont," Sebastian exclaimed. Banging on the roof of the carriage, he thrust his head out of the window and shouted up to his coachman, "Haines, I need to call on Dudley."

Although Dudley had been woken from his bed at midnight, a relatively early hour for the likes of Delmont, he did not show any signs of irritation. Nor did he demand an explanation. Instead, he sat patiently, in his robe and bare feet, and listened to Sebastian swiftly relate the events of the evening.

"And you let him accompany you?" Dudley asked astounded, casting Delmont a look to suggest he was lucky to be alive. "Did you not castrate the last man who betrayed you?"

Had it been in any other circumstances, Sebastian would have regaled them with a host of fabricated details, just to make Delmont squirm. "Forgive me, but we do not have much time," Sebastian urged. "I need the address of the warehouse in Wapping, the one owned by the same company as Labelles."

"You believe Dampierre has taken your wife to a warehouse?" Delmont asked with some apprehension as he sat in the corner like a boy no one wanted to play with.

Dudley raised a brow and gave Sebastian a sanctimonious grin. "It would make sense," he nodded. "He could not take your wife to Labelles," he continued, stressing the matrimonial connection. But then he paused. "Wait, there is a house."

Sebastian jumped up from the chair as Dudley rushed over to the desk and rifled through some papers. "Here it is," Dudley said, scribbling the directions. "It's in Burr Street."

"Burr Street," Sebastian repeated. "Near the docks?" If he was correct in his assumption and Dampierre was using his ship to transport women, then he would have planned to ship out at the earliest convenience. The tide would be high for another few hours. But Sebastian could not assume he would wait until the afternoon, let alone another day.

"Give me a minute and I shall come with you," Dudley said.

Sebastian placed his hand on Dudley's shoulder. "Stay here. Charlotte needs you. Besides, Delmont will assist me, won't you Delmont?"

"Of course," Delmont inclined his head. "It is the least I can do."

Dudley examined Sebastian's domino. "Well, at least let me get you a coat."

As his carriage rattled along the narrow streets, Sebastian removed the mahogany box from under his seat and loaded the pistol.

"I take it you have a plan?" Delmont said, sounding a little more at ease than he had done previously.

"Of course," Sebastian glanced up and smiled. "I'm going to kill him."

"I meant something a little more structured," Delmont replied with a shake of the head. "You can't shoot a man in a street. Someone will call a constable."

"Who said anything about shooting him," Sebastian countered, reaching down into his left boot and pulling the hunting knife from its sheath. "I'm going to use this." He turned it around in his hand, and it glinted in the lamplight.

Delmont appeared alarmed and swallowed deeply.

"What?" Sebastian said. "Are you telling me you would not do the same for the woman you love?"

Delmont shrugged. "I have never been in love. Well, perhaps once, a long time ago," he said, his tone melancholic.

And there it was, Sebastian thought, the reason behind Delmont's disreputable conduct. "Do you know why you're sitting there? Why I have not strung you up from a tree somewhere?"

Delmont simply shook his head.

"Well, other than the fact you're the only one who can identify Dampierre. I speak from experience when I say, sometimes good people do bad things, and more often than not for justifiable reasons."

Delmont sneered. "And you have decided I fall into such a category."

"We shall see," Sebastian said, placing the knife back in its sheath. "Now, as to my structured plan," he mocked. "As we have to ride past Burr Street, we'll check the house first. I'll wait in the carriage on the corner of Nightingale while you knock the front door. If they're there, you are to say you do not believe the marker to be genuine, and you wish to discuss the matter with Dampierre." Sebastian considered his companion. "Can you do that?"

"Of course," Delmont replied with a hint of arrogance.

The moment they pulled up on the corner of Burr and Nightingale, Sebastian was almost certain Dampierre had not brought Sophie to the house.

Despite the hour, there were still a few men lying on the pavement outside the King's Arms tavern. The street was also home to a vast number of sailors, some of whom were only just making their way home to their lodging houses.

Delmont confirmed his theory when he returned to the carriage. "The house is empty," he said, slightly breathless. "I knocked twice. And then the woman next door lifted up the window, poked her head out and shouted sling yer hook. That was until she noticed the quality of my clothes and then she asked if I could spare a few shillings. She is probably rousing her husband as we speak in the hope of stealing my handkerchief."

Sebastian almost smiled. Delmont could be quite humorous, but his mind was occupied with more important things. He opened the carriage door but did not get out. Instead, he used it to lean on so he could speak to Haines perched upon his box seat.

As Sebastian closed the door and sat back in his seat, he relayed the arrangements he had made with Haines. "The warehouse is off Green Bank. Once we're certain they're inside and have made an assessment of the situation, we will proceed as before ... with you providing the distraction."

Delmont shrugged. "Well, I am regarded as rather adept when it comes to creating amusing diversions."

CHAPTER 27

*S*ophie had been taken to a small warehouse somewhere near the docks, a damp brick building containing numerous stacks of wooden crates, a makeshift bed with tatty blankets and a few old chairs scattered about. Both windows had been boarded up. The only light came from oil lamps which hung from metal chains flung over the rafters. The air was pungent with the smell of tobacco, mingled with the sickly smell of sugar and the potent fumes from rum.

Having made numerous attempts to flee, Sophie had been dragged into the warehouse and forced to sit on a chair in the middle of the room, while Marie paced back and forth, hugging her stomach.

"Forgive me," Dampierre said as his lackey, a rather cold, hard looking man with a protruding forehead who went by the name of Morgan, tied her hands to the back of the chair with rope. "But you will insist on struggling." He inclined his head to the side as he studied her, his gaze slithering over her like a snake.

She would rather kill herself or throw herself overboard than submit to him.

She wondered what Dane was doing. Was he tearing

Delmont's mansion house apart looking for her? Sophie's heart went out to him, for he would blame himself. He would find a way to punish everyone and everything—which was why she needed to escape. There was no point crying and pleading. Dampierre was a callous, cold-hearted man and so she would need to find another way to be free of him.

"Please, Victor," Marie cried, "is all this necessary?" She walked over to him and placed her hand on his arm. "Take the necklace, but let Miss Beaufort go home. I will come away with you," she pleaded as she caressed his arms. "We could go to Jamaica." She touched his cheek.

Dampierre pushed her away, and she tumbled back, hitting her head on the floor. "My sons cannot be born to a whore."

Sophie held her breath, waiting for a sign that Marie was not hurt. Even Morgan stood up straight and took a few hesitant steps towards the limp body.

"Get up, Marie," Dampierre shouted. When she moved her arms, he repeated his instruction as if she were a child merely seeking attention.

Morgan walked over to one of the other chairs and brought it into the middle of the room. He strode over to Marie, placed his hands under her arms, lifted her off the floor and dumped her onto the chair.

"Do you see what I must endure, Miss Beaufort," Dampierre said with a languid flick of the wrist. "Such weakness, such whining and whimpering after a gentleman, it is … degrading." He walked over to Sophie, ran his finger slowly down her cheek and across her bottom lip. "How is one supposed to feel like a man when it is all offered so … so freely?"

As Dampierre stepped away, Sophie glanced across at Marie, who appeared to have recovered from her injury. Marie looked up at her, held her gaze and silently mouthed, "I'm sorry."

"No," Dampierre continued as he paced the floor, his hands clasped behind his back. "It is the fire burning deep within that I find so … so alluring."

In this meditative mood, Dampierre appeared far more egotistical. Yet his movements, his manner, his words felt contrived and calculated, as though driven by some strange deep-rooted obsession. It went beyond a simple carnal craving or a depraved appetite. It had something to do with proving his worth as a man. But could she use it against him, Sophie wondered? Could she weaken his position enough for him to make a mistake? It was worth a try. Perhaps he had been repressed or intimidated by a woman. Perhaps that's where his hunger for power and control came from.

"I have decided to call you Victor," Sophie said firmly, surprising everyone in the room for she had said very little until now. "You will have no objection?" It was both a question and a statement depending upon how one perceived it.

"No, no objection," he replied, albeit somewhat hesitant as he considered her request. "We are to be married, after all."

She heard the apprehension in his tone, noticed he used the word marriage to intimidate. "Well, as to that, Victor," Sophie replied arrogantly. "I have decided not to accept."

Dampierre sniggered and was about to offer what she suspected would be a peremptory reply.

"I do not want to hear what you have to say on the matter," Sophie continued, raising her chin. "Your opinion is not important, not to me, not to anyone."

The Comte de Dampierre stood in the middle of the room, his mouth slightly open as he stared at her. "We will be married," he repeated, anger brimming beneath the surface.

Sophie glanced at Marie, who was watching her intently, before focusing her attention directly at Dampierre. "How can you say that when you know your lineage is lacking? Who was your mother?" Sophie was guessing this was the root cause of his vile obsession. When he did not answer, she raised her voice. "Well, who was she?"

He appeared visibly shaken and then stuttered and stumbled

over his words. "My father was a gentleman. He was the son of—"

"I did not ask about your father."

Just when Sophie thought she was making some progress in unsettling the comte, someone banged loudly on the iron door. Dampierre froze. When it became apparent the person was not about to leave, he gestured for his man to deal with it.

"If you call out, Miss Beaufort," Dampierre warned, regaining his vitality, "I shall be forced to hurt Marie."

But Sophie did not have the opportunity to do anything, for the person barged into the warehouse determined to cause a scene. It was not until Morgan retreated further into the room, that Sophie identified the caller as being Lord Delmont, brandishing a pistol.

"Forgive me for intruding on this little party," Delmont said, examining his surroundings with a look of disdain. "But as you went to so much trouble to spoil mine, I thought it only fair."

Delmont glanced in Sophie's direction but did not reveal any identifiable emotion. He appeared taller than she remembered, his golden hair much darker, and he looked vastly more sinister in such crude surroundings.

"What do you want?" Dampierre's words cut through the air like a knife. "How did you know to come here?"

"Has anyone ever told you it is preferable to invite more ladies to a party than gentlemen?" Delmont replied, giving Dampierre a smug grin. He pushed his free hand through his golden locks. "The numbers have been evened somewhat, as the two men you posted outside have decided to take a swim. Still, I believe I stand a better chance with these ladies than you two miscreants."

Sophie sat in stupefied silence, wondering what on earth Lord Delmont was up to. Why had he raised his voice when they were all just a few feet away? She noticed Dampierre glance back over his shoulder, to the walking cane he'd left on top of a crate.

"You have your marker," Dampierre said with contempt. "You will get nothing more from me."

Delmont laughed. "I would agree if the marker was authentic."

So his only reason for following them, his only reason for storming into the warehouse and waving his pistol about, was money. And when satisfied, was he just going to walk right out again and leave her tied to the chair?

Dampierre took a step towards Delmont. "Are you questioning my honour?"

"I am," Delmont nodded confidently, pointing his pistol a little straighter. "And as I appear to be the only man who is armed," he shouted as if to exaggerate his point. "I do not suppose there is much you can do about it."

There was a faint rustling sound in the far corner of the room. Dampierre heard it too and narrowed his gaze, peering beyond Lord Delmont's shoulder.

Sophie noticed the flicker of a shadow and watched helplessly as Delmont lost focus and made the foolish mistake of turning to look. Sensing it was his prime opportunity to alter the turn of events, Dampierre lunged forward and knocked the pistol from Delmont's hand. Morgan hurled himself at Delmont, grabbing him around the neck, pulling him to the floor and pounding him with his fists until he was practically unconscious.

"No," Sophie yelled. Not because she gave a hoot what happened to Lord Delmont, but because it meant Dampierre would have a weapon and another means with which to threaten.

Like a man possessed, Dane charged out of the darkness in an attempt to reach the pistol before Dampierre could get his hands on it. But he was too late. And, once again, they found themselves in the precarious hands of the Comte de Dampierre.

"You will stay where you are," Dampierre shouted, his arm shaking from exertion as he pointed the pistol at Dane. When Dane ignored his threat and took another step forward, Dampierre switched direction and aimed at Sophie's head.

Her heart skipped a beat, but she did not believe Dampierre would pull the trigger. Somewhere in his warped mind, he believed he needed her. Else why would he have gone to so much trouble? Dane, on the other hand, must have believed him capable of carrying out his threat and so stared at her, his face ashen, his eyes wide and fearful.

Sophie's throat grew tight, her vision blurring as tears welled. Perhaps it was because of Dane's tortured expression, or Marie's look of guilt and remorse, or Delmont's body lying battered and beaten on the floor. Whatever the reason, tears trickled down her cheeks, and she shook her head in an attempt to make them stop.

"Sophie," Dane whispered, but that one word sounded like a heart-wrenching apology.

Dampierre flicked his gaze towards her. "Stop it," he yelled. His eyes conveyed contradicting emotions: fury and fragility. Anger was the only emotion Dampierre understood or had the capacity to cope with.

The more tears that fell, the more volatile Dampierre became. At one point he stepped closer, grabbed Sophie by the arm, the pistol wavering between her heart and her head.

"Don't," Dane pleaded, his handsome face etched with pain.

"Shut up." Dampierre turned the pistol towards him. "Perhaps if I shoot you, then we can continue as before. It would not take much to finish Lord Delmont." He gazed at the large body slumped on the floor.

As the tension in the air grew more palpable, Marie jumped to her feet. "What has happened to you, Victor? You must stop all of this," she said wearily. "For goodness' sake, listen to what you are saying. You can't just kill them."

Dampierre aimed the pistol at Marie. "No? Then perhaps I should shoot you, Marie. You think you have fooled me with your protestations of loyalty. But you are the traitor here. And now you have tainted Miss Beaufort with your little sobs and snivels."

Sophie noticed Morgan edge closer to Marie, and she shouted out, "Please, sit down, Marie," in the hope of warning her. Morgan looked like a man who would beat a woman as easily as he had Lord Delmont.

Ignoring Sophie's plea, Marie cried, "I cannot take any more of this." She opened her arms wide, providing the perfect target. "Shoot me, Victor. Shoot me, for I swear to you if I leave here, you will never set eyes on me again. Now, I am going to release Miss Beaufort—"

A loud crack resonated through the air as the Comte de Dampierre fired the pistol.

Sophie screamed. Unable to cover her face with her hands, she closed her eyes as she could not bear to look into the cold, lifeless eyes of her friend, Marie.

In that second of silence, as the acrid smell of burnt sulphur invaded the room, Sophie promised herself she would see Dampierre hang for what he'd done.

"Morgan!" Marie screamed, and Sophie opened her eyes to see Dampierre's man lying on the floor, blood gushing from a wound to chest as he gasped his last few breaths. Marie scrambled to her feet, and Sophie guessed that Morgan must have pushed her out of harm's way. Marie sank back down to the floor by Morgan's side and stroked his brow and cursed him for being so stupid, telling him to hold on and everything would be fine.

Dane used the distraction to attack Dampierre.

Tackling him to the ground, they fought and struggled as Dampierre threw away the now useless pistol in a bid to reach his cane. For what seemed like an eternity, they wrestled on the floor, with Dampierre showing surprising resilience when Dane punched him in the face and stomach. In desperation, Dampierre kicked out, sending Dane flying back. As Dane reached into his boot and pulled out his hunting knife, Dampierre got to his feet. He grabbed his cane, ripped the sword from its sheath and

Sophie barely had time to blink before the sharp point was at her throat.

"Slide the knife across the floor to me," Dampierre cried amidst breathless pants. "Do it now or I will kill her."

Without any hesitation, Dane did as he asked, but the knife slid past Dampierre, who was not in any position to attempt to retrieve it.

"If you harm a hair on her head, I will kill you," Dane warned, but the threat only roused Dampierre's ire.

"What is she to you?" he asked with some irritation. "That you would risk your life in such a manner." He lowered the sword until the point fell just above Sophie's breast, just above her heart. "Tell me," he yelled, pricking Sophie's skin with the tip of the blade.

She refused to cry out, even when she looked down to see the small drop of blood escaping.

"She is everything to me," Dane replied abruptly, gradually coming to his feet.

Dampierre gave a condescending snort. "And does Miss Beaufort know you frequent my establishment? Does she know you've been intimate with Antoinette?" He spat on the floor by way of an insult. "You dishonour her with your filthy words, for it is you who has allowed her to parade around so disgracefully, you who has sullied yourself and now think to sully her by association."

From the floor behind him, Marie looked up from Morgan's dead body. Patches of blood as dark as claret stained the front of her dress, her hands, and her cheeks.

"Hypocrite," Marie shouted. "It is you who defiles everything you touch. You who vilify."

In a fit of rage, Dampierre turned slightly but became distracted when Delmont—who had rolled on to his side—moaned, coughed and spluttered.

"Shut up!" Dampierre cried, growing more agitated as his gaze flew from Lord Delmont to Dane and then to Sophie.

"Murderer!" Marie yelled. "Murderer!"

"Shut up!" he spat, hitting his head with his free hand. His countenance suddenly improved when he whipped the tip of his sword to rest on Dane's heart. "If I kill you, then I shall be free to leave here with Miss Beaufort."

"Don't," Sophie cried. "I promise you … I shall leave with you, just don't …"

The Comte de Dampierre stared at her for a moment as he considered her words. "You care for him," he said bluntly. "Therefore, I cannot let him live."

Dampierre pulled his arm back slowly, ready to thrust the sword into Dane's chest. Marie ran to him and tugged his arm but Dampierre batted her away, and she fell to the floor behind him.

As Dampierre pulled his arm back once more, Marie got to her feet and charged at him, growling as she hit him in the back.

Everything went strangely silent for a few seconds.

Sophie looked at Dampierre, who stood frozen to the spot, staring out into nothingness—then he coughed, a gurgling sort of sound as blood bubbled and frothed from his mouth. The sword fell from his hand and clattered on the floor. As he sank to his knees, Sophie had a clear view of Marie, standing with wide eyes, the knife in her hand smudged with Dampierre's blood.

When Dampierre collapsed to the floor and finally stopped heaving and spluttering, Marie whispered, "We are free."

CHAPTER 28

*H*aving untied the ropes binding Sophie's hands, Sebastian took her in his arms and kissed her repeatedly on the temple. He stepped back and scanned every inch of her, checking for cuts and bruises, pushing away the tendrils of hair from her face.

He stopped and examined the ebony curls, his brow raised in curiosity. "What happened to your wig?" he asked as he caressed her cheek.

"I lost it," Sophie replied, placing her hand on top of his. "Morgan knocked it off … well, pulled it off, when I tried to escape."

He forced a smile, brought her hand to his lips and kissed her fingers by way of a distraction. He did not want to think about what had happened to her during the last few hours, what could have happened to her.

"I need to alert a constable," he said with some trepidation. "Haines will take you and Madame Labelle home while I stay here and deal with this."

He looked over his shoulder and gestured to the two bodies sprawled out on the floor. Morgan was lying face up; his vacant eyes open as he stared at the ceiling, his chest an island of deep-red blood amidst a sea of clothes. Dampierre lay face down, his head resting on his arm as though sleeping.

"I'll stay with you," Sophie insisted. "I can explain what happened. I can tell them—"

"No," Sebastian snapped. He took a deep breath and then softened his tone. "I need you to escort Madame Labelle home."

"Her name is Marie. Somehow, I don't think she'll ever be Madame Labelle again."

Sebastian glanced back at Marie, who was sitting in the chair, her bloodied hands resting in her lap, her face pale and listless.

"Haines will take you to Labelles. I want you to help Marie pack her things. Do you feel able?"

"Yes," she whispered. "I'll do anything to help."

He placed his hands on Sophie's bare shoulders, dismissing the urge to trail his fingers over the smooth, creamy-white skin, dismissing the urge to stroke and caress her worries away. "Marie must say nothing about what has happened to Dampierre or Morgan."

Sophie looked soulfully at Marie. "What will happen to her?" she whispered. "You cannot let her hang for this, Dane."

He thought for a moment. "She has suffered enough at the hands of Dampierre," he said. "But if I am to lie for her, then I need to know she will not contradict my story."

"But how will you explain all of this?" Sophie asked, nodding to the dead men, an anxious frown marring her brow.

"I will have to make it look as though Morgan stabbed Dampierre and before he fell, Dampierre shot him in retaliation. Lord Delmont will corroborate the story. No one will question the word of two peers."

Sophie glanced at Lord Delmont, who had managed to sit upright, albeit with a groan. "You should go to him," she urged. "He's in a bad way."

"Wait here," Sebastian said as he turned and left the warehouse. He used the bird call to alert Haines, and when the carriage rumbled into view, he returned to Sophie. "Haines will take you now." He bent down and brushed his lips against hers. "Be as quick as you can at Labelles and then return to Red Lion Square."

Sophie pursed her lips and nodded. He watched her walk over to Marie, rubbing the red marks on her wrists where the rope had dug in. "Come, let me take you home." She put her arm around Marie and lifted her up from the chair.

Marie made no comment and simply allowed Sophie to escort her from the building.

Sebastian stepped over Dampierre's lifeless body and knelt down next to Delmont. His right eye was black and swollen; he had a split lip and a deep graze on his forehead.

"Delmont," Sebastian said softly, placing his hand on the man's arm. "Do you feel well enough to stand?"

With his breathing slow and measured, Delmont turned to Sebastian, grimacing as he gave a weak smile. "The next time … you invite me to … to one of your gatherings," he said, wincing as he held his arm across his abdomen, "remind me to decline."

Sebastian bit back a chuckle. "I believe you invited yourself." He was surprised Delmont could still deliver one of his witty quips with his face so badly beaten. "I need to call at the Thames office to fetch a constable and a doctor to look at your injuries."

"The only thing injured," Delmont panted, "is my pride … and perhaps a rib or two." He glanced at Morgan. "You could have warned me … I'd be up against a champion boxer. The man was an animal."

"An animal with a heart, apparently. He saved Madame Labelle's life."

Delmont gestured towards the comte's listless body. "I take it Dampierre shot him. But who killed Dampierre?"

"I did," Sebastian replied without hesitation. He did not

know Delmont well enough to trust him with the truth. "I did not think it necessary to involve the ladies, so I sent them home."

Delmont's eyes scanned the floor and settled on the blood-stained handle of the knife. He examined Sebastian's clean hands and coat and offered a dubious frown. "I understand you do not wish to embroil your wife in a scandal. But how will you explain ..." Delmont paused and put a hand to his ribs, "how will you explain our presence here?"

Sebastian raised a brow and with a sly grin said, "Well, that's where you come in. I thought we could say Dampierre kidnapped you with the intention of—"

"Kidnapped me!" Delmont cried. "Kidnapped ... I shall never be able to show my face in my club again." Delmont shook his head. "Can you not think of some other reason, something more heroic?"

"There was nothing heroic about the way you escorted my wife out into the mews and left her alone to deal with Dampierre," Sebastian growled, reminding Delmont he had still not forgiven him entirely for the part he had played.

"I understand that, but ... but to say I was kidnapped." Delmont thought for a moment. "Could you not say Dampierre discovered me helping this Madame Labelle? Perhaps she was running away, and I had met her here to pay for her passage to ... well, you could think of somewhere."

Sebastian considered the request. If Madame Labelle went abroad for a while, it would add credence to their story while ensuring she did not confess to the crime out of a sense of guilt. He could send her to France, to stay with Marcus Danbury, just for a month or two.

"Very well," Sebastian agreed. "You were helping a poor woman flee the country and paid for her fare to France. I came along to assist, and we were both held against our will. Dampierre will have gunpowder on his hands, so we'll say an argument broke out when we offered Morgan a substantial sum of money to help us. Morgan stabbed Dampierre, who swung around and shot him. It's best if you say you can't remember much. One look at your face and no one will dare argue."

"And I suffered these injuries while protecting a lady," Delmont added. "I've always wanted to play the hero. When word gets around, the ladies will hang from my arms like fruit bats."

CHAPTER 29

*M*arie had not spoken a single word during the carriage ride from Wapping to Marylebone.

Before they entered Labelles, Sophie gave Marie her gloves to wear and draped the blue cloak around her blood-stained dress, so as not to draw undue attention. Luckily, the patrons had either retired to the privacy of the upstairs rooms or were too engrossed in their activities to pass comment.

It was Sophie who packed Marie's things, choosing a couple of dresses and undergarments, just enough for a few days away. The only item Marie picked up was a small leather Bible, which she clutched to her chest instead of packing it with the rest of her things. When they were about to leave, Marie paused and rushed back up the stairs to her bedchamber. She returned a few minutes later, carrying a square wooden box.

"Do you have everything you need?" Sophie asked, wondering what was in the box. With her gaunt face and empty expression, Marie appeared fragile and lost and not at all like the confident, composed woman she had met in Leicester Square.

"Yes." Marie nodded. "But the girls … what will happen to them?"

"Lord Danesfield will take care of it," Sophie reassured her.

Dane took care of everything. He was the most solid, most dependable man she had ever known, and she had been foolish to think otherwise.

Marie was just as quiet on the journey to Red Lion Square and upon their return had asked to go to her room. Sophie had no such luck as James insisted on hearing every horrifying detail. A whole hour passed before Sophie was able to go and check on her.

She met Amy on the stairs, carrying a bundle of clothing. "What would you like me to do with her dress, miss?" Amy asked, glancing down at the blood-stained garment.

"Burn it," she replied. "But you must never mention it to anyone." Sophie took a few more steps and then turned and asked, "Did she say anything to you?"

"No, miss. She's not said a word. She just lay in the bath, staring up at the ceiling."

Sophie offered a weak smile, thanked the maid and continued up the stairs, deciding to change out of her masquerade gown before calling in on Marie.

Having changed into her breeches and shirt, as they were the first thing to hand, Sophie tapped on Marie's door and waited for a response before entering.

Though the hour was late, Marie was not in bed. She sat curled up in a chair in front of the fire, wearing a plain cotton nightgown. The room was far too warm, but she got the feeling Marie's shivers had nothing to do with the cold. Even so, she picked up a blanket from the end of the bed and draped it around her friend's shoulders. Moving the chair from the dressing table, Sophie placed it in front of the fire and sat down.

"How are you feeling?" Sophie asked even though she knew it was a stupid question.

Marie stared into the flames. "I thought I would feel relieved, happy," she said softly, still clutching the Bible in her hand. "But murder … it is just one more sin to add to a list of many."

"It was not murder, Marie. You were defending yourself," Sophie corrected. "He would have killed you. He would have killed us all."

Marie looked down at the Bible and stroked the cover. "My father would not have seen it that way." She sighed. "One day, I will answer for it. I will answer for it all."

Sophie shook her head. "You're wrong. You saved my life and Annabel's, too."

Marie shrugged. "Perhaps."

They remained silent for a few minutes. Sophie followed Marie's vacant gaze to stare at the flames and became lost in her own tumultuous thoughts.

This would be the last night she would spend under Dane's roof. She'd spent the last six years being angry with him. How would she survive the next six years feeling nothing but love? In truth, she would never fully recover from their separation; she would always feel a little less than whole, always feel empty and incomplete.

As though sensing the reason for Sophie's disquiet, Marie asked, "Will you return to your village now that the matter is concluded, now Victor is … is dead?"

Sophie looked up and met Marie's gaze. "I have nowhere else *to* go," she replied with some amusement.

"But surely your marquess will offer for you?"

Sophie snorted. "Under the circumstances, he probably believes he should marry me. But it is not the same as wanting to. Besides, he needs to marry someone a little more refined and a little less headstrong."

"Call me naive," Marie countered, "but you have not mentioned love. If he loves you, surely that is more important than anything."

Sophie stood, walked over to the hearth and poked the fire. She could not even bear to consider the thought that Dane had feelings for her in that regard. It would only make walking away all the more difficult, all the more painful.

"Love plays no part in the marriages of the nobility," Sophie replied, stabbing at the coals as though they were to blame for all things considered unfair. "You have seen the proof with your own eyes."

They were interrupted by a knock on the door, and Sophie opened it to find Dane waiting outside. Her heart skipped a beat.

"You're back." She stepped out into the hall and closed the door gently behind her. "What happened?"

Dane scanned her casual attire with interest and pulled her into his arms, where he kissed her with a desperate urgency.

Panting, Sophie broke away first. "You cannot kiss me like that with my brother in the house," she protested weakly. "What if he should see us?"

Dane's hands settled on her waist, gripping the loose fabric to pull her closer to his warm body. "I do not care who sees us," he whispered in her ear. "I want to feel your naked body next to mine."

Please, she begged silently. Please say no more.

"I want us to be together, Sophie. Always. I want us to—"

"We cannot talk about it now," she replied softly so as not to cause alarm, but she needed to change the subject and quickly before the tears began to fall. "I fear Marie is not herself and needs our help."

Dane dropped his hands and stepped back. "Forgive me," he replied, shaking his head. "I am being insensitive." He nodded towards the closed door. "About Marie, I have an idea. Let us go and see if she approves."

Dane began by relating the story he'd told the constable and the magistrate. He also told them of his plan for Marie to leave the country for a month or two. "You should have seen Delmont," he mused. "The man should be on the stage. There is not a person in the whole of London who would dare question his version of events." He smiled at Sophie. "Indeed, it is a shame I had not known him sooner, for there has been many a situation where I could have done with a man of his talents."

"So they believed this story of yours?" Marie asked, still somewhat apprehensive.

"The magistrate had no choice. Delmont raved on about how disgraceful it was that two peers could be assaulted in such a fashion and demanded to know what was going to be done about it. Besides, the fact that the magistrate still appeared somewhat at odds, having been roused from his bed at such a ridiculous hour, helped matters."

"But if they believed your story, then Marie can return to Labelles," Sophie said.

Dane pursed his lips and shook his head. "I'm afraid you can never go back there, Marie. Dampierre must have been working with someone else, someone abroad who brokers his deals. I'm sure once his partner hears of his death he will come to stake claim to his business."

"But Marie has a claim to the business," Sophie said. "Surely she should not be—"

"Lord Danesfield is right," Marie interrupted, raising her hand by way of an apology. "I own nothing and have no claim to make. Victor did have a contact abroad. I have heard him mention a man, heard tales of his cunning, of his cruelty." She placed a hand on Sophie's arm. "I will go to France and stay with Mr. Danbury until it is safe for me to return."

"Danbury is a good fellow, a little rough around the edges, but he is more than capable of handling the situation," Dane said convincingly. As though guessing Sophie's next question, he added, "Haines will accompany you. He knows Danbury and will see you settled before returning home."

Marie gave a weak smile. "Thank you. I will not forget your kindness. But I must ask, what will happen to my girls?"

Sophie turned to stare at Dane. "You will do something for them, won't you?"

Dane smiled at her, and the warmth in his eyes warmed her to her core. "Of course. I will see to it that they are provided for and given an opportunity to improve their status, should they so wish." He patted Marie's arm and added, "I will write to you and keep you updated on their progress."

Marie stepped forward took his hand and kissed it. "Thank you, my lord."

Sophie could not have loved him any more than she did at that moment. Her heart was bursting, her body inflamed.

"I shall leave you to get ready while I write two letters to Danbury. I shall send one immediately and give you another, should there be any problem." He took Sophie to one side and whispered, "We must leave in ten minutes. I shall see them safely to Dover and return as quickly as I can. I have spoken to James. He is happy to wait here until my return."

This was going to be the last time she would be with him like this, Sophie realised. She could not stay and wait for him to return. She could not hear his offer of marriage as she did not have the strength to decline. She was too weak when it came to her feelings for him, and she would crumble as soon as the words left his mouth.

"Take care," she said, throwing her arms around his neck and hugging him tight. When her lips began to tremble, she relaxed her arms and kissed him softly on the mouth.

"I'm only going as far as the coast," he said with a chuckle as they stepped apart.

I love you, she whispered silently. I shall always love you.

"I know." She shrugged. "I had best go and help Marie."

Sophie breathed deeply when she heard the door close and distracted herself by helping Marie dress. When she was ready to go, Marie took Sophie by the hand and sat her down on the edge of the bed.

"Once, you asked me why I had not run away from Victor," Marie began, "and I implied I had nowhere to go. Well, that was not entirely true." She picked up the wooden box she'd taken from Labelles and placed it in Sophie's lap. "Here, I would like you to take this, for the time being. Until I have use of it."

Sophie met her gaze. "What is it?"

"Open it," Marie urged.

Sophie opened the box. Inside she found a long, black iron key, a large quantity of folded notes and a diamond brooch.

"The brooch was left to me by my great aunt," Marie began. "Other than my Bible, it is all I have that connects me to my other life, the life I had before Victor." She reached down into the box and removed the key. "This represents a dream," she continued, twirling it between her fingers. "A foolish dream I thought would never come to fruition. It is the key to a small cottage, a cottage I bought without Victor's knowledge. It is in the village of Marlow, just outside High Wycombe, a beautiful village where I spent many happy years. I could not go there while Victor was alive, for he would know exactly where to find me."

"But you could go there now, you could live your dream," Sophie replied eagerly.

Marie smiled. "And I will, when I return. But in the meantime, I would like you to take care of it for me. Only if you want to."

Sophie did not know what to say.

Marie handed Sophie the key. Then she fastened the brooch to the inside of her dress and began counting out the notes. "I prayed for the day when I would be free from Victor." Separating the notes into two piles, she folded the larger pile and thrust it down the front of her dress, before handing the other pile to Sophie.

"I cannot take this," Sophie objected.

"You will," Marie said firmly, putting the notes into Sophie's hand and covering it with her own. "You have given me back my life, and now I must make amends for all the wrongs I have done."

Sophie jumped up and hugged Marie. She was so grateful to have somewhere to go, somewhere where she would not have to suffer the pain of seeing Dane. Even if it was just for a few months. It would suffice, just while she decided what she was going to do.

"I want you to have a choice," Marie said. "Lord Danesfield is a good man, but you have to be true to yourself. If you decide to go to Marlow, you will find Hope Cottage on the lane to the right of the church." She kissed Sophie on the cheek, picked up her bag and then walked to the door.

"I will not come down as I could not bear to wave goodbye," Sophie said. "Please tell Lord Danesfield I was tired and have gone to bed."

"Very well," Marie nodded.

"And promise me you will not say a word about the cottage."

Marie hesitated and then said, "I promise."

*a*t the sound of a gentle rap on the study door, Sebastian
lifted his head off the desk, the hard surface being a
most unsuitable place to sleep. He brushed his hands through his
hair and bid the caller to enter.

Dudley Spencer poked his head around the door and asked in
his usual amused tone, "Is it safe to come in?" When Sebastian
replied with a grunt, Dudley stepped into the room and closed
the door. "I thought Haines was exaggerating when he said all
you do all day is growl and grumble." Dudley drew a chair up to
the desk and sat down. "It seems we can add grunting to your
newfound repartee. As you've come back to town, I take it you
have still not found your wife?"

"You know very well she is not my wife. Still you insist on
tormenting me." His bitter tone reflected his mood.

Dudley inclined his head. "I must admit I am not used to
seeing you so out of sorts. I find I rather like it. It makes me feel
vastly superior, knowing you have made such a mess of
everything."

"What do you want?" Sebastian barked, which was a polite
way of saying *leave me the hell alone*.

Dudley raised a brow as his mouth curved into a sardonic

grin. "I merely came to update you on the progress of our new finishing school."

"It is not a finishing school," Sebastian corrected. He sat back in the chair and folded his arms across his chest. "And if you think I am writing another letter to Marie to relay more good news about the social advancement of her girls, you can think again."

Indeed, the woman had refused to offer any insight into Sophie's whereabouts. A whole month had passed since he'd returned home to discover Sophie had already left for Marchampton.

He had raced on ahead of James, driven by a need to be with her, to hold her in his arms and claim her as his own. He should have known something was wrong when he discovered she had left before breakfast and without her brother's knowledge. If he had bothered to check her room, he would have known she had taken nothing other than the clothes she had arrived in. If he had bothered to stop and call in at the mews, instead of insisting that Altair be brought out quickly, he would have known she had not taken Argo.

Instead, he had ridden all the way to Marchampton to discover, to his disappointment, that she was not there. He had waited three days, three days of pacing and worrying before James rode over to Westlands with the letter. A letter she had written and sealed in his blasted study. He must have read it fifty times or more and still it did not make any sense.

"I take it Marie still refuses to say a word about Miss Beaufort's mysterious disappearance."

Sebastian stretched across the table, picked up the crystal glass and swallowed what remained of his brandy. He did not bother to ask if his friend cared for any refreshment. "Miss Beaufort has not disappeared." He sighed in agitation. "Her letter stated quite clearly that she had enjoyed her freedom in town so much, she did not wish to return home. She wants to break free from society's constraints and live independently."

Dudley pursed his lips but could not prevent a small snigger from escaping. "You mean she found you far too domineering. I always knew you would have to settle for one of those wall-flower types."

Sebastian jumped up out of his seat. "How can you sit there and jest about such a thing when you know my feelings on the matter? I'm in love with her, damn it," he said, prodding his own chest. "Me, the man who is always practical, the man who was going to choose a bride based on status and wealth and a host of other stupid notions. The man who would choose any reason to avoid making the same mistake as my father." Sebastian dropped back into the chair and sighed. "Yet here I am, suffering a pain that rips and tears at my heart, suffering in the knowledge I have lost everything." He was quiet for a moment and looked past Dudley to an invisible point on the wall. "If she walked through the door, I do not know whether I would strangle her or kiss her until she could not breathe."

Dudley cast him a pitiful look. "The problem is you do not know how to deal with women."

"If that's all you've come to say, you can go."

Dudley ignored his blunt reply. "You expect Marie to break an oath she made to a friend. Would you break such a confidence? No, you would not," Dudley continued, answering his own question. He sat back in the chair with a smug grin. "You should have been far more cunning in your approach to the matter. Indeed, with a campaign involving a degree of delicate moves, it was not difficult to discover that Miss Beaufort has hidden herself away so you may marry someone deemed more worthy. Marie provided the opportunity for her to do so."

Sebastian's mouth fell open, and he sat up straight. "What? How do you know this?" he asked, with some impatience.

"Marcus told me," Dudley replied. "I stressed the importance of the situation and he obliged by persuading Marie of the seri-ousness of your suit."

"But why would she tell Marcus?" Sebastian asked somewhat bemused.

Dudley raised a brow and shook his head. "Please tell me you are not that naive. Marcus was always useful when it came to beautiful women although I fear Marie is not such easy prey."

Sebastian recalled a comment made by his coachman. "Haines did say she slapped Marcus across the face for being too familiar when they first met," Sebastian sniggered. It was the first time he had laughed in a month. "Perhaps it was my fault for telling him she was the madame of a brothel."

"I don't know," Dudley said, "living in an old monastery does strange things to a man." He removed a letter from his pocket and handed it to Sebastian. "The details are all in there. If you hurry, you could be with Miss Beaufort for luncheon."

Sebastian could not stop smiling. He scanned the letter. "Dudley, I don't know what to say … High Wycombe! She's been in High Wycombe all this time."

"I know," Dudley laughed, "and I thought you were adept at locating runaways." He held Sebastian's gaze and said in a more serious tone, "Do not forget, Miss Beaufort believes herself unworthy of you. I would hate for you to say the wrong thing and ruin all my hard work."

"Your hard work," Sebastian mocked, patting his friend on the shoulder as he hurried towards the door. "What about Marcus?"

"I have it on good authority Marcus Danbury has thoroughly enjoyed pursuing this particular line of enquiry," Dudley whispered to himself as he heard Sebastian's footsteps bounding up the stairs.

Trowel in hand, Sophie stepped back from the border and admired her work. It had been a laborious task, clearing the neglected garden, but it had kept her busy, kept her mind from straying to thoughts of Dane.

She wiped her brow with the back of her hand and then rubbed her lower back. Being bent over for such long periods had taken its toll. It would take too long to heat enough water for a bath, so she would settle for a cup of tea instead and then perhaps a long walk. That would straighten her out, she thought, as she cleared away her tools and basket and nipped inside to wash her hands.

As lovely as the cottage was, with its thatched roof and quaint little windows, Sophie could not see Marie living happily in such seclusion. Even someone used to a rural way of life, as Sophie was, would find it quite lonely at times. Oh, the days were fine, as there was always plenty to do. It was the nights that were the most difficult; it was the nights when all the memories came flooding back.

She'd always known it would be a challenge, but the hole left by Dane's absence was growing bigger by the day, swallowing her up bit by bit. Sometimes, she would wake at night and imagine him lying next to her, imagine the warmth radiating from his body, enveloping her. Sometimes, she would catch his masculine scent in the air, but when she tried to locate the smell, it always faded away, dissolving into nothing.

The lengthy absence had proved one thing: her soul would be forever entwined with his. No matter where she went or what she did, she would never feel complete again.

After dabbing at her eyes with the pads of her fingers, she looked out through the window. An image of Dane formed before her, of him standing tall and strong as he tied his horse to the post next to the gate. Her foolish heart skipped a beat, and she cursed.

Was it not enough that her visions disturbed her dreams? Was she now going to be taunted during her waking hours, too?

In a fit of temper, she marched over to the cottage door and flung it open in the hope such a torturous image would disappear so she could be left alone in peace.

"Am I late for luncheon?" Dane lowered his hand as though he had intended to knock.

Sophie placed her hand over her heart as she studied the magnificent form filling the doorway. "Dane," she whispered, sounding breathless. She touched his blue coat, the tips of her fingers barely grazing the material. "Is it really you?"

Dane glanced over his shoulder. "Who else were you expecting?" He removed a glove, lifted a hand and wiped something from her cheek. The feel of his warm fingers proved too much to bear, and she suddenly felt dizzy. She put her hand to her head and blinked in a bid to dispel the sparks of bright lights flashing before her eyes.

Then everything went black.

When Sophie opened her eyes, she was lying on the bed and immediately thought she'd imagined the whole thing—until Dane walked into the room carrying a cup of tea. He'd removed his hat and coat, and as he placed the cup on the bedside table, a lock of hair fell over his brow. Straightening, he brushed it back and offered her one of his boyish smiles. It lit up his face, and he had never looked more handsome.

"I shall end up with a permanent stoop after a week of living here," he said jovially as he glanced up at the ceiling but an inch or two above his head. "I have hit my head three times or more."

Sophie simply stared at him. "How did you know where to find me?"

Dane folded his arms across his chest and grinned with smug satisfaction. "Marcus Danbury wrote to Dudley. Apparently, he tortured Marie until she told him."

Sophie gasped. "If he's hurt her—"

"When I say torture, I do not mean in the literal sense. Danbury can be very charming and extremely persuasive. He is renowned for his expertise with women."

"I cannot believe Marie would be so weak as to fall prey to

such a libertine," Sophie replied, attempting to sit up so she could drink her tea.

"Weak!" Dane exclaimed stepping forward to offer his assistance, but she dismissed him with a wave of the hand. "It has taken him the best part of three weeks to accomplish something he would normally achieve in an afternoon. Under the circumstances, I believe Marie has been exceptional in her attempt to defy him." He glanced towards the end of the bed and said, "May I sit?"

Sophie nodded reluctantly, for to be in such close proximity would only cause more pain and disappointment. She took another sip of tea and placed the cup back on the table. "What did you mean when you said you would develop a stoop living here?"

"Exactly that," he replied. Examining the bed, he added, "Perhaps I should spend an equal amount of time lying down. This bed is rather on the narrow side, but it shouldn't be a problem. I am sure you—"

"You cannot stay here," Sophie interrupted, overcome with a wave of panic. "We cannot continue as before." Although there was nothing she desired more.

Dane smiled. "I know that," he said softly, his warm brown eyes melting her heart. "But I am not leaving, not now, not ever."

Sophie wanted to throw her arms around him, to draw him down, to feel the weight of his body, to plead with him to keep his vow. But she held her resolve. "And do I not have a say in the matter?" she said coolly.

Dane searched her face, and his gaze came to rest on her mouth. "If that beautiful mouth of yours would just speak the truth. If those sumptuous lips would convey what was in your heart instead of what is muddling around in your head, then I would gladly listen to what you have to say."

He was still staring at her mouth, and she moistened her lips.

"I have told you, told you in my letter. I want to be left alone, left to live independently and away from—"

Dane leant forward and placed his finger on her lips to silence her. "No, you don't," he whispered. "Do not be afraid. Do not be afraid to be yourself with me. I know what you want, what you desire. I know what you need because you live inside me." He placed his hand over his heart. "Our lives are entwined whether you wish it or not."

Sophie placed a trembling hand on his arm. "Do you not think I know that? Do you not think I feel it, too?" she cried, allowing her emotions to run free. "But you must think of your responsibilities. You have not worked all these years to be saddled with a hothead. I am wild, impetuous, and untamed and would probably cause you no end of embarrassment."

Dane gave a frustrated sigh. "Sophie, there is no woman in this world I admire and respect more than you. You were willing to sacrifice yourself for your family. What man could ask for more from a wife? What child could ask for more from a mother?" He leant forward again, this time, to wipe a tear from her cheek. "I love you. I have loved you from the moment I pulled you down from your horse. I have loved parrying words with you in my study, loved the look of wonder on your face at Rockingham Pool. I particularly love your passion for secluded carriage rides."

His words enveloped her like a warm blanket on a cold winter's night.

"It's because I love you, so very much," she cried, "that I cannot let you make such a sacrifice. There is but a pittance of a dowry. I have nothing to offer—"

"I do not need money, Sophie," he laughed incredulously. "Dudley and I, we were sensible enough to invest our earnings in order to provide a yearly income. I shall never need to think about money again. Besides, if you care anything for the welfare of little Mary Hodges and the rest of my tenants, you have to marry me."

Sophie raised a brow and smiled coyly. "Oh, and why is that?"

"Because, without you, I am afraid I may resort to buying diamond-encrusted watches or be forced to start a collection of rare snuff boxes, all in the hope of dulling the pain." He shuffled forward and cupped her cheek, his thumb tracing the outline of her lips. "I cannot live without you. I am even prepared to write to Bertram and offer him the running of Westlands if you'll let me stay here with you."

Her heart skipped a few beats, and a lump formed in her throat. He would sacrifice everything he had ever worked for, everything he had achieved, for her. She could not live without this man, and he could not live without her. Somehow she would make it work.

"There will only ever be one Mr. Shandy at Westlands," she replied, "and it will not be your second cousin Bertram."

He took her hand in his. "Say you'll be my wife?" Too impatient to wait for her answer, he pulled her up into his arms and kissed her deeply. "Marry me."

"Yes," she whispered. "I'll marry you."

Amidst breathless kisses, the words *I love you* passed back and forth between them until Dane suddenly stopped. "Wait here." He rushed out of the door and returned with the red velvet pouch. "It was to be a wedding present, but I find I cannot wait."

Sophie's eyes widened. "Is it my mother's necklace?"

"No," he corrected. "It's your necklace." He removed it from the pouch and held it out to her. "Here let me put it on. I have spent a whole month dreaming of you wearing this."

"I can't wear it with this dowdy old dress," Sophie exclaimed, gesturing towards the brown muslin.

Dane cast a lascivious smirk. "My thoughts exactly." He gestured to the bed behind them. "And I believe we have some catching up to do."

EPILOGUE

EIGHTEEN MONTHS LATER

*S*ebastian opened his eyes, stretched and turned to drape his arm over his wife's warm body—except the bed was empty. Assuming she had gone to the nursery, he yawned as he pulled the coverlet up around his shoulders and drifted back off to sleep. Indeed, it was some time before he was woken by his valet walking jauntily into the room with a breakfast tray.

Sebastian propped himself up on his elbows and glanced at Claude with some amusement. "I take it Mrs. Bernard is in a good mood this morning?" he asked. Although looking at Claude's happy disposition, he knew the answer to his question.

"She is still talking about Lord Delmont's personal compliment regarding the smooth running of the garden party," Claude answered, placing the tray on the bed next to Sebastian without so much as a glimmer of discontent. "I fear we shall all be hearing about it for months."

He should invite Delmont more often, Sebastian thought, giving a chuckle as he glanced down at the tray. His stomach rumbled upon witnessing the delicious sight of sliced ham and eggs. "And what good deed have I performed to deserve such a treat?"

Claude bowed. "Lady Danesfield felt that you would need sufficient sustenance for your excursion today."

Like a man who had just regained consciousness after a serious drinking bout, Sebastian frantically searched his mind in the hope of remembering what was significant about the day. "Did she happen to mention where we are going?"

"It is all in the letter, my lord," Claude said as he offered a bow. Noticing Sebastian's confused expression, as there was no sign of a letter on the tray, Claude added, "You must finish your meal before I have permission to hand it over."

Sebastian smiled. Once again, Sophie had piqued his interest. He could barely contain himself during his meal as her unpredictability always roused an element of excitement, coupled with an element of fear.

"There, all gone," Sebastian said, swallowing down the last morsel and sounding somewhat like a boy in the schoolroom. "The letter, if you please." He held out his hand.

Claude bowed, handed over the sealed note and removed the tray from the room.

Sebastian leant back against the pillows and read the cryptic note, smiling when he got to the part that said, *"Having experienced feelings of rapturous pleasure in every room in the house, I suddenly realised there is a case of unfinished business that requires our attention. Should you wish to bring this business to fruition, you will know where to find me."*

Jumping out of bed as though the sheets were ablaze, he didn't wait for Claude to return and dressed with haste while he considered the note.

What possible unfinished business could they have?

Scanning through once more, he acknowledged the seductive undertone. He hoped she didn't expect him to travel all the way to High Wycombe. Although from his recollection, there was nothing left unfinished from their time there. No, wherever she'd gone, it couldn't be more than a few hours ride. Then inspiration struck, and he hurried down to the stables to find Haines.

Coming to an abrupt halt at the sight of one of the stable boys brushing down Altair, Sophie's current horse of choice, Sebastian called out to Haines and the man in question came lumbering out of a stall. "Which horse did Lady Danesfield take this morning?"

"She has gone out in the gig, my lord," Haines replied, scrunching his weathered brow. "She was going to ride Cronus as Altair needs a new shoe but then decided on the gig."

"And you did not think to stop her?"

"I don't expect Lady Danesfield would take instruction from a coachman," Haines informed him in a tone that made Sebastian feel stupid for even asking the question.

"I wouldn't worry, Haines. She does not take instruction from her husband either," Sebastian sighed. "Did she mention where she was going?"

Haines' mouth straightened into the beginnings of a weak grin. "I'm afraid I can't say, my lord. But know that Haines always keeps his eyes on the road, always looks straight ahead, even when he arrives a little too early with a chattering maid in tow." He turned and looked over his shoulder and whispered, "But I'd best not say chattering now that she's my wife."

"Thank you," Sebastian said, patting him on the shoulder.

Sophie heard the thunderous pounding on the dusty road but did not sit up. She was lying on a blanket, her hands cupping her head, looking up at a perfectly blue sky when Dane dropped down beside her.

"I remember feeling overwhelmed by the beauty of this place." She propped herself up on her elbows to look out over Rockingham Pool. "And it is just as spectacular now."

"I'm afraid I cannot comment on its beauty," he replied still a little breathless from his journey. "Nothing could compare to the look of pure pleasure on your face when I brought you here. I have never forgotten it." He glanced down at her breeches and let his fingers trail along the soft curves of her thighs.

"It is a special place for me." She looked up at him. "I tried to fight my feelings for you, but it is impossible not to love you. Everything changed the day we came here."

Dane smiled. "Everything changed for me, too. I am just sorry that the memory was tainted by me hurling you into the carriage."

She sat up and put her hand on his cheek. "Which is why I think we should finish what we started," she said, blushing slightly. "There is a secluded spot just to the right, behind those trees."

He pulled her into his arms and kissed her with unbridled passion. "Have I told you how much I love you, how much I want you?"

"Every day." She sighed with pleasure. Getting to her feet, she took hold of his hand and pulled him towards the trees. "Come, it would not be wise for you to be seen kissing Mr. Shandy, and little William desperately needs a sibling to keep him company."

Dane inclined his head. "But next time, do you think you might wear a dress? I find breeches so cumbersome."

Sophie gave a coy smile. "Next time, it is your turn to surprise me. But know I've always found a military uniform rather appealing."

"What about a pirate? I've often fancied setting sail on the high seas in search of treasure."

She pulled him behind the trees and devoured his mouth while her hands ravaged his body. When they broke for breath, she said, "Did you ever hear the story about the prince and the pirate princess?"

"I can't say I have."

"Well, the princess was forever stealing into places unnoticed," she said, stripping off his waistcoat and running her palms over his shoulders. "I should have a care. One day you may come home to find she has captured your study."

"Now my mind is busy concocting all sorts of lascivious images. Should such a scandalous event ever occur, there must be some way I'd be able to reclaim it."

"Oh, she has her price. But you will have to wait to find out what it is."

The End

Thank you!

Thank you for reading *What You Desire.*

If you enjoyed this book please consider leaving a brief review
at the online bookseller of your choice.

**Read Marcus Danbury and Marie Labelle's story in
What You Propose**

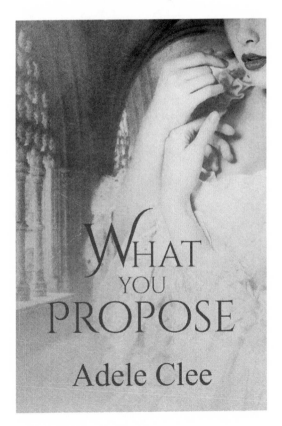

CHAPTER 1

A VILLAGE NORTHEAST OF SAINT-BRIEUC, FRANCE, 1820

Marcus Danbury raced through the cloisters, the clip of his boots echoing along the ancient corridors.

"Tristan." He stormed through the arched doorway out into the courtyard. The usually peaceful recreation area provided little comfort today. "Tristan."

Where the bloody hell had he got to?

Marcus placed his fists on his hips as he scanned the row of small windows set into the stone wall. He would wager twenty gold francs his friend still lay snoring in his bed.

They had drunk far too much wine last night. So much so, Marcus had been forced to dunk his head into the gardener's barrel in the hope the cold water would waken his numb brain.

Despite his frustration, he had to chuckle at the irony of his situation.

One would expect a monastery to be a haven from the trials and temptations of loose women. Who would ever have thought he'd offer sanctuary to the madam of a bawdy house? Although he hadn't exactly offered to play host; the request had been more akin to bribery, and he'd had less than a day's notice to get used to the idea. Had it not been for the debt he owed to the Marquess of Danesfield, he would storm down to the rusty gate and inform

Dane's coachman to turn around and take the strumpet straight back to England.

An image of a well-rounded woman with a huge powdered wig and heavily rouged cheeks flashed into his mind. She would have a fake mole, of course, close to the lips, which would alter in size depending on how drunk she was when she applied it. No doubt her generous bosom would be bursting out from the strict confines of her dress, wobbling and jiggling about when she walked, just to torment him.

God, it had been weeks since he'd last settled between a pair of soft thighs, which was why he supposed he should be grateful to Dane. After numerous years in service, he was confident this Madame Labelle possessed all the necessary skills needed when it came to giving pleasure. Should her countenance be so dreadfully unappealing, he would just have to close his eyes.

"Tristan."

The sound of a window opening caught his attention, and he spotted a mop of golden hair and a pair of beady eyes peering out of the tiny gap.

"What is it?" Tristan shouted. With his bare arm hanging from the handle, Marcus knew he had only just dragged himself out of bed.

"The carriage is waiting at the gate."

"What carriage?"

"Madame Labelle's or Miss Labelle's or whatever the hell her name is."

In his letter, Dane mentioned the woman had been in partnership with a Frenchman yet they'd never married. In the eyes of the Lord, she must be as good as wed to a hundred men. Marcus shook his head. Hypocrisy was a trait he despised; no one deemed him virtuous or moral and so he could hardly cast aspersions. Indeed, he had often wondered if living in an abandoned monastery was a form of penance.

Tristan opened the window fully. "So why haven't you sent someone down to let her in?"

"I thought you could go."

Most of the servants had gone to the market and on Thursdays Andre distributed alms in the village. Selene would be busy in the kitchen, and he'd be damned if he'd go.

In London, Madame Labelle might be the ruler of her domain, but he refused to pander to her whims. Here, she would answer to him. Here, he was the master and as such he refused to do anything to weaken his position—including acting as the hired help.

Madame Labelle could sit in her carriage for the rest of the day for all he cared.

Perhaps living in a monastery might provide enlightenment, might make her reconsider her disreputable ways. To be virtuous, one must first learn patience. Thirty minutes sitting in a stationary carriage would certainly help her do that.

"Give me a few minutes." Tristan sighed. "I need to dress."

"There might be a reward in it." Marcus chuckled to himself.

One look at Tristan's handsome features and the bawd would be offering to pay him for his services, although he had yet to see Tristan succumb to any woman. He didn't hold out much hope for a haggard, middle-aged matron of a brothel.

After waiting for fifteen minutes, Tristan met him in the chapter house. Marcus had stripped away all decorative objects and used the room as a study, a library, and a private sanctuary.

"Perhaps it is wise I do go down and let them in," Tristan said, scanning Marcus' relaxed attire. "You do realise your shirt is wet around the collar, and your breeches look as though a donkey has slept on them. Will you not at least wear a coat?"

"No. This Madame Labelle creature can take me as she finds me." He brushed his hand through his hair in a bid to tame the wild, unruly locks. After spending years servicing the aristocracy, the woman would probably find him rather crude and uncouth, which pleased him greatly and he snorted with amusement.

"Well, she will find you have the clothes of a beggar and the look of a libertine."

"Good." He waved his hand down the front of his friend's fitted coat and pristine cravat. "You will more than make up for my inferior apparel and shoddy manners."

Tristan chuckled. "Did Dane tell you why he's sent her here?"

"He was somewhat vague. He said the woman offered him assistance."

"I'm sure she did."

"He wants to keep her out of London for a while."

"Yes, but for how long?"

Marcus shrugged. "I have no idea. But if she's staying here, she can damn well earn her keep."

Tristan's eyes grew wide. "You don't mean to—"

"I mean she can work in the kitchen," he interjected with a grin. "She will learn that there are no airs and graces here. She cannot flash her fleshy wares in the hope of securing a warm bed and a hot meal for the evening. If she wants to eat, she works. Just as we all do."

"Andre could do with some help in the garden."

Marcus grabbed his friend's shoulder. "Well, there you have it. Madame Labelle will be the new gardener. We shall see if the woman's fingers are as nimble as her profession demands."

Marcus spent the next ten minutes pacing the floor. A strange feeling settled in his chest. The woman's presence would create a shift, unsettle the equilibrium; it would involve them all making changes, certain allowances. She may have experience running a bawdy house, but she would play no part in running his house.

Should he greet her at the door, let her feel the sharpness of his tongue, let her know of his indifference to her plight? Should he sit behind his large desk, busy scratching away with quill pen and ink and pay her no heed?

Damn it.

He could hear the carriage wheels rattling over the stone bridge.

Madame Labelle needed to feel the weight of his authority. She needed to know he would not tolerate any interference.

With that in mind, he strode out through the cloisters and crossed the garth to the entrance located in the west wing. With the bar already raised, Marcus pushed the reinforced oak doors just as the carriage rumbled to a halt outside. His gaze darted to the box seat of the conveyance, to see Tristan perched on top sporting a wide grin.

"Look who's here," Tristan cried with genuine excitement.

As the coachman removed his hat, Marcus sucked in a breath. "Haines." He rushed forward. "By God, I'm surprised Dane sent you. How was your journey?"

Marcus expected him to raise a weary brow and offer a grim expression as he jerked his head towards the carriage.

"It was a good crossing," he said without showing the slightest sign of irritation. "Spent the time playing cards and supping too much ale. The lady kept to her cabin mostly. I don't think the motion suited her stomach if you take my meaning."

More like she'd decided to earn a few guineas and used sickness as an excuse to stay abed.

"How long will you stay with us?"

"Only for a day or two. Just until the lady's all settled."

Marcus could not recall a time when he'd heard a man refer to a whore as a lady. Haines was probably just being polite. The man had a heart as large as his stocky frame. Either that or he had developed a *tendre* for the woman during the journey.

"Talking of which," Tristan said. "I should get down and help her out."

Tristan wore a smug grin. Or perhaps Marcus was mistaken. Perhaps his friend was simply pleased to be reunited with the man who had once saved both their lives.

Marcus took a few steps back, squared his shoulders and

raised his chin. He may dress as a peasant, but he knew how to convey the countenance of a duke.

Tristan opened the carriage door and let down the steps before offering his hand to the occupant.

As Madame Labelle descended the three tiny steps with all the demureness of a duchess, Marcus almost expired from a distinct lack of air. He sucked in a breath in an attempt to inflate his gasping lungs, fought hard to maintain his arrogant facade.

Bloody hell!

For all that was holy. He considered rushing into the chapel, dropping to his knees and giving thanks. Indeed, it took a tremendous amount of effort not to look to the heavens and give a knowing wink.

Madame Labelle was certainly no middle-aged hag. The woman could be no more than five-and-twenty.

There were no hideous moles or warts. Her pure porcelain skin needed no paints or powders. His gaze drifted up to her honey-gold hair. It hung loosely around her shoulders, and he imagined the ends were long enough to brush against the base of her spine. An image of her lying naked in his bed flashed into his mind. He cursed Dane for not warning him he would be giving sanctuary to the goddess Venus.

The woman ran a bawdy house he reminded himself, mentally shaking his head. Although looking at her plain, simple gown, she looked more like a vestal virgin. Oh, he had no doubt she could keep the sacred flame in his hearth alight.

Damn it. He couldn't just stand there staring. He was going to have to say something.

"Madame Labelle. Let me welcome you."

She glanced at him briefly, not bothering to look at his unconventional choice of attire. As a woman skilled in the art of seduction and titillation, he expected a flirtatious comment or a suggestive wiggle of the hips. But he received neither.

"You are Mr. Danbury, I presume?" she asked, raising her chin.

Her voice sounded too haughty, too lofty for his liking. She could stop with the pretence. He was not a randy lord seeking proof she ran a higher class establishment.

"I am," he replied, intrigued by the smile that touched her lips as she scanned the exterior of the ancient stone building.

"And this is a monastery?"

"It was a monastery, but now it is my home."

"Is there still a chapel?"

"A small one."

Why did she ask so many questions?

"Excellent," she beamed, her face alight with pleasure and he had to blink from being blinded by the sheer brilliance of it all.

Marcus shuffled uncomfortably on the spot.

Perhaps it would have been easier if she had been an old hag with a crude mouth and a saggy bosom. The thought forced him to focus on her petite frame. In stark contrast to her steely composure, she appeared delicate and fragile, and he guessed her small breasts would fit nicely into his warm palms.

Roused by a sudden suspicion that this was a trick concocted by Dane for his own amusement, Marcus chose to be rude. "You seem eager to visit the chapel. Have you come here to repent?"

"Perhaps." She eyed him suspiciously but showed no sign she had taken offence. "In any given situation, one must make the most of the opportunities presented before them."

Marcus considered her cryptic words. Was she referring to her scandalous past? Did she consider him an opportunity to line her pockets? By God, he'd be tempted to pay just to satisfy his curiosity.

He stepped closer. It had been years since he'd felt such a strong pulse of desire.

"Perhaps I should follow your philosophy and make the most of the opportunity standing before me," he said with a smirk. He decided it best to be blunt for he had no intention of playing her mind games. "It's been a while since I've had the opportunity to bed a woman as fetching as you or with half the skill when it comes to pleasing men."

The slap came quick, sharp, stinging his cheek, albeit temporarily.

Tristan gasped but then raised a brow to suggest Marcus deserved nothing less.

That did not stop his blood boiling and bubbling away inside, and he clenched his jaw for fear of growling.

Who the hell did she think she was? Perhaps the woman had forgotten that she spent all of her working hours on her back.

"Let me make a few things clear, Mr. Danbury, before we proceed any further." Her blue eyes flashed a hard frosty stare. "My name is not Madame Labelle. That name was given to me, forced upon me and I have borne it for far too long. I do not know what Lord Danesfield has told you. But from your crude and presumptuous manner, I can only guess. You should know I have left that world behind me, too." She exhaled deeply, a tired, weary sound and a frisson of guilt coursed through him. "Now, let me thank you for your hospitality and for offering me a place to stay."

She held out her hand. He didn't know whether to kiss it, turn his back or drop to his knees and swear undying loyalty.

He took her bare hand, ignoring the sparks of desire flitting through him and brushed his lips against the soft skin. It took a tremendous effort not to linger over it as the sweet smell of almonds flooded his nostrils.

"Forgive me, if I caused any offence. If you no longer wish to be known as Madame Labelle, how would you prefer to be addressed?" He could not hide the note of contempt in his tone.

As she glanced up at Haines, the coachman offered a reassuring smile and nodded his head as though encouraging her to continue.

"My ... my given name is Anna." The words stumbled from her lips but then she repeated with a little more confidence, "My name is Miss Anna Sinclair."